The SURROGATE

PENELOPE WARD

Penelope Ward
First Edition
Copyright © 2023
By Penelope Ward

Editing: Jessica Royer Ocken
Proofreading and Formatting: Elaine York,
Allusion Publishing, www.allusionpublishing.com
Proofreading: Julia Griffis
Cover Design: Letitia Hasser, RBA Designs

The SURROGATE

To every reader who asked me
for this beautiful, broken man's story—
this one's for you.

CHAPTER 1
Sig

Track 1: "Rhinoceros" by The Smashing Pumpkins

I might as well have had a rhinoceros in my bed. That snoring had to be what a rhino would sound like.

I never let women stay over at my London flat—ever. But Monica had fallen asleep when I'd gone to the toilet after our encounter last night. I hadn't had the heart to wake her. And considering her snoring had kept me up most of the night, I'd paid heftily for that decision.

As with the other handful of women I'd slept with in the nearly five years since my wife died, there had been no real spark between Monica and me. In fact, that was *exactly* how I preferred it. I had no interest in building anything with anyone after Britney. I'd lost my one true love, and no one else was going to compare. I didn't need to get emotionally involved, nor did I have it in me anymore. So, I intentionally sought out women I knew had no expectations and with whom the chemistry was merely physical.

When Monica's snoring had first reared its ugly head, I'd tried rolling her over, but to no avail. I'd ended up moving to the guest bedroom. How could someone's incessant snoring disrupt everyone's sleep but their own?

I pondered that while staring blankly at the coffee machine, until a knock at my door interrupted my thoughts.

Who the hell is knocking this early?

If I'd known who would be standing on the other side of that door, I would never have opened it—especially since I wasn't wearing a shirt, and there was a half-naked, snoring woman in my bed.

"What are you doing here?" I asked them as I opened.

"Nice to see you, too," Phil chided.

My in-laws, Phil and Kate Alexander, stood in the hallway. While they lived in the US, they came to England from time to time to visit Britney's grave and see me. We'd stayed quite close over the years. Phil had purchased an apartment here that he rented out as an Airbnb, but he kept it open for the weeks he and his wife would visit the UK.

"Why didn't you tell me you were coming?" I asked.

"We emailed you about our trip," Kate answered. "You never responded."

I hadn't checked my personal email account in over a week. "You should've texted."

Phil looked me up and down. "Aren't you going to invite us in?"

I supposed I had to do that, didn't I? *What choice do I have?* "Sure." I stepped aside. "Of course. Come in."

After they entered, Phil looked toward my bedroom. "What is that sound?"

"It's a woman," I reluctantly admitted.

"Ah. You devil. I should've known." He smacked my arm and turned to his wife. "I told you we should've called first."

"I'm sorry." I cleared my throat. "This is terribly uncomfortable for me."

"Nonsense." Kate waved her hand. "You shouldn't be uncomfortable. It's been almost five years. You think we don't realize you have women over from time to time?"

"I've never had someone spend the night, actually. But I'd also never had anyone fall asleep before I could call them a ride."

"You must've entertained her quite well." Phil smirked.

I cleared my throat again. "She's been snoring all night, but I haven't had the heart to wake her."

"Shall I do the honors, then?" Phil wriggled his brows.

I shrugged. "Go for it."

He proceeded to yodel for several seconds. Kate and I just looked at each other. Phil was always a bit of an oddball character, so neither of us was surprised. When he stopped, I peeked into the room to find that while Monica was stirring, she hadn't woken up.

"She's still asleep," I announced. "Care for tea?"

"I would love some," Kate said.

Phil and Kate took seats at my kitchen table.

After boiling some water, I poured their tea and brought two cups over.

A minute later, Monica sauntered in. "Oh." She scratched her head. "Hello."

"Monica, these are my in-laws."

"Your *in-laws*?" Her eyes widened. "You're married?"

Phil pretended to be surprised as he looked over at me. "You bastard!"

Monica looked ready to blow.

3

"He's only joking. He's a ballbuster," I assured her.

"I apologize for my husband's behavior." Kate whacked Phil on the arm. "Our daughter was married to Sig, but she passed away several years ago. We're just visiting. We didn't know he had anyone over."

"Oh." Monica's expression softened as she looked over at me. "You didn't say anything about..."

I sipped some tea. "We didn't say much to each other at all, though, did we?"

"Right." She looked down at her feet. "Uh...I'd better get going."

"Alright, then." I stared into my teacup without making eye contact.

"You have my number," she said.

"I do." I nodded once.

Monica left the kitchen. The three of us were quiet as we listened to the sound of her exiting my apartment.

After the door slammed closed, Phil turned to me. "She'll never hear from you again, will she?"

"Not unless I have the sudden urge to be kept awake all night."

Kate sighed. "You can't live like this forever, bringing home women you barely even talk to."

"I have no interest in anything more."

"That's because you're intentionally not letting the right people in," she scolded.

"I appreciate your opinion, but I know what I need, and it's *not* a relationship."

"Britney would want you to find happiness. You know that, right?"

Britney would want to be alive. That's what she would want. I cleared my throat. "Anyway, what brings

4

you to town? You couldn't possibly have come over this early to chastise me about my personal life."

They looked at each other.

Suspicious, I lifted a brow. "What's going on?"

Kate set her cup down. "There *is* something we want to talk to you about."

"Alright…" I took a sip.

"We came to London for the hospital fundraiser, but we figured we'd kill two birds with one stone while we were here." She paused. "Phil and I have been talking, and…" She took a deep breath. "We'd like to use one of the eggs. We think it's time."

I nearly spit out my tea, and the room swayed as the meaning of *eggs* registered. I knew my wife had frozen her eggs before she'd started cancer treatments. That was before we'd even met. She'd mentioned it to me, and it had always been at the back of my mind, but I tried not to think about it. The eggs on ice were something she and I had only talked about in the context of us having a child together once she got through treatments—alive. I couldn't fathom any other use for those eggs.

I sat in silence as Kate continued.

"We've debated it for a long while. Britney was our only child. We're in our late fifties, so obviously I can't have another biological child, but we'd like to raise our grandchild."

"You think this is what she would want? For her child to come into the world without its mother? Britney had intended to be around for that child when she harvested her eggs."

"Yes, I know." Kate nodded. "But when it became clearer to us that she might not make it, I asked what she

5

wanted me to do with them. She said she wasn't opposed to the thought of living on through a child. She signed the eggs over to us, but she made me promise I would clear it with you first. She didn't want us to do anything to upset you. That seemed to be a dealbreaker."

I narrowed my eyes. "Why didn't she mention any of this to me?"

"I don't think she ever wanted to believe she wouldn't be around, Sig. I had to bring up the subject. Because it had to be discussed, knowing she was likely going to..."

Die.

My stomach knotted. How could I, in good conscience, keep this from happening if it was what Britney wanted? There was nothing I wouldn't do for her. This would be a chance for my wife to live again, indirectly—or at least a part of her. If her parents were willing to care for the child, who was I to stop them? It didn't feel like my decision to make, even if Britney had been adamant about my approval.

I rubbed my thumb along the mug. "So, you're looking for my permission..."

"Well, not just your permission." She paused. "We want you to be the father, of course."

Oh.

Fuck.

Why the hell hadn't *that* occurred to me? If I'd thought the room was swaying before, it was spinning now.

"No," I said, starting to perspire.

"No?" Phil arched a brow. "You'd rather we use a random man's sperm?"

Uh...

No.

My stomach turned. When he put it that way, I couldn't imagine any other man fathering the child. "No way would I allow that."

"Then using your sperm is the only option," Kate said. "But if you don't want to, we won't. We won't move ahead with anything."

"Just to clarify again, you wouldn't have to *raise* this baby, Sig," Phil added. "It would be ours. But at the same time, if you ever decided you *wanted* to raise it, we wouldn't stand in the way. We'd fully help raise him or her and give them the best life we possibly can."

My chair skidded as I got up. "Excuse me. I need a moment."

I went to my room and sat on the edge of the bed. With my head in my hands, I took a moment to ground myself. I would've given anything to go back just an hour, when I was listening to rhinoceros sounds and not dealing with the bomb they'd dropped.

The thought of having a child without Britney here was excruciatingly painful. To know she'd never have a chance to experience being a mother. But I had to trust that Kate was telling the truth about Britney's last wishes.

After a few minutes, I'd calmed down enough to re-join them in the kitchen. "I need time to process this," I said.

Kate nodded. "Of course. Take as much time as you need. The eggs aren't going anywhere. We're the only ones getting older." She chuckled. "Phil and I need to do this while we're still young enough to responsibly care for our grandchild."

I swallowed. "I understand."

Kate took a sip of her tea. "There's one more thing we need to discuss."

"What?"

"The surrogate."

My brain must have been operating at a slower speed today. Maybe it was the lack of sleep, because not only had I not initially realized they would want me to father the baby, but the fact that someone would need to *carry it* had also skipped my mind.

Before I could respond, she added, "We think we've found someone."

My eyes went wide. "Without discussing this with me, you found someone?"

"You would have the final say. We wouldn't do anything without your approval."

"Who is this person?" I asked, my guard up as far as it could go.

"One of Phil's oldest and dearest friends has a daughter. She'd never met Britney because they grew up in different states, and she's a bit younger. But Phil and I were visiting Roland and his daughter recently in Rhode Island. We confided in them about our situation, never expecting her to offer to help. I know we should've discussed it with you first, but I got really emotional one night and well, the floodgate opened. Like I said, I never expected that she would—"

"Who in their right mind would offer something like that after one conversation?"

"She's a wonderful girl with a big heart," Kate explained.

"I don't buy it." I crossed my arms. "What does she want?"

Kate's forehead wrinkled. "What do you mean?"

"Money. How much is she asking?"

"That wasn't even discussed," Phil answered.

"Well, that's insane. Who agrees to do something like this without discussing money?"

"Because it's not only about money for her," Kate said. "Of course she knows it will come with compensation, but she genuinely wants to help us."

"How old is this person?"

"Twenty-five," Phil answered.

"Twenty-five, and she wants to give up a year of her life? She doesn't sound right in the head."

My mother-in-law crossed her arms. "I doubt there's anyone you would deem fit for this task, Sig. Because you're not open to it yet. Once you've had time to think, you can meet her. I already told you we won't do anything against your wishes. If you don't like her, we can find someone else. What you want is what matters most."

What I *wanted* was for this entire situation to disappear.

What I *wanted* was to have Britney back.

And that would never happen.

CHAPTER 2

Sig

Track 2: "How Can You Mend a Broken Heart" by The Bee Gees

A couple of days later, feeling anxious, I left work before noon, which I almost never did. I drove to the countryside to my cousin Leo's home. I wanted to discuss this latest development with him and his wife, Felicity.

Leo Covington was the Duke of Westfordshire, a title passed on to him when his father died. While Leo was my first cousin, I was not an aristocrat myself. Leo's father was married to my mother's sister; we were the non-aristocratic side of the family. I'd spent most of my younger years reaping the benefits of my association with Leo, however. And in addition to being my cousin, Leo had always been my best mate, confidante, and travel partner.

Leo and Felicity lived on a property known as Brighton House, which had been passed down in the Covington family. They had an obscene number of animals inhabiting the surrounding acreage, including a Shetland pony Leo had purchased for Felicity when he was wooing her in America nearly a decade ago. They'd named him Ludicrous, which pretty much summed up that entire transaction.

Ninety minutes after bolting from my office, Leo, Felicity, and I sat around the center island of their massive kitchen, which featured French doors overlooking acres of farmland. I'd just finished recalling my conversation with Kate and Phil.

Felicity slid a tray of crackers, cheese, and fruit over in front of me. "I think it's really precious that they want to do this, Sig."

"Precious or insane, depending on how you look at it," I said, popping a cube of cheese in my mouth.

Her eyes glistened. "Imagine getting to hold Britney's child. How incredible would that be?"

My chest tightened. "Excruciatingly painful would be more like it."

She nodded. "I guess I can see that perspective, too."

I stuck a toothpick into an olive. "The past couple of days, I've felt like the star of a miserable made-for-television movie I would never willingly subject myself to."

Leo clapped my shoulder. "I give you credit for even considering it, cousin. I think I'd have the same reaction you do, honestly."

"I could say no to the whole thing, but...Phil and Kate lost their entire world when Britney died. They've been nothing but good to me. I won't stop this, even if it tears me up inside."

Leo nodded. "So you've already made your decision, then. You're going to say yes."

"Well, I suppose 'yes' is only *one* decision. There are other things that need to be worked out."

"Like whether you'll father it?" he asked.

"No, that's a given. I can't stomach it any other way."

"Wow." Leo nodded. "Alright."

Felicity rubbed her pregnant belly. "So I suppose the final decision would have to do with choosing a surrogate."

"Well...they *think* they've already found someone."

Felicity tilted her head. "Why do you say it like that? You don't trust their judgment?"

I flicked some crumbs away. "I don't trust anyone who'd agree to something so fast. Apparently, they had one conversation with a friend's twenty-five-year-old daughter, and the next thing you know, she's offering up her womb."

Leo poured some Prosecco. "Who is this person?"

"I don't know much except that her father and Phil are old mates. This girl must be crazy to offer to do this."

"I don't think it's a crazy thing to offer," Felicity said. "I mean, there are kindhearted people out there. Britney's story is tragic. I could see myself getting wrapped up in the emotions of it all and offering to help, if my life situation were different."

"Well, you're insane, too, then, Ginger."

"It's been nearly ten years, Sig. Are you ever gonna stop calling me Ginger?"

I winked. "Never."

Ginger was a nickname I'd given Felicity back when she'd first met Leo because of her red hair. I'd called her a lot of names in jest over the years, ballbuster that I was. My cousin and I had been on a three-month jaunt around the US a decade ago when he'd met Felicity on the last leg of our trip in Narragansett, Rhode Island. (I was completely unhinged that summer, by the way. It was before I'd met Britney, and let's just say I had *a lot* of fun on that trip.)

Leo and Felicity had taken quite a long road to get to where they were now. Felicity was currently pregnant with their second child, a daughter they planned to name Britney. Needless to say, I'd pretty much lost it the day they told me that. Their other daughter, Eloise, was three and a little whippersnapper. She was at nursery school at the moment, otherwise she would've been circling my legs, trying to get me to play with her.

Leo sipped his Prosecco. "Okay, so what's the next step, then?"

"I have no idea." I sighed.

"I do," Felicity said.

I turned to her. "Do tell, Ginger."

"You need to invite the potential surrogate here. Meet this woman and make your decision based on *actually* getting to know her, rather than assumptions."

"She's hardly a woman. Who the hell knows what they want to do with their life when they're twenty-five?"

"Wasn't Britney twenty-six when you met her? You thought she was pretty mature, didn't you?"

"That was different. She knew she could be dying. That matures you real fucking fast."

Felicity nodded. "But let's face it, Sig. You're never gonna feel like anyone is good enough to carry this baby. If this is going to happen, you need to be a bit more open-minded."

"What I'd like is for this entire situation to go away so I don't have to deal with it at all."

I'd had no desire to have kids until I met Britney. And after she died, I vowed I would never have children with anyone else, which was fine because I'd never planned to have kids anyway, never wanted them with anyone but her. But I hadn't accounted for a situation where she and I would conceive a child without her being here. The one thing I knew? I wouldn't be able to handle raising that child myself.

"I've already decided Phil and Kate should be the ones to take care of it. I'm not suited."

"Okay." Felicity nodded. "Good that you can admit that, if that's how you feel. But you'll always be its father. You won't be able to change that."

Father.

Me?

I couldn't fathom it.

On the way back from Leo's, instead of returning to my place in London, I decided to spend the night at my other residence, a bed and breakfast known as The Bainbridge on the other side of Westfordshire.

I'd met the innkeeper, Lavinia, several years ago when Felicity had stayed there during a trip to the UK to visit Leo. At the time, Leo had asked me to look after Felicity since she'd been a stranger in a new country; his obligations had meant he couldn't be with her at all times. That had been shortly after Britney died, and I was a walking zombie in those days. With nothing better to do, I'd stayed at the bed and breakfast with Felicity, never expecting that

I'd remain good friends with the old woman who owned it. Lavinia had become like a second mother to me, which was convenient since my actual mother wasn't the easiest to get along with.

Lavinia's bills had become a struggle over the years, so I'd bought the inn from her and taken over the expenses in exchange for her continuing to run it. She still lived there and hosted occasional guests, which lately had been few and far between. She was growing frail, so the guests were pretty much on their own when it came to carrying their bags or changing the sheets, though a housekeeper I'd hired deep cleaned once a week. I kept a room at the inn and stayed there whenever I was in the countryside. I was in London most of the week, since that's where I worked.

Lavinia had also become a confidante over the years. Although there were forty-five years between us—eighty-two versus thirty-seven—we got on quite well. I appreciated that the inn was a no-judgment zone, unlike my parents' house, where I was frequently criticized for my life choices. While Lavinia, too, offered her opinion on things I didn't want to hear about, she never shoved anything down my throat.

Lavinia sat alone in the dark in the kitchen when I arrived from Leo's early that evening. A single candle was lit in front of her.

I went straight for the cabinet where she stored the liquor. "Turn on some lights, woman."

"I'm meditating."

"Looks like a horror show in here."

She laughed. I liked making her laugh—and busting her balls. Two of my favorite things.

"What's got you down tonight?" she asked.

"How could you tell?"

"Well, you usually say hello before you grab the gin."

"Yeah," I muttered. "Sorry." I lifted the bottle. "Care for one?"

She nodded.

"Gin by candlelight. How special," I said as I poured us each a drink. I took them over to the table and filled her in on the visit from Phil and Kate a couple of days ago.

Lavinia sat with her eyes wide, soaking in every word, as if this was the most exciting thing to happen to her in years.

"What is this woman's name who offered to carry the baby?" she asked.

I looked away. "Would you believe I don't know? I never asked."

"Well, I think it's high time you found out. And she can stay here if you invite her to Westfordshire."

"You want a front-row seat to this shitshow, eh?" I narrowed my eyes. "Anyway, why would I invite her here?"

"Well, you'd have to meet her first, wouldn't you?"

"Felicity said the same thing. I haven't thought it through. I definitely wouldn't want her staying with me in London. That would be awkward." I rubbed my temples. "I don't need the added stress of this. Work's been busy."

A couple of years back, I earned my MBA and took over the management of several of Leo's properties. *Yes, continuing to ride those coattails.* My cousin couldn't handle all of his businesses himself and needed someone trustworthy to count on, but I refused to accept handouts, and I didn't take the job until I'd finished my schooling

16

and gotten the experience I'd need for the position. Since then, I'd taken over several more of the responsibilities at Covington Properties. Not to toot my own horn, but profits had skyrocketed since I'd come on board. Leo certainly couldn't complain about that.

Lavinia frowned. "There's more to life than work, you know."

"I've been slowly getting my life back over the past five years. Work has been a major part of that."

"Taking strange women to your apartment in London and then kicking them out is hardly getting your life back," she cracked.

"I'll have you know, I kindly ask them to leave, not kick them out."

"Same thing."

"Anyway, I don't *always* kick them out." I tossed back half of my gin before slamming the glass down. "There was that one rhinoceros..."

"What?"

"Never mind." I chuckled.

"What's the real issue here, Sigmund? Why are you so troubled by this, if Britney's parents offered to take care of the child?"

I had to ponder that. "The real issue is Britney." I looked into my glass. "I wonder if it's what she *truly* would've wanted, despite what she told her mother in her final days. She might not have been of sound mind when she was on multiple medications." I swallowed. "I can't ask her, and that kills me."

Lavinia touched my arm. "Do you think you'll ever be able to let her go?"

"I'm not trying to let her go." I shook my head. "I don't *want* to let her go."

"That was probably the wrong terminology," she corrected. "I meant, do you think you'll ever be able to let *someone else* in?"

"That's not something I want, either."

"I suppose you can't mend a broken heart." Lavinia sighed. "Maybe there's only meant to be one—one great love."

I stared into the distance. "It's hard to imagine that I hadn't even known her a year. It felt like a lot longer."

"I didn't realize that." She tilted her head. "Remind me how you two met?"

My eyes widened. "How is it possible that you don't know? I thought I told you everything."

"You might've, dear, but I'm going a bit senile, so tell me again."

I took a deep breath to gear up for the emotion of the story. I'd keep it short so as not to go off the rails tonight. "Britney was traveling to the UK for medical treatments. But I didn't know that at first—she certainly didn't look sick. She and I met at an airport in the US. I was heading back home from a trip to the States. We bickered about something, and I think I fell in love with her smart mouth almost instantly. I teased her about being short, and she called me an obnoxious giraffe. We had immediate chemistry like I'd never felt in my life. We ended up sitting next to each other on the plane, but she insisted that we needed to separate once we landed. I couldn't accept that, never seeing her again. She wasn't ever able to get rid of me, much to her dismay."

"What happened after the flight?"

"I followed her to her hotel room—where her parents were waiting. That's when I found out the truth. Phil and Kate were already in town to accompany her to her treatments. They were in the UK because that's where the doctor conducting the clinical trial was located."

"And you stayed…"

"Spent every single day of the next six months with her—lots of hard days, but lots of beautiful ones in between. Fell in love, got married…" I paused, feeling an ache in my chest. "And then she died." I downed the last of the gin, which burned the back of my throat. "Six months. That's all we had." I sucked in a shaky breath. "Changed my life forever."

Lavinia reached for my arm. "It's so tragic, but so beautiful, Sigmund."

"Those months were the greatest gift of my life. I don't need to fall in love again, Lavinia."

"Perhaps you don't. But you *do* need to have this child. A piece of you and her. *That* will be your greatest gift."

CHAPTER 3

Abby

Track 3: "Crash" by The Primitives

I called my father from the road on the way to the inn.

"This place looks like something out of a movie, Dad. Rolling hills, stone architecture. I can't believe I never thought to visit the English countryside before."

"Well, I'm happy you arrived in one piece and that it's off to a good start. Please keep me posted on everything. If something doesn't feel right, you come right back home, you hear me?"

I swerved to avoid oncoming traffic. "Thus far, the only thing that doesn't feel right is driving on the left side of the road."

"Oh, don't tell me that. I'm worried enough as it is."

"It's a pretty narrow country road, too. But it's fine. I'm getting used to it."

"Okay, well, don't talk while driving. Concentrate. And call me when you get there safely."

"I will, Dad. Love you."

"Love you, too."

It didn't matter how old I was, my father would always worry about me, especially when I was far from home. I'd only been out of the US once before, to Mexico with a group of people during my high school years. My mother had been alive then, so Dad had a distraction. Now, with her gone and my sister across the country, his focus was mainly me.

Two weeks ago, Phil and Kate had called to say Britney's husband wanted me to come to the UK to meet him before he agreed to the surrogacy. He'd offered to send a ride to get me from the airport, but I preferred to have a car while I was here so I could explore the sights. He'd ordered me a rental instead, which I'd picked up before driving to the countryside. He'd messaged me the name of the inn where I'd be staying, The Bainbridge in Westfordshire. Apparently, it was run by a friend of his. I had no idea when I'd be meeting the man himself. I didn't even know what he looked like—not that it mattered, but it would've been nice to have some idea going into this. I hadn't wanted to be rude and ask Phil and Kate for a photo. A Google search had turned up nothing, aside from a fuzzy photo of him and his aristocrat cousin in a gossip rag from years ago. There'd been some kind of scandal involving the cousin... Anyway, the idea of meeting this guy for the first time was nerve-wracking, despite my excitement to be visiting a new place.

I rolled down the car window, breathing in the scent of grass and something that smelled like chamomile. Or maybe that was the daffodils that had popped up everywhere along this road. My hair blew in the wind as I soaked in the fresh air. A week would not be enough to enjoy this magical place.

I had about a mile left to go when I came upon an open field of what appeared to be hundreds of sheep. It was like all the sheep I'd counted in my head to get to sleep as a child suddenly came to life. A living dream. *Wow.* Simply breathtaking. My car slowed...

Boom!

Oh no.

No.

No. No.

I'd been so distracted by the sheep that I'd slammed right into the car in front of me. Thankfully, I hadn't been going fast, but I could already see a small dent.

Shit. Shit. Shit!

The car pulled over to the side of the road, and so did I.

A tall, dark-haired man got out. He was strikingly handsome, which made this whole thing so much more embarrassing.

I got out, too, noticing barely a scratch on the front of my rental car.

"What the hell?" he demanded.

"I'm sorry. I took my eyes off the road for just a split second and—"

"Clearly. What in God's name were you looking at, your phone?"

"No." I pointed to across the road. "The sheep. They're so beautiful. And there were so many. I got distracted."

He narrowed his eyes. "Sheep."

I swallowed. "Yes."

"Well, there are sheep everywhere here. So if you get distracted that easily, you're going to get yourself killed."

"I've never hit another car in my life. I'm so sorry."

"How lucky am I to have been the target of your first sheep-watching calamity."

God, the accent. So gosh-darn sexy. The wind blew a waft of his masculine scent toward me. We were in a rural area, yet this guy looked plucked straight from the city. Very *London*, if you asked me, wearing a fitted, ribbed black turtleneck that complemented his shiny, black hair and a chunky, expensive watch. And he was so wonderfully tall.

I caught myself staring and cleared my throat. "I have insurance. But I'm from the US. I don't know how this works if I'm driving a rental in another country. I—"

"Don't worry about it." He held his palm out.

Baaaa... I heard in the distance. "Are you sure?" I rummaged through my purse. "I have to give you something."

"What are you going to give me? Nail polish to touch up the damage?" he cracked. "Just keep your eyes off the sheep and on the bloody road before you kill someone."

Before I could say anything further, the man returned to his car and got in. If this was how the rest of the trip was going to go, I was in trouble. At least he'd let me go, and I wouldn't have to tell anyone I'd be meeting about this.

I pulled onto the road again, noticing that the guy had waited for me to take off first. As I drove away, I could see his car behind me through the rearview mirror. He'd probably let me go first because he was paranoid to drive in front of me again. Couldn't say I blamed him.

When the GPS alerted me that I'd arrived at my destination, The Bainbridge Inn, I was surprised to see the man I'd hit also pull into the driveway.

We both exited our cars, and a sense of dread filled me. "Did you follow me here?" I asked.

He didn't immediately answer, and his expression was hard to read. He looked a little disoriented. "I did *not* follow you here, no."

"Then why did you pull in after me? You changed your mind about taking down my information?"

"This is my destination," he said, stone-faced.

"You're staying here?" I shook my head. "Oh." I laughed nervously. "I'm sorry. What are the chances? That's...unfortunate."

"Unfortunate why?"

"That I hit you while you're on holiday."

"I'm not on holiday. I *live* here."

Just then the front door opened, and a sweet little old lady emerged. "You must be Abby."

I straightened. "I am, yes."

"I see you've already met Sigmund."

My jaw dropped.

Sigmund?

Ugh!

This is Britney's husband.

Crap.

Great.

Just great.

His full name was Sigmund Benedictus, but Phil and Kate called him Sig.

I turned to him. "Well, this is embarrassing. Did you know it was me this whole time?"

"When you pulled into the inn, I figured it out. But I had my suspicions after you rammed into me and I heard your accent. I feared it was you."

My cheeks burned. "Why didn't you say anything, if you suspected?"

"I wanted to observe you in your natural element, I suppose."

That kind of pissed me off. He was testing me? "Learn anything interesting?" I cocked my head.

"You're a bad driver."

There was an awkward silence as we stood across from each other. A brisk breeze blew my long, brown hair around. His stunning looks were unnerving. I hadn't been prepared for this. Not that his appearance mattered—I wasn't coming here to date him. But I might've been less tense if he wasn't so intimidatingly good-looking.

The old woman stepped between us and held out her hand to me. "I'm Lavinia."

I took it. "It's nice to meet you. Thank you for having me." I turned to Sig. "I didn't realize you *lived* here."

"Only part time."

"He's being humble," Lavinia interrupted. "Sigmund actually *owns* The Bainbridge. He bought it from me when I couldn't afford to keep it any longer. He saved this place from being shut down."

I looked over at him. "That's commendable."

"Not really. I needed a place to crash when I'm in Westfordshire. And Lavinia is a good drinking chum." He looked out toward the road a moment. "I won't be staying here this week, however."

"You live in London normally, right?"

25

"Yes."

This guy was not going out of his way to make me feel welcome. He did *not* seem comfortable with me being here, and I had to wonder if Phil and Kate had steered me wrong.

"Well, let's not all stand here in the middle of the driveway." Lavinia waved toward the stone structure, covered in vines. "Come on in. Make yourself at home."

As I followed her into the house, I could hear Sig's footsteps behind me.

The walls in the living room were painted dark green. There was a fireplace in the center and gnome statues scattered about the room. The coffee table looked hand-made, as if someone had chopped down a tree outside and carved it.

We passed a small piano that looked like it had been collecting dust on the way into the kitchen. When I breathed in the spicy aroma of something cooking on the stove, my stomach grumbled.

"I've put on a pot of stew for dinner," Lavinia announced. "Do you eat meat?"

"I do. It smells delicious. Thank you so much for doing that."

The kitchen cabinets were painted light green, and there was a small center island in the same color with a wooden butcher-block countertop. Porcelain figurines were arranged on fixed-bracket wall shelves.

"We'll eat about six, if that works for you," she said.

"That sounds perfect." I nodded, having no idea what time it was.

Sig finally spoke. "Lavinia has to limit her trips upstairs. I can show you to your room."

"Don't give away my weaknesses so soon, Sigmund," Lavinia said from behind me.

I smiled at her and turned to him. "That'd be great."

He picked up my suitcase and ascended the stairs. I followed, unable to escape the view. Through his dark jeans, I could see Mr. Benedictus had quite a nice ass. Totally inappropriate observation to make about Britney's husband? Maybe. But Sig was a beautiful man—on the outside, at least. And he was definitely older than me, maybe somewhere in his thirties.

He opened one of the rooms and set my suitcase in the corner. The bedroom had floral wallpaper and a four-post bed. The large window offered a view of the narrow road at the front of the house and farmland in the distance.

"This room has the nicest view and its own loo." He walked to the other side of the space. "There's a small wardrobe if you wish to hang up your things."

He made it seem like his job was to give me a quick tour of this place, rather than get to know me. It was as if he'd forgotten *why* I was actually here. The man hadn't made eye contact with me since we arrived, and I had to wonder if he was still upset about me hitting his car.

"I feel like we got off on the wrong foot, Sig," I blurted.

"Why ever would you think that?" He raised a brow as he finally looked at me. Not even a hint of a smile, though.

"Okay. Well, hopefully you'll lighten up as the week progresses."

"Is your being here contingent on that? Because I'm not known for my bright and cheery demeanor. I'm more of a miserable fuck, in general."

"I can see that. You're not exactly giving a welcoming vibe. But I can't figure out if it's because I hit your car or something more." When he continued to remain silent, I got straight to the point. "Are you not okay with the surrogacy thing?"

"If I weren't okay with it, you wouldn't be here," he said, looking out the window.

"Then it's *me* you're not happy with?"

"I don't even know you."

"Okay." I rolled my eyes. "Good talk." I looked down at my shoes.

"I'll let you unwind." He took a few steps back. "See you at dinner."

"Yeah," I murmured. "See you then."

CHAPTER 4

Abby

Track 4: "Mean" by Taylor Swift

Feeling jittery, I sat down on the bed and bounced my legs. I found my phone and texted my dad to let him know I'd arrived safely. I didn't have the energy to fill him in on anything more than that, so I opted not to call. I had very little nice to say so far, and I didn't want to worry him. I could only hope this cold reception would change as the night progressed.

After a few minutes, I walked over to the window and looked out toward the beautiful green hills across the road. Then I spotted him. Sig was outside, right near the weathered sign with gold lettering that spelled *The Bainbridge.* He paced a few times before planting himself on a stone ledge at the point where the driveway met the road. He dropped his head into his hands for a moment before looking up at the sky. His legs bounced, and he seemed anxious and upset.

Suddenly all I wanted to do was flee this place—get the hell out of here as fast as possible. This was *not* what

I'd signed up for. It wasn't that I'd expected a red carpet, but this felt like the rug had been pulled from under me.

Why did you ask me to come here?

Moving away from the window, I tried to forget what I'd just seen, instead forcing myself to take a much-needed hot shower in the adjacent bathroom before dinner.

After I emerged, I dressed in comfy clothes: leggings and a Rhode Island-themed T-shirt that said *Feed Me Hot Wieners and Tell Me I'm Pretty*. I might've dressed nicer if I'd felt it would be appreciated, but screw it. If I had to endure his attitude, I at least wanted to be comfortable.

It was a few minutes before six, and I didn't want to keep the sweet, old lady and her stew waiting. So, I put one foot in front of the other and willed myself to go downstairs, even if I would have preferred to bury myself under the covers.

The wooden stairs creaked as I descended before making my way into the kitchen. My stomach dipped when I found him there, pouring an amber-colored liquid into a glass.

When he turned to me, he lifted the bottle. "Care for something to drink?"

I wondered if this was some sort of trick, like maybe he wanted to see if I drank a lot, so he could use it against me in his "assessment." No way was I falling for that.

"I'm trying to limit alcohol right now." I held my head up high. "I'll just help myself to some water."

"The glasses are in that cupboard, dear." Lavinia pointed to a cabinet as she stood at the stove, stirring the stew. "And there's a jug of filtered water on the table."

"Thank you, Lavinia."

"I don't cook so much anymore, but this is a special occasion." She smiled at me.

At least one person was attempting to make me feel welcome. "What do you normally eat, if you don't cook?" I asked.

"Sigmund cooks when he's here, or I make a large batch of something and freeze it. I also frequent the pub down the road more than I probably should."

"Ah. You'll have to take me there. I'd love to treat you to dinner before I leave to thank you for your hospitality."

"That would be lovely."

The three of us eventually sat down at the table, quietly eating the stew, the occasional clanking of our spoons the only sound.

"What is your surname, Abby?" Lavinia finally asked.

"Knickerbocker."

Sig's eyes shot up from his plate. "Knicker...like knickers?"

I knew *knickers* was the term Brits used for underpants. "Yes." I gritted my teeth. "Spelled exactly that way, actually."

He chuckled.

"You've been quiet this whole dinner, and that's the first thing you think to say to me? Benedictus is a bit of an odd name, too, you know." My blood boiled. "So is Sigmund, for that matter. You don't look like a Sigmund Benedictus."

"What's that supposed to mean?"

"It was actually a compliment."

Lavinia snorted.

Sig shot daggers at her. "What is it that you do, Abby?" he asked.

31

I sat straighter in my seat. "I graduated with a degree in English from the University of Rhode Island. At the moment, I'm between jobs, but I'm in the process of trying to reopen my mother's store. After she passed away, I kept it afloat for a while, but the economy tanked, and we had to shut down."

He swirled his drink around in his glass. "What type of store?"

"Rhode Island-themed trinkets and souvenirs."

"That's where that hideous T-shirt you're wearing came from, I assume."

I ignored his comment. "We live in a sea town and get an influx of people in the summer months. But even with that, we weren't able to keep things running for too long after my mother died."

His tone softened. "What happened to your mother?"

I swallowed. "She died of cancer three years ago."

He frowned. "I'm sorry."

"Thank you."

After a moment, he spoke again. "So, if you're trying to reopen the shop, you need money. That's why you're interested in the surrogacy, I take it."

I couldn't tell if that was supposed to be an insult. "Well, the money won't hurt, but there are *much* easier ways to make quick money than to be pregnant for nine months."

"So, you don't *want* to be pregnant?" He drew in his brows. "Why offer?"

"I didn't say that at all. My point is that no one would offer to do this *just* for the money. You have to want to help someone."

"Why do you want to help Phil and Kate?" Sig leaned back in his chair and crossed his arms. It seemed our casual dinner had transformed into a formal interrogation.

His sleeves were partially pushed up. My eyes fell to his wrist as I noticed three lines tattooed around it, one thicker than the other two. Did he have any other ink beneath that black turtleneck? I must have been crazy for wondering such a thing at a time like this.

"Phil is a good friend of my dad's, as you know," I finally said. "They grew up together. Even though I never met Phil and Kate's daughter—your wife—I felt for them when she passed away. And when they came to visit us recently, I got to spend time with them. I was very touched. And I feel strongly in my heart that I should at least offer to bring their dream to fruition."

"Sounds to me like you're telling me what I want to hear and not why you *really* decided to do this."

I put my spoon down. "You think I'm lying?" My blood pressure rose. "First you accuse me of only being in it for the money. And now you don't believe anything I say at all?"

He stared right through me. "What's missing in your life that you feel the need to make this sacrifice for someone else? What are you running away from?"

"What's missing in *your* life that you feel people always need to have an ulterior motive or some messed-up story in order to want to help?" I leaned in. "Do you trust *anyone*, Sig?"

He pushed his napkin aside. "Very few people, honestly...and with good reason."

I straightened in my seat again. "Well, I've got news for you. You're not going to find someone with purer intentions than mine. But I'm not going to spend the next week bending over backwards to prove that when you clearly made up your mind about me before I said a word."

"Yes, your debut was a *smash* hit, I must say."

It felt like steam was coming out of my ears. Lavinia flashed a look of sheer disappointment in Sig's direction.

"I can't prove myself to someone who wants me to fail. Clearly you invited me here to mess with me, and for that, you can fuck off." My chair scraped against the hardwood floor as I shot up from my seat. "Lavinia, thank you so much for this delicious stew. Truly. But I've had a long day and would like to rest."

"Of course, dear," she muttered.

I stormed up the stairs and picked up the phone to dial Phil and Kate.

Kate answered, "Abby! We were just wondering how—"

"This isn't going to work out."

CHAPTER 5

Sig

Track 5: "Save Your Tears" by The Weeknd

A little while after dinner, I was upstairs in my room at The Bainbridge when my phone rang. It was my mother-in-law, calling from the US.

Rubbing my temples, I picked up. "Kate..."

"What the hell did you say to her?"

Abby had apparently wasted no time reporting back to them. I massaged the tension from the back of my neck. "Well, I guess that didn't take long."

"How did you manage to piss her off in the first couple of hours?"

"It's one of my special talents."

"Sig..."

I sighed. "I wanted to know her intentions. I wanted honesty. And I didn't feel she was delivering."

"Not everyone is dishonest. She has no reason to lie."

"I would've had more respect for her if she'd told me she was doing this for the money. At least that would be

35

more truthful than the righteous explanation she'd have me believe."

"Look, Sig. I know you have mixed feelings about this whole thing. I understand. No one is going to be good enough in your eyes for this task. But at the very least, you trust Phil and me, right? We wouldn't choose someone *we* didn't fully trust. So you need to trust our judgment here."

Deep down, I knew she was right. I was sabotaging the situation. It wouldn't have mattered who walked in that door today. "It's not Abby, Kate. It's me." I pulled my hair as I paced. "I don't think I'm ready for this."

"Why didn't you say something before she traveled all the way there, if that's how you feel? We would've never encouraged her to come meet you now. We would've waited or—"

"I wanted to do it for you. But meeting her made me realize that everything is…happening so fast."

"Okay." She exhaled. "I'm glad you said something. Maybe we need to take a step back."

My chest hurt. I hated disappointing them. They'd been through enough.

"Abby wants to leave the UK early," she said.

I nodded. "I suspected that."

"Well, that's what you wanted, isn't it?"

Shutting my eyes, I muttered, "I'm sorry, Kate."

"You can't help how you feel, Sig." She exhaled. "You don't need to apologize. We'll figure this out, okay? I'll call you again soon to check in."

After we hung up, I stared at the wall for several minutes before deciding to go back to London. I'd just need to say goodbye to Abby. On the way down the hall, I passed the open door to her empty bedroom.

When I got downstairs, I found Abby sitting on the couch in the living room with Lavinia. She had Lavinia's legs up on her lap while she painted her toenails.

They hadn't noticed me, so I stood at the base of the stairwell, watching them.

Despite the fact that I'd upset her earlier, Abby was all smiles. She spoke softly to Lavinia, who seemed to be in heaven with the pampering. There was no denying that this girl was quite fit. I hadn't expected her to be such a bombshell. She was one of the most beautiful women I'd come across in a long while. Her chestnut brown hair fell to the middle of her back, and her features reminded me of a younger version of the actress Diane Lane. A tall, gorgeous brunette had been exactly my type before I'd met my wife—who ironically had been short with blond hair, resembling Tinkerbell.

I cleared my throat to announce myself. "I thought you were leaving."

"Who told you that?" she asked without making eye contact as she continued to paint Lavinia's toes.

"Kate called."

"I hope she gave you a piece of her mind."

I rubbed my chin scruff. "She wasn't thrilled with the current state of affairs."

Abby looked up at me. "Well, unfortunately, as much as I would love to escape this uncomfortable situation, there are no available flights until tomorrow night." She resumed applying the paint. "Thank goodness Lavinia is cool as hell because the rest of the company here is no bueno."

Lavinia turned to me. "I complimented Abby on her toenail color, and she offered to do mine since I can't bend anymore. Sweet as pie, she is."

"Rhubarb pie, maybe." I smirked.

"You just can't stop yourself, can you?" Abby grinned through her teeth.

She seemed to be taking it all in stride now. She wasn't going to put up with my shit, and I had to say, that was definitely a point in her favor. It was the same quality I'd appreciated about my wife.

"Have you always been such a pill, *Sigmund*?" she asked, my name rolling off her tongue like an expletive.

"Not when you get to know him," Lavinia chimed in. "He's been through a lot, but that doesn't give him an excuse to be an arse."

I glared at her. "Thanks for your assessment, Lavinia."

"Well, it's the truth. I have your number, Sigmund. I know you better than most."

Abby blew on Lavinia's toes before closing the bottle of polish. "I think we're good to go, but stay here for about fifteen minutes to let them dry. Take the time to relax."

"I feel like a queen." Lavinia beamed.

Abby got up from the couch. "I'll walk you out, Sig," she said, striding past me as if she were the owner of this place and not me.

Once outside, we stood in front of my car in the chilly evening air. We faced each other in tense silence for a few moments.

"I just wanted to say goodbye, since I probably won't ever see you again," she told me. "We got off on the wrong foot, but I know your attitude isn't about me. It can't be. I've done nothing wrong." She chuckled. "Well, besides crash into your car. I'll take full responsibility for that."

I nodded. "As you should."

She hesitated. "I also noticed you outside earlier, shortly after I arrived. You seemed deep in thought and upset. That's when I realized the problem is much bigger than me."

I scoffed. "How do you know I wasn't mourning the pristine condition of my car?"

She seemed unamused by my attempt at humor. "I don't know exactly what you're going through, Sig. I can't imagine what it's like to lose a spouse. But I *do* know what it's like to lose someone. And it sucks. It changes a person. I'm just... I'm really sorry for you." Abby's eyes began to water.

"Save your tears. I'm fine."

She wiped her cheek. "You don't seem fine."

I had the immediate urge to get in my car and take off, but leaving her here, with her glistening eyes begging me to say something more, didn't feel right. She'd come all this way. At the very least, I owed her a proper thank you for making the journey. Before I could figure out the appropriate words, she spoke again.

"You were right, actually."

"Right about what?"

"There is a bit more to my motivation." She wrapped her hands around her arms to stave off the cold. "I've been feeling lost for the past few years. I lost my grandmother,

39

then my mother, and then the store, which was their legacy. My boyfriend then decided he didn't want to be in a relationship anymore. After losing almost everyone who meant something to me, I realized my happiness had always been derived from other people." She looked up at the sky. "That was a hard realization. I had no clue how to be satisfied with just myself and no one else. If happiness comes from within, I've yet to figure out how to achieve that." She exhaled. "So I figured the next best thing is to make *others* happy until I can get there on my own. Offering to be a surrogate was my way of making that happen and also giving myself a purpose when I don't seem to have one. The way I saw it, I had two choices. I could sit around and waste another year trying to figure my life out, or actually do something to make a difference in someone else's." She shook her head. "But none of that matters, because it's clear *you* aren't ready for this."

I stared into her eyes. "You're right."

"Why did you agree to it?"

I exhaled. "I suppose, like you, I wanted to make others happy. I didn't want to let Phil and Kate down."

"This is a big decision. Even if they raise the baby, it would be life-changing for you. You don't owe anyone anything, Sig."

"I owe it to my wife to do what she would've wanted."

"She would've wanted you to be happy and at peace more than anything else."

In my heart, I knew Abby was right, and her words gave me surprising relief. She seemed to be on my side and understood where I was coming from—that calmed me a bit. I'd been rushing to get this over with, because I feared if I slowed down, I'd change my mind and disappoint my in-laws. I felt obligated and stuck. But I should've given myself time to figure out whether having a child was something I could handle.

"Thank you for your words. They're very insightful."

She raised her brow. "Are you mocking me?"

I laughed. "Given my behavior today, I can understand why you would assume that. But no. That was probably the most genuine thing I've said all day."

She chuckled. "Well, I never know with you."

I blew out some air, my breath visible in the chill of the night. "You came all this way. You shouldn't have to fly back so soon. At the very least, give yourself a holiday. Stay at the inn. Lavinia fancies you. It'll be good for her, too."

"I never actually changed my ticket," she admitted. "I considered it and checked on alternate flights, but I decided to stay the week and go somewhere else in England. I'm not going to let you rain on my parade, Benedictus." She winked. "But if you don't mind, I'd love to stay here with Lavinia."

"Of course. Enjoy it. She'll welcome the company."

"Thank you."

"And I'll stay out of your hair." Our eyes locked for a moment before I moved toward my car. "Very well, then. I'd better get going."

"Okay." She took a few steps back toward the door. "Have a good night."

"You as well." I nodded. "Good luck to you."

CHAPTER 6

Sig

Track 6: "Royals" by Lorde

Granting myself permission to take a step back gave me a newfound peace about the situation. Remarkably, I slept fairly well. Abby had managed to hit upon something last night, and for the first time, I no longer felt a sense of urgency or pressure.

I woke up the following morning feeling less anxious than I had in more than two weeks. And with that came clarity. It felt a bit wrong leaving Abby high and dry, alone at the inn with Lavinia when I was the one who'd demanded she come to England. She was here because of me, and I'd done a total one-eighty.

I decided to suck up my pride and call the number she'd given me in our initial email correspondence.

She answered, her voice a bit groggy. "Is this the one and only Sigmund Benedictus calling my phone? Emphasis on the dick?"

"Real mature. Now you're showing your age. But I suppose I deserve that." I sighed. "Did I wake you?"

"No. I've been up for a while, poking needles into my Sigmund Benedictus voodoo doll."

I chuckled. "Is he as handsome as I am?"

"He came complete with permanent scowl and dented car."

"You must be running out of needles."

She laughed. "What's up? I didn't think I'd hear from you again, let alone first thing in the morning."

"I've changed my mind."

"About the surrogacy?"

"No. About the car accident. I'd like to get your information to charge you for the damage," I teased.

After a few seconds of silence, she said, "Seriously?"

"I didn't take you to be so gullible."

"Well, I've come to expect anything from Mr. Hot and Cold."

Tell her you're sorry, you dumb arse. "Actually, the real reason I'm calling is to apologize for my behavior yesterday. I should've been more welcoming, regardless of my personal feelings."

"Regardless of your personal dislike for me?"

"That's not what I meant. I was referring to my hesitation about the entire situation. As you surmised, my attitude had nothing to do with you personally, though I know it didn't feel that way."

"I get that you were trying to sabotage the arrangement. Lucky for you, I have thick skin and accept your apology. But do I get a refund for yesterday? I'll take payment in the form of one adorable sheep at my door by six tonight."

She'd managed to make me smile. "Funny enough, another reason I'm calling involves sheep," I said.

"Well, now you've got my attention."

I began to pace. "It occurred to me that given how much you seem to like animals, you might be interested in visiting my cousin's farmhouse while you're in the countryside."

"Would that cousin be Leo, Duke of Westfordshire?"

"I see you've done your research."

"Well, I don't just learn about people through blatant interrogation like you do. I do my research quietly."

"Yes. This would be Leo's house."

"Then no," she said.

"No?" I stopped pacing. "Why?"

"That's too much pressure."

"How so?"

"Would I have to curtsy or something?"

She can't be serious. I bent my head back in laughter. "He's not King Charles, Abby. You don't bow to a duke. Although, I'm upset at myself for not lying and telling you to do it. Would've been worth it just to see Felicity's face."

"That's his wife?"

"Yeah. She's American—from Rhode Island like you, actually. After all these years, she's still not comfortable with her title. And I think someone bowing to her would just about put her over the edge. Whatever you do, don't call her *your grace*. She detests it."

"I wasn't planning on it. And thank you for not setting me up for embarrassment."

"The day is still young." I opened the shade and looked out at the cloudy London sky. "Anyway, if you're not interested, that's fine. I just figured—"

"Not interested in sheep? Or getting to play *Downton*

Abbey for a day? Are you kidding? I would love to visit the farm. Lavinia is a sweetheart, but she doesn't have the energy to get out and do things with me. I'd like to take her to the pub for dinner tonight, though. Already promised that. Will we be home by then?"

"Yes. Leo's house is not too far from the inn. Just on the other side of Westfordshire."

"Great. Okay. Then I would love to take you up on your offer."

Felicity took to Abby immediately, as I'd imagined she would. Both being from Rhode Island, they seemed to have a lot in common.

My cousin's wife had whisked Abby away to show her around the grounds while I hung out with Leo inside. It was the only opportunity I'd have to speak to him in private about the latest happenings.

He worked to open a bottle of Cabernet Franc. "She seems like a nice girl."

"Not sure how you can know that after meeting her for ten minutes."

He popped the cork. "You're telling me you don't like her?"

I swallowed. "The verdict is still out."

He poured a glass. "You're doing your best to sabotage the situation, I take it? Her looks are probably freaking you out even more."

"What do you mean by that?" I knew damn well what he was referring to.

"Come on, Sigmund. She's *exactly* your type. Or at least what your type used to be. Must make an already uncomfortable situation even *more* uncomfortable for you, eh?"

There was no denying how beautiful Abby was, so I didn't even try. "Her above-average looks are inconsequential, Leo. Given the nature of the situation, she's totally off limits."

"I'm certain you brought her here to meet us today to distract from how awkward you've been toward her."

"Awkward? No. Rude and standoffish? Yes. It's a miracle she's still here."

"True to form, I see." He rolled his eyes. "What's acting like a knob going to achieve?"

"Well, for one, it caused her to almost leave. Which, of course, was what I'd wanted. I don't know what the hell we're doing at the moment, though. Last night, I admitted to her that I don't feel ready to move forward with the surrogacy. Then I felt bad for wasting her time, so I tried to make up for it by bringing her here since she loves animals."

"So, this visit is one big distraction?" He handed me a glass of wine.

"Pretty much, yes." I took a sip.

"Are you really not ready, or are you just scared?"

I stared out the French doors, where I could see Abby in the distance standing next to Leo's daughter, Eloise, and petting one of the animals. Her joyous smile warmed even my cold heart. "Her being here just made it all too real."

"I don't think you'll ever feel completely ready, cousin. You made your decision to go ahead with it. It just started to feel scary because things are actually moving. If Phil and Kate believe Abby is the right person for this, you might not want to let your fear stand in the way. You could lose her and end up with someone you dislike even more."

I looked out again to find Abby lifting Eloise into the air.

The problem was, I *didn't* dislike Abby at all. I wished I did. It would've made it a lot easier to send her home.

CHAPTER 7

Abby

Track 7: "3 Sum" by Mark Dohner

You've heard the term *died and gone to heaven*? Well, if I died today, and I could choose my heaven, I'm pretty sure Brighton House would be it. This huge farm was like a dream, from the wide-open fields to the plethora of horses, sheep, and pigs. And Felicity was an unexpected slice of home—of normalcy—in this otherwise foreign place. She became an instant friend.

"I can't thank you enough for showing me around today," I said as we reentered the house. Her daughter, Eloise, ran ahead of us to greet her dad.

"The pleasure was all mine," Felicity said. "I can't believe how much we have in common. It's like looking at myself in the mirror—you know, if I were suddenly tall and gorgeous."

"Oh, you're too nice." I felt myself blushing. "And are you kidding? You're stunning."

Felicity had wild red hair and freckles. She was absolutely beautiful inside and out, and I wished I had more time here to get to know her.

She grinned. "I mean, two girls from Rhode Island seaside towns together in the English countryside? Pretty cool, if you ask me."

"Did you ever spend time in Massasoit?" I asked.

"My foster mother used to take me to the beach there occasionally. It's not too far from Narragansett, where I grew up."

"Do you remember a store called Little Rhody? Purple on the outside?"

"That's the souvenir shop by the beach? The one that served ice cream?"

I nodded. "That's my family's business."

"No way."

"Well, it was. It closed when the economy got bad. I'm in the process of trying to reopen it."

"Ah, I see."

When we entered the kitchen, Sig and Leo were standing there talking. "Were your ears ringing, Sigmund?" I teased.

"Why is that?"

"I *might* have been talking about you to Abby," Felicity said.

"And Abby's still here? You must've not told her the full truth." Sig sniffed the air. "What's that stench?"

It hadn't registered until he mentioned it, but boy did I smell it now. I lifted my foot to examine the bottom of my shoe. "Shit!" I looked up at him. "*Literally.* I must've stepped in manure outside."

"It happens! Stay put," Felicity said, running off. "I'll get you something."

Eloise pointed at my shoe. "Poop!" She ran after her mother.

I shrugged, turning to Sig and Leo. "Way to make a debut, huh?"

"You seem to attract small disasters, Abby Knickerbocker." Sig turned to Leo. "I never told you about the minor car accident."

I chuckled. "And here I was thinking the shittiest thing about this trip was your attitude, Sig. Apparently I found something shittier."

Leo snorted. "I like her."

"Thank you, your majesty." I bowed before winking over at Sig. "Kidding!" I told Leo. "I know I'm not supposed to do that. This one tried to set me up and tell me I was, though."

"I wasn't setting you up. I was merely *wishing* I'd done it." Sig smiled over at me. That was rare. But he had a beautiful smile.

Felicity returned wearing rubber gloves and holding a spray bottle and some cloths. This was so embarrassing. We ended up having to take my shoe over to a bathroom sink since the cloths weren't cutting it.

After I was as clean as could be expected under the circumstances, she and I returned to find the guys standing on the back patio off the kitchen. Leo held Eloise as they talked. We joined them outside.

"Can you stay for dinner?" Leo asked.

"Actually, we need to head back to take Lavinia to the pub tonight," I said.

"Aw, that's sweet." Felicity grinned. "Isn't she the best?"

"I love her," I admitted.

"She really helped me out one summer years back when I was visiting and things got complicated with Leo," Felicity said. "She was my lifesaver. So was Sig." She turned to him. "That's when he and I became close."

"Stop lying. You've *always* loved me, Ginger. From the very beginning." Sig winked.

She smacked him on the shoulder. "Actually, I pretty much *hated* you the first summer I met you."

"So there's hope for me after all?" I chided.

Sig glared at me, and I loved it. What was wrong with me that I found him so damn attractive despite everything? It was wildly inappropriate. Not to mention, I had no clue where things stood with the surrogacy; the only thing I knew for sure was that having a crush on Sig would get me a ticket to nowhere.

After we said goodbye to Leo and Felicity, Sig and I hopped in his car and went back toward the inn. As always, the scenery through the countryside was mesmerizing, especially with the sun setting.

"Thank you again for bringing me out here today. Felicity is basically my spirit animal."

"You two seemed to have a lot in common."

"We do. It's a little scary." I turned to him. "And oh my goodness, the Shetland pony Leo bought in Rhode Island all those years ago? The fact that they still have him? My heart nearly melted."

"Ludicrous. They certainly gave him the appropriate name."

"Someday I'm going to tell the love of my life that I've always wanted an extravagant animal, just to see if he buys it for me." I laughed.

"Or he could think you're crazy and ignore the request."

"Worth a shot." I shrugged.

"What would you choose?" he asked.

"For my animal?"

"Yeah."

"I'd have to think about it."

"It wouldn't be a sheep, by chance?" He arched a brow.

"No. It would have to be something crazier. Like an ostrich or something." I chuckled. "Speaking of crazy, I learned a lot about you from Felicity today. Certainly more than I've learned from you."

"Anything interesting?"

I squinted. "Two Marias? Really?"

He rolled his eyes. "I see she didn't hold back."

"I'm just teasing. But yeah, she told me all the juicy stuff from back in the day."

Felicity had told me the first summer she met Sig, he'd been dating two women at the same time—both named Maria. The women apparently knew about each other and had threesomes with him.

"I liked to party in my younger years. So sue me."

I held my hands up. "No judgment here."

"Someone had to have fun on that trip. Leo spent the last part of it miserable, whipped, and fawning over a woman he thought he could never have."

"Do you still have threesomes?" I asked, feeling brazen.

"The only thing worse than one woman I'm not all that interested in would be two. So no."

"I've never had a threesome," I offered.

"Thanks for sharing."

"I'd be too jealous," I admitted. "I'd never be able to enjoy myself."

He glanced over at me. "There's an art to it."

"In what way?"

"Making both women feel equally desired. It's hard work, but effective if you know what you're doing. Nothing I have the energy for anymore, though." He sighed. "What else did Ginger recklessly divulge about me?"

"Nothing bad. She said you're an amazing cook and echoed what she said on the patio about you being there for her when she was going through tough times with Leo." I paused, recalling what Felicity had told me about her tumultuous romance with Leo before they finally sorted things out. "They have quite the story, those two."

He chuckled. "More drama than a Korean soap opera."

My eyes widened. "You watch K-dramas?"

His expression softened. "Britney used to like them."

"Ah." My heart clenched. "What do you watch?"

"I don't watch the telly much."

"What do you do for fun?"

"I work long days during the week. By the time I get home, shower, and cook dinner, it's fairly late. I collapse into bed and do it all over again the next day."

"That doesn't count as fun. What about on weekends?"

"Depends where I am. Some weekends, I go to Westfordshire and hibernate at the inn. Others I stay in London."

"If you have a date, you stay in London?"

He shook his head. "I don't really date."

"But you hook up with women."

"Occasionally..."

"You never let them sleep at your apartment, though."

"Felicity told you that, I presume."

"Yeah."

"Ginger has a big mouth."

I kept prying. "Are you not open to more than one-night stands at this point?"

"Are you not open to minding your business?" He grimaced. "I haven't met a single person worth having more with."

"Are you *looking* for more, though?"

"I'm absolutely not."

"So you're gonna live the rest of your life alone? You're only thirty-seven."

"I suppose Felicity divulged my age, too."

"You're older than I thought. You look much younger. I'd guessed about thirty-two."

"Must be all the gin keeping me youthful."

"That's gotta be it." I chuckled.

Sig turned the tables. "I thought you were the one who preached about finding happiness from *within*. Why do I need someone to be happy?"

"Finding happiness from within doesn't mean you shouldn't strive for human connections. You need to be happy inside, but sometimes another person can enhance that. I feel like you don't have either of those things."

"Well, thank you for your miserable take on me. Considering you've known me all of two days, it will be taken with a grain of salt."

When the car in front of us stopped abruptly, Sig slammed on the brakes and reached his arm out in front of me, as if to keep me from plunging forward. The palm of his big, masculine hand pressed against my ribcage, causing what felt like a bolt of electricity to shoot through me.

My God, I'm hard up. My voice shook. "What was that?"

"Some people can't drive." He flashed me a mischievous grin. "*You* of all people should know that."

I sighed, laying my head back on the seat. Putting his arm out to protect me had been completely instinctual. He was rough around the edges, but there was clearly a caring and protective side in there.

I straightened in my seat. "Anyway, I'm done interrogating you about your personal life."

"Fantastic."

We drove in silence for a couple of minutes before I turned to him. "You're welcome to ask me anything you want. You know, if this whole trip is still an interview of some sort. I don't know where things stand on that."

"I haven't made a decision one way or the other."

"Did something change to make you consider moving forward again? You said you weren't ready just yesterday..."

"You said you were leaving, and yet…you're still here."

Crossing my arms, I sank back into the seat. "I'm probably insane for that."

"I agree."

I shook my head. "I love how you deflect whenever you're asked something serious."

He sighed. "I'm still unsure about things. I may never *feel* truly ready. What I need to decide is whether I want to go through with it despite that."

"I hear you…" I looked out the window at some cattle grazing in the distance. "Well, no pressure from me. I just wanted some clue as to what we're doing. The offer will stand, even if it's months from now."

He arched his brow. "That's not really true, though, is it?"

"What do you mean?"

"You're at a point right now where you can carry the baby, but if even one thing changes, that won't be the case."

"Like what would change?"

"If you met someone and he didn't like the idea—something like that."

"Well, he'd have to accept it, if it was what I wanted."

"I wouldn't easily accept my woman carrying someone else's child."

"Even if it was for a good cause?"

He scratched his chin. "No, probably not."

"Well, my track record is such that I don't have to worry about meeting Mr. Right anytime soon." *Instead, I'll just sit here crushing on Mr. Not A Chance in Hell.*

CHAPTER 8

Abby

Track 8: "When Will I See You Again" by Three Degrees

After driving back from Brighton House, we pulled up to the inn and found Lavinia waiting outside for us. She wore a purple hat adorned with a flower and a long, crushed-velvet black coat.

"Oh my God. Lavinia's so cute. Does she always get all dressed up and wait outside like that?"

"Patience is not her strong point." Sig chuckled.

I rolled down my window, and she stuck her head in. "Hello, loves. I figured I'd get some fresh air while I waited for you to come back."

"Just admit you have ants in your pants," he teased.

"You're coming with us, Sigmund, yes?" she asked.

He shook his head. "I wasn't planning on it. I need to get back to London."

I was bummed to hear that.

Lavinia stuck her head farther into the vehicle. "You must come. You know I can never finish my fish and chips.

It doesn't heat up the same way at home and makes the whole house smell like fish. I need you around to clean my plate."

"You want me to join you for dinner because I'm your human waste disposal..."

"Come on," I urged. "You need to eat anyway, right?"

Sig exhaled. "Fine."

It was a nice night, so Sig parked, and the three of us walked down to the pub—the only restaurant within walking distance of Lavinia's house. Despite her frail appearance, Lavinia did pretty well walking the few blocks there, albeit at a slow pace.

McPhee's Pub, like many of the buildings in Westfordshire, had a stone exterior. It was an old building, and the inside featured a dark ambience, with cherry-wood booths and small jarred candles set out on the tables. It had a very homey feel. There were lots of framed photos on the walls and various trinkets hung everywhere. It seemed like an extension of the inn.

A waitress came by and placed menus in front of us. "What do you fancy to drink?"

"I'll have a water," I told her.

"You said you're limiting alcohol." He raised his eyebrow. "Why?"

"Because I don't want to give you yet another reason to veto me."

"That's stupid." He turned to the waitress. "Bring us each a pint of lager, please."

Thank goodness. I could really use it tonight.

After she came back with our beers, I took a long, much-needed sip.

"They make their own beer. How do you like it?" Sig asked.

"It's so good that you're seeming nicer by the second." I winked.

"Drink up, then." He grinned.

I asked Lavinia to suggest something on the menu, and she insisted I get the fish and chips. Sig agreed, and the three of us all got the same thing.

As the waitress set the plate in front of me, I felt my eyes go wide. "This piece of fish is bigger than my forearm."

"That's why Sigmund always finishes my scraps." Lavinia laughed.

"Well, Sig, you might have to finish me off, too."

His eyes widened.

Oh goodness. I didn't mean it to come out that way. "I mean finish my plate." My face must have turned fifty shades of red.

He cleared his throat. "It's what I'm here for, apparently."

Things turned quiet for a bit as we dug into our food and I recovered from my embarrassment.

Lavinia turned to me with her mouth full. "Did you have a good time today at the Covington estate?"

I wiped my lips. "It was *so* amazing, Lavinia. An animal lover's dream. Felicity and I really hit it off."

"So glad you loved my girl," she said. "Felicity is darling. And so are you."

Lavinia and I did most of the chatting during dinner while Mr. Grumpypants stayed quiet. But at one point, I looked over at Sig to find his eyes fixed on me. He quickly looked down at his plate, but it was too late. I'd seen him staring. I didn't know what to make of it. Usually I could sense whether or not someone liked me—not in a romantic sense, but in general. Not with him, though. So I wondered why he was observing me so intensely. The beer had given me just the right amount of buzz to not care at the moment, however.

After Sig *finished off* all of our plates, the three of us walked home. The stroll back was even nicer than the first one, as there was something so calming about walking in the dark. I was full, though. I think I was practically waddling.

When we arrived at The Bainbridge, Lavinia went inside while I lingered and walked Sig over to his car. "Thank you for today."

"I'm glad you enjoyed it," he said.

"Will I see you again?" I dared to ask.

He looked out toward the street. "Work is a little busy this week. But I'll try to return to Westfordshire at some point."

Well, if that wasn't noncommittal, I didn't know what was. "Okay."

He was about to enter his car when I stopped him. "Sig…"

He looked over at me. "Yeah?"

"Whatever you decide, it's okay. I won't take offense. And I won't consider this a wasted trip either way. Even just these two days have been an amazing experience. I didn't realize how much I needed a change of pace. And I have you to thank for it."

"I'm glad." He nodded once and got into his car, offering one last wave goodbye before he started the engine.

I walked backwards toward the entrance to the inn as I watched him drive away. *Was that goodbye forever?*

CHAPTER 9

Abby

Track 9: "Sweet Dreams (Are Made of This)" by The Eurythmics

Sig never returned to Westfordshire after that night at the pub, and I didn't see him again before I returned home to the US.

On my last night there, he'd called to apologize for not having come back out to the countryside. He'd given work as his excuse and thanked me for making the trip to the UK. But he hadn't given me any clue what he was thinking about the surrogacy.

I'd relayed all of this to Phil and Kate, of course, who seemed just as perplexed as I was about where things stood.

At the very least, I'd made a lifelong friend in Lavinia from the trip. Actually, *two* friends, since Felicity and I had also exchanged information. She and Lavinia had given me open invitations to come back and visit sometime in the future. And I planned to do so someday. I had to return to that beautiful place.

I'd been back home in Rhode Island for two weeks when I received a phone call from Kate one morning.

"Hey, Abby. How are you?"

"I'm good."

"Good. Good." She took a deep breath. "So...Phil and I spoke to Sig last night. He called us."

My heart raced at just the mention of his name.

"He indicated that he'd like to move ahead with the surrogacy." She paused. "And he'd like you to be the surrogate."

That knocked the wind out of me. "Really?"

"Yes."

"Well, I'm shocked, to say the least. Especially with the way the visit went."

"Apparently, he's been quiet because he needed time alone to reflect on the situation. We were just as surprised as you that he came to this decision, given his prior behavior." She paused. "Are you still interested in being our surrogate?"

I swallowed. "Yes. I am."

"Well, we're very grateful for that. But there's something else we need to discuss."

Pacing, I licked my lips. "Okay..."

"There's a condition he put forth, something I wasn't expecting. This might change things for you."

Condition? I stilled. "What is it?"

"He'd like everything to be done over there, in England. And he'd like you to move there if you become pregnant—only until the baby comes, of course."

Wow. Okay. Moving to the UK wasn't something I'd considered. I'd imagined being near my dad throughout this process. "Did he say why he wants me to move there?"

"He wants to be there for the appointments. I think he needs to have some control over the situation. He also mentioned a position for you at the property management company he runs, so your time isn't wasted while you're there. He knows you're in between jobs right now and thought you might appreciate the income."

He wants to offer me a job? "Do you think moving to the UK is the best step here?" I asked.

"Well, how do *you* feel about it? That's what matters."

I stared out my window. "I'd have to leave Dad alone for nine months, which isn't something I was expecting."

"I know. That's why you'll need to think about it."

"But at the same time, having regular work would be great. And logistically, I suppose it makes sense for me to be there so Sig could be involved in the appointments. It hadn't occurred to me that he'd want to be."

"Then there's the implantation," Kate pointed out. "It makes sense for you to go to the UK for that as well. He's going to need to give a sample. And of course, if the first one doesn't take, we would need to try again, if that's something you agree to. That means it could be a bit longer than nine months. So something to consider. We're open to whatever you want. Traveling back and forth for the implantations is an option, too. And of course we'll cover all costs."

I took a moment to breathe. "I guess there's a lot we still have to work out, huh?"

"Take some time to think about what you're willing to do, Abby, before making a final decision. Again, there's no pressure. We appreciate that you're even considering this."

"Okay, I'll think about everything and get back to you soon, Kate."

"Great." She sighed. "One more thing."

My heart couldn't take much more. "Okay…"

"Sig asked that you call him."

I decided it didn't feel right to make a final decision without at least speaking to Sigmund first, so I was glad he'd encouraged that.

And a couple of days later, I was ready to make that call. It had taken me a while to mentally prepare myself. I'd also wanted to discuss the situation with my father first.

It was around 8 PM UK time when I called, on a weeknight, so I figured Sig would be home. I felt jittery as I waited for him to answer.

"Hello?" His deep voice vibrated through me.

"Hi." I could hardly get the words out. "It's Abby."

"I know."

"You have my number programmed into your phone?"

"I do."

"You must have expected me to call, then."

"I did."

"I see you're just as talkative as always."

"And you're just as smart-mouthed."

Falling back into our argumentative rapport brought me some comfort. "What made you decide to move forward?" I asked. "You pretty much ghosted me before I left England. I put my money on never seeing you again."

"Despite being busy with work, as I previously explained, I was giving you space to enjoy the last of your trip."

"But the purpose of my trip was for you to get to know me."

"You can't really know someone in a week anyway."

"So you're still unsure about me? You didn't answer my question. What made you say yes to this?"

"I'd made the decision to go through with this before I met you, as you know. I've concluded that it doesn't matter whether I'm ready, because ultimately, I'm not doing this for me. I'm doing it for Britney and her parents. I won't stand in the way." He paused. "And I agree with Phil and Kate's choice of surrogate."

"I passed your test, then?"

"I still think you're a bit bonkers. But you're genuine. I'll give you that. And you're right... I doubt I'd ever find anyone better."

I waited for the punch line, but it never came. Warmth flowed through my body. "That's very kind. I sort of thought you didn't trust me."

"Well, I wouldn't let you drive me anywhere."

I laughed. "I have to say, though, I was surprised by the requirement that I move."

"Is that not something you're open to?"

"I didn't say that. I just wasn't expecting it."

"It makes the most sense, don't you think?"

"Yeah, I suppose it does. I talked to my dad. He's encouraging me to do it, especially since you've offered me a job, which is most appreciated."

"You need your father's permission?"

"Not at all. But I'm his only family here. My sister lives on the West Coast. I'd be leaving him alone for more than nine months, so I wanted him to be okay with it. That matters to me."

"Well, good, then."

"Do you have any siblings?" I asked.

"No. I'm an only child."

"I see." I cleared my throat. "Anyway, the fact that you've offered me a position at your company is very gracious."

"The job won't be brain surgery. But we're in need of someone who can help on the customer-service end of things. We manage a lot of properties where things are constantly going wrong. You'd be drafting responses, taking calls, and keeping track of any open-ended disputes with clients and contractors until they're resolved. It requires someone who can write and communicate well. I figured as an English major you must be able to write, yes?"

"Yes. That sounds like something I can handle." I lay down on my bed and stared at the ceiling, having a bit of an out-of-body experience. "Where would I be living?"

"I figured you'd want to stay with Lavinia."

"Wouldn't that be too far from your office in London?"

"About an hour-and-a-half commute. But you'd only have to report to the office once or twice a week to show face. I could send a car for you on those days. You can work from home the rest of the time. Once you're properly trained, it's an easy job to do remotely because it's all phone calls and emails."

"That sounds like a dream, honestly—aside from you being my boss."

"You won't be working directly under me and probably won't see me much. You'll report to our customer relations manager. Most of the tasks you'll be taking on belong to him currently. But he's going to be helping us with some new acquisitions, expanding his role a bit, thus the need for support on the customer-service side."

"Ah, okay. Good to know. Probably better that I won't be reporting to you." I hesitated a moment. "Will we...tell people what's going on? Why I'm really in the UK?"

"No, I don't think that's necessary. It's none of anyone's business."

"Okay. So they'll just think I'm a single mom or something?"

"I haven't gotten that far, Abby."

"Okay."

"Any other questions?" he asked.

"When does this all start?"

"Whenever you're ready."

Am I ready for this? I felt a mix of fear and excitement—but more excitement. "Sig?"

"What?"

"Are *you* ready?"

"I told you, I'll never feel fully ready."

"Yeah, but something made you bite the bullet..."

After a brief pause, he said, "I found a gray hair."

I smiled. "Is that the truth?"

"It helped me realize I don't have forever to make this happen for them. They're getting older, and frankly, so am I. Sometimes you have to wager your best guess on the decisions you make, even if it doesn't feel a hundred-percent comfortable."

"Fair enough." *Wow. This is really happening.* "When should I plan to come out there?"

"There's no immediate rush. You can let me know when to book your ticket."

"Okay. Will do." I looked out my window. "I'll see you soon, I guess."

"Yeah." He sighed. "I'll let you go."

"Goodnight."

"Sweet dreams," he said before hanging up.

"Sweet dreams." That gave me butterflies.

Which was unsettling.

I was about to embark on the craziest journey of my life. But the butterflies were because I never thought I'd see *him* again. And now I would.

CHAPTER 10

Sig

Track 10: "Too Late to Turn Back Now" by Cornelius Brothers and Sister Rose

The past month had been a whirlwind from the moment I decided to move forward with the surrogacy. Balancing the usual stress of work with anxiety over this situation had been a challenge.

I'd given a sperm sample, which was then used to create embryos with Britney's eggs. Abby had started taking medications to prepare for the transfer while she was still in the US. She'd arrived here a few days ago, and today we'd just completed the transfer of a single embryo. We'd have to wait two weeks before a blood test could determine whether that had resulted in a pregnancy.

There was something surreal about walking out of the doctor's office in London with Abby after the procedure. I'd opted to sit in the waiting room while she was in there, and it had seemed to happen very quickly.

"How are you doing?" I asked.

"Fine," she assured me. "I don't feel any different or anything."

"Was it painful?"

"Not at all. Just a little bit of pressure. Nothing I couldn't handle."

"Good." I nodded, feeling a knot in my stomach. "It seemed quick."

"Yeah. You'd think something so monumental would involve more than opening your legs for a matter of minutes." She smiled hesitantly. "Though I suppose that's how the natural way works, too."

I opted not to touch that one. "What do you need to do now?" I asked.

"I'm supposed to take it easy today, but the doctor said I don't have to be on bed rest. Just no running marathons or anything too crazy."

"Let's get you back to the inn, then. I can make supper."

She searched my eyes as we faced each other in the car park. "You're stressed."

"What are you talking about?"

"Lavinia told me you always cook when you're stressed."

"In this case, I'm cooking because *you* should rest. Not because I'm stressed."

"We could get takeout."

"Not necessary. I like to cook," I said as I unlocked the car.

"Okay. Whatever you need." She got into the passenger side. "I'm glad we're doing this at the end of the week. That way I can relax this weekend and be ready for work on Monday. What time should I be ready?"

"I'll send a car for you around seven AM," I told her as I pulled into traffic. "I've already alerted our customer relations manager that you'll be there for training. You should plan to come into the office every day for the first couple of weeks."

"I won't see you there?"

"Likely not." I'd make sure of it, since seeing her at the office would be a distraction I didn't need.

"Okay, well...I can't wait to get started."

After we got to the inn, I immediately left for the food shop. The breather felt good—an opportunity to live in denial for a bit. It was too late to turn back now, but I hadn't fully accepted that yet. I still wanted to pretend none of this was happening. Abby was handling everything like a champion; the problem, as usual, was me.

When I returned with the groceries, Abby and Lavinia were watching a film.

"Exactly how many people are eating here tonight?" Abby asked when she saw the bags I'd brought in.

"I'm making some things and freezing them for you since I won't be here the next few days."

"You didn't have to do that," she said. "But thank you."

I got to work in the kitchen, hoping they'd give me space. I wanted to get lost in the process. But that was difficult when Abby approached and leaned over to watch every move I made.

"Do you always slice that fast? You're gonna take one of your fingers off, Sig."

"Hopefully not the middle one. I need that quite a lot." I slid the onion pieces aside and began dicing garlic, as if in a race against time. "Haven't you heard the rule about never disturbing the chef?"

"I'd like to help, if you'll let me."

"You're supposed to be resting."

"She just said I needed to take it easy. She didn't say I couldn't stand and chop vegetables." She moved in closer. "Seriously, what can I do?"

Her flowery scent caused my body to react. I couldn't even look at her, because I knew I'd soften if I caught a glimpse of her beautiful face or looked into her always-curious eyes.

"I appreciate the offer, Abby, but I prefer to cook alone, if you don't mind." *Or rather, your nearness is making me uneasy.*

"Sure. No problem," she muttered, disappointment in her voice.

She didn't deserve my cold demeanor. Abby was clearly trying to connect with me, and I'd put a block up. I wouldn't be able to manage the situation this way for the next nine months, but this was what I needed for tonight.

I prepared three different trays of dinner: a vegetable lasagna, a chicken and mushroom casserole, and a shrimp, pesto, and pasta bake. I popped the shrimp dish in the oven for tonight and placed the other two meals in the freezer.

Once dinner was baking, I went into the living room, where Abby was showing Lavinia something on the telly.

Lavinia patted the spot next to her. "Sigmund, come sit. Abby is showing me her family's shop."

I stepped farther into the living room.

Abby paused the telly and looked up from where she sat with her legs crossed. "A local news station did a feature on our store a few years back, when my mother was still alive. It's posted on YouTube. I pulled it up to show her."

"Ah." I sat down.

She pressed play again. A brown-haired woman who looked an awful lot like an older version of Abby was being interviewed. The reporter followed her around a shop that seemed to be exploding with T-shirts and knickknacks.

I looked over at Abby. She was quiet, her eyes glued to the screen. She looked like she was about to cry. I realized that she, like me, truly understood loss. That might have been why she had so much patience with me. Like Britney, Abby's mother had been too young to die.

"When you reopen the shop someday, I have first dibs on the giant lobster hat," I announced.

She turned to me and smiled. "You got it." Her eyes lingered on mine. She was trying to read me, probably wondering why I'd decided to joke around after having been a miserable prick most of the day.

But I couldn't handle it, the intensity of her eyes. The only thing worse, perhaps, was when she'd caught *me* staring at her that night at the pub. For many reasons, I quite liked looking at her. Which was unsettling. It wasn't just because she was pretty. That was the obvious reason. But I also liked to *listen* to her. Her voice was pleasant. And when in conversation, she spoke with conviction, always connected to what the other person was saying. I liked to observe that, even if it was my dirty little secret. It had to be done stealthily. I'd vowed never to let her catch me doing it again.

I cleared my throat. "Well, the timer is set for dinner. It should go off in about thirty minutes. I'm going to head back to London."

The light in Abby's eyes dimmed. "You're not staying to eat with us?"

"No," I said as I grabbed my coat. "You two enjoy it."

CHAPTER 11

Sig

Track 11: "Memories" by Maroon 5

That night, desperate to drown out the day, I decided to arrange a meet-up with a woman I'd met some time ago on a dating app. I'd hooked up with Alaina once, and I wasn't normally one for encores, but quick and easy was what I needed tonight—something to ensure that I felt nothing, least of all the emotion of what had taken place today.

When Alaina showed up at my flat, she looked ready to pounce, dressed in a tight, red getup and thigh-high leather boots. "I'm surprised you called," she said as she entered. "I didn't think I'd hear from you again. What's been going on?"

"I'm not in the mood to talk, if that's okay."

Her eyes lit up. "Fine with me." She tossed her purse. "The last time we *didn't* talk was one of the most memorable nights of my life, so..."

I pulled her toward me, kissing her hard and willing myself to escape into this forced connection. *This* was it, the life I was used to. Empty. Meaningless. Worry free. No fears for the future. Just...numbness. Moving my lips over hers with greater force, I somehow felt worse with each second that passed. Feeling nothing was the goal, yet this had the opposite effect, causing me to feel negative emotions like disgust. I'd wanted this woman here to take my mind off of today, yet there was no part of me that actually wanted *her*.

My phone chimed. "One moment..." I pulled away from the disaster I'd started, rubbing my bottom lip before reaching for my phone.

It was a text from Abby.

Abby: The shrimp dish was really good. Thanks for making it. I do wish you'd stayed for dinner, but I understand why you didn't. Today must have been a lot for you. It was a lot for me. More than I imagined it would be. I hadn't watched that video of my mother since before she died. This was the first time I'd seen her or heard her voice. It was heartbreaking and beautiful all at once. But I needed my mom today. We try to hide from memories because it hurts. But sometimes what we really need is to remember.

I let her words soak in. She was right. What I needed to fix my problem was not escape but to allow in everything I'd been trying to push away. I'd been blocking thoughts of Britney, because going there for even a second made me tremendously sad—for all she had missed out on today, for all she'd be missing out on, in general. But the effort of blocking her from my mind was probably more exhausting than just letting everything in.

"What's wrong?" Alaina asked.

"Huh?" I felt dazed, still staring down at Abby's text.

"Is everything okay? You look like someone died."

Someone did die. Just not tonight. "Yeah, uh..." I finally looked up from my phone. "I'm sorry. I...I can't do this tonight."

"What?" Her face reddened. "Why did you call me, then?"

"I thought I needed it, but..." I shook my head. "It wasn't what I need."

"Well, *I* needed it," she spat. "Thanks for wasting my time."

"I'm sorry," I muttered, turning away. It was an arsehole move. She had every right to be pissed at me. I just didn't have the mental capacity to care at the moment.

Alaina grabbed her coat and stormed out the door, leaving a trail of muttered expletives in her wake. I deserved each and every one of them.

I stared at the door for a full minute before I texted Abby back.

> **Sig:** I'm happy you enjoyed the meal. You're right. Today was a lot, and I have a tendency to run from emotions. The stronger they are, the faster I go. I try not to feel anything most days. It's a practice I've almost perfected. But today, I failed. It became unbearable. I owe you an apology—again. It wasn't you. Please know that. You were the best part of today.

My chest felt raw. It felt odd to be so...honest. I probably shouldn't have admitted that last part, but it was true. Abby's calm demeanor had helped balance the panic I'd felt from the moment she went in for the procedure. As difficult as this situation was, she made it better.

The three dots moved around as she responded.

Abby: We'll get through this. One day at a time. Have a good night, and it's okay. I understand why you left.

I sensed she really did. That's why she'd texted me. It had been just what I needed to hear. My finger lingered over the keypad. Part of me yearned to continue the conversation, to release some of these trapped emotions. With her, I thought I could do it. But instead, I put my phone away.

That night, before I went to bed, I took my phone out again—not to text Abby back, but to do something for the first time in the five years since Britney died. I watched a video of her and me jaunting around London before she'd gotten too sick. It wasn't as painful as I'd thought it might be. I even managed to smile as it brought many more positive feelings than negative ones.

Maybe I could watch it again sometime.

CHAPTER 12

Sig

Track 12: "Fast Car" by Tracy Chapman

The following Monday, Abby had completed her first day of training at Covington Properties. Not wanting to micromanage, I'd left it to my customer relations manager, Art Schumacher, to show her the ropes. I did, however, offer to drive her from London back to Westfordshire that night rather than call her a car so I could address any questions she had at the end of the day.

I hadn't seen her at all, since my office was on another floor, but I'd asked her to meet me outside at 6 PM, and I pulled my car around to the front of the building to wait. It was a mild May evening, dry without a raindrop in sight.

When I spotted her walking toward me, my heart skipped a beat. Abby looked different than I'd ever seen her before. She wore a form-fitting, pinstriped dress with an edgy diagonal neckline. While businesslike, it was a more provocative wardrobe choice than I might've imagined for her first day on the job. Simply put, she looked smoking hot, and I knew a few of the wankers who worked for us must have had a field day ogling her and drooling. I supposed I was one of them right now.

"Hey." She smiled as she got in and fastened her seatbelt. "Thank you for offering to drive me back."

Clearing my throat, I started the car and took off down the road. "How was your first day?"

"There's a ton to learn, particularly with navigating the database, but I'll be able to handle the responsibilities no problem once I get the hang of the technical side of things. Like you explained, it's mostly writing responses and handling phone calls, both of which I'm very good at."

"Was Art helpful in explaining things?"

"He actually had to leave the office unexpectedly, so I didn't get to work with him much."

I narrowed my eyes. "What?"

"Yeah. Some kind of family issue. I thought you knew."

"No, I didn't." I glanced over at her. "Who the hell was training you, then?"

"Alistair Jones."

I scowled. *Great. Just fucking great.* Alistair Jones was a known philanderer who loved women, and I was certain he'd try to dig his claws into Abby. Sadly, he reminded me of myself a decade ago, only worse. "He's not qualified to train you properly."

"He works under Art, doesn't he? He seemed to know what he was doing."

"He's *not* qualified." I gritted my teeth. "I'll work with you tomorrow if Art isn't back."

"Okay," she muttered, likely confused by my reaction.

Ask her how she's doing, for fuck's sake. She could be pregnant. I had a tendency to forget that, or maybe it was more that I tried to forget. "How are you feeling?"

"Fine," she said. "No different than normal."

Trying to calm myself, I took a deep breath and nodded. "Good."

"Those two dinners you left in the freezer were really good. We had each of them over the weekend."

"I'm glad."

I'd just pulled onto the motorway when she turned to me. "So...I was thinking..."

"That's dangerous," I taunted.

She rolled her eyes. "I'd like to have a car while I'm here, Sig. It would make it easier for me to go to the market to buy stuff for Lavinia and me. Calling a ride every time I have to leave the house isn't practical. I'm not asking you to pay for it. I just wanted you to know I don't want to have to depend on anyone for rides, so I plan to get something of my own."

"Don't be ridiculous. You can't afford to buy a car when you're only here temporarily."

"Sure, I—"

"I have a car for you."

She blinked. "Really?"

"It's parked at Leo's. It's not being used currently."

"Wow. Okay. That's awesome."

"I purchased it as a gift for Felicity, actually."

"That's quite an expensive gift."

"Well, she's been a good friend. And it's sort of an inside joke. I couldn't pass it up when I found it." I checked the rearview mirror as I switched lanes. "Anyway, I'm cer-

PENELOPE WARD

tain she'll have no problem with you using it while you're here. It's only been collecting dust in their garage. It would actually be good to have it driven once in a while."

Her face brightened. "That would be great."

"Shall we head over there now and pick it up?"

"Do you think they'll mind if we pop over unannounced?"

"Wouldn't be the first time I dropped in on them, but I should probably call. If they're not there, their house manager, Nathan, can let us in. He's an old chum of mine."

"What does the house manager do?" she asked.

"Normally, someone of Leo's stature would have an entire staff twenty-four/seven. But Felicity insisted she didn't want to live that way—with virtual strangers in their home. So they compromised. They operate with the bare minimum: security at the gate to their property, one house manager, and one part-time housekeeper. It's about one-tenth of the staff Leo had growing up."

"It's hard to imagine that anyone needs that many people roaming around their house, fluffing their sheets and fanning them." She laughed. "I'm with Felicity."

I rang Leo on the way to fill him in. He told me he and Felicity weren't home, but I was welcome to enter the garage and take the car. I had all the security codes to his property, and Nathan was apparently off tonight, so there would be no staff there.

When we arrived, Abby seemed surprised to find six cars parked inside the garage. We passed the luxury vehicles to get to the one she'd actually be driving. I chuckled at the shocked expression on her face when she saw it.

"Wow, this is..."

83

"Small?" I offered.

"Yeah, but it's perfect." She brushed her fingers along the hood. "A Fiat, right?"

"Yep. My legs barely fit inside," I said. "But it should suit you just fine."

"Lime green. Quite the color." Abby opened the door and got in. "What's the story behind it?"

"Felicity drove an older version of this car when Leo and I met her in Rhode Island. I used to tease her about how ridiculous it looked. After she moved here, she was always mentioning how much she missed that car, so I found one and gave it to her on her birthday."

"Wow, Mr. Moneybags, that was quite a gift." She rubbed her hands along the leather steering wheel.

"Seeing her face when I drove up that day was worth every penny."

"I love the relationship you and she have." Abby played around with the seat, adjusting it back and forth.

I leaned against the open door. "You can drive this car on one condition."

She looked up at me. "What?"

"Just use it to get around town. I don't want you driving something this small on the motorway."

"I'll be fine on the motorway."

"Because you're such a good driver?" I arched a brow. "Non-negotiable, Abby."

"Okay. Fine. Backroads only." She sighed. "That's all I need the car for anyway, to get around town."

"Very well, then." I grabbed the keys from a hook at the other side of the garage and walked them over to her. "Here are the keys."

Abby exited the car and stuffed them into her purse. "Thank you."

"We should get going," I said.

"Wait. Since we're here, do you think we could say hello to the animals?"

"I should get back to the city."

"Okay." She frowned. "I understand."

But the disappointed look on her face overshadowed my better judgment. *How can I say no?* "Maybe just a quick visit out back before it gets dark."

CHAPTER 13

Sig

Track 13: "Mind Your Business" by will.i.am and Britney Spears

A quick visit turned into an hour jaunt around the property, during which *I'd* stepped in dung this time and gotten my balls busted for the better part of thirty minutes as a result. After going inside and cleaning up, we resumed hanging out with the animals.

Now I thought we were finally headed inside to lock up, but instead Abby grabbed my arm and led me into a small barn. She plopped down in a giant pile of hay.

"Feel free to make yourself comfortable."

"A pile of hay just begs to be jumped in, doesn't it? I've been eyeing this ever since we peeked in here earlier." She waved me over. "Come join me, you hardass."

I reluctantly walked over and lay down next to her. "You've already made me extremely late getting back to London, not to mention the excrement I wouldn't have stepped in had I not let you convince me to stay here. I need to get going."

"To what? Your empty apartment?"

"My sanity is waiting for me back there, yes."

"Being around me makes you insane?"

"My sanity resides wherever I happen to be alone."

"You know, since it's late, you could sleep at the inn instead of going all the way back to London. We could drive together to work in the morning. Then you wouldn't have to call me a car."

"Or I could not waste time sitting in this pile of hay and instead get back to London at a decent hour."

She ignored me. "Close your eyes for a moment and just breathe, Sigmund. Listen to the sounds of the animals in the distance."

Not sure why, but I listened to her. I closed my eyes and pulled air in and out. It was rare that I took the time to pause and experience being in the moment. While I generally preferred being alone, I rarely allowed my mind to quiet. This felt foreign but not unpleasant, and perhaps needed, particularly because I was focused on the sounds of nature outside rather than my internal monologue.

When I opened my eyes, Abby still had hers closed. She really was stunning, the nostrils of her perfect, up-turned nose flaring a bit with each breath she took. Her lips parted.

When she opened her eyes, I turned away. *Why do I always get caught staring at her?*

"Why were you looking at me?" she asked. "You were supposed to close your eyes."

A rush of heat traveled from the base of my neck to the top of my head as I said nothing.

"Did you even close your eyes at all?" she asked.

"I did. Then I got bored. You're more interesting than the darkness, I guess."

"What a compliment. A step up from pure darkness."

"While I like being alone, I don't like quiet. It was nice for a while when I was listening to the animal sounds. But then I lost focus."

"It's too powerful, right? No distractions? Having to reflect and *feel* without turning to anything else?"

"That's precisely why I can't do it for long."

Her eyes seared into mine. "Tolerating stillness is an art form. Something I'm still working on. I was actually struggling myself."

"Struggling with drowning out your thoughts?" I asked.

She nodded. "Yeah."

"What were you thinking about?"

"I was trying to gauge whether the fact that I don't feel any different means anything when it comes to the implantation. I've always suspected I would somehow know if I were pregnant. But I feel exactly the same." She turned toward me. "Are you secretly hoping I'm not?"

I pondered that, knowing I owed her an honest answer. "I don't know what I'm wishing for, Abby. On some level, I'd be relieved if you weren't, but not entirely. It's complicated. But it doesn't matter, does it, if we're going to try again anyway?"

"What if none of them work? There are only a limited number of embryos."

While the prospect of that brought me some relief, it was also heartbreaking. Truly heartbreaking. Because once they were gone, that was it.

"If it doesn't happen, it wasn't meant to be," I said.

Her mouth curved downward. "I feel like that, too. But I would be really sad for Phil and Kate."

"It's not worth speculating about something that hasn't happened, though."

My phone rang, and I looked down to find it was Lourdes, a woman I'd hung out with over a year ago. She'd been texting me lately to get together, and I'd been ignoring her messages. I silenced the ringer.

"Who was that?" Abby asked.

"Someone named—none of your business."

"A woman? Is that why you're in such a rush to get back to London?"

"Trust me, I haven't met anyone worth rushing anywhere for."

"Well, excuse me, Mr. Picky."

I rolled over a bit to face her, resting my chin on my hand. "You think it's odd to be selective?"

"I don't think you're being selective. I think you're closed off to *everyone*. There's a difference."

"You seem to have me pegged, but what about you? Why are *you* single?"

"I had a bad experience, as I think I've mentioned, and haven't felt like having my heart toyed with again."

"How long ago was that? The guy who broke up with you..."

"Nearly three years now."

"But you've dated since that breakup."

"Yeah. There've been a few brief..."

"Hookups?" I arched a brow.

"I guess I can admit that now that you're not actively assessing my character."

"Why would I judge you for that? Sex is natural—necessary for survival, if you ask me."

"You just don't want to have anything to do with the women after."

Unable to deny it, I shrugged. "There haven't been *that* many women since Britney. At least nothing compared to when I was younger. Most of the time, I meet someone and decide not to go through with anything. But of the encounters I *have* had, yeah, it's never mattered whether I saw them again."

"What was different about Britney? I mean, when you met her? How did you know she was the one?"

My chest constricted. "I'd love to be able to give you a less cliché answer—because I *hate* clichés—but I just knew. After about an hour together, I never wanted to be apart from her."

"Fair enough. They say that's what happens sometimes. You just *know*."

"You've never experienced that?"

"Nope." Abby shook her head. "Still waiting for it to happen to me." She smiled. "Anyway, for the record, I don't just hook up with people randomly, like *some* people." She elbowed me. "I have to know them first."

"Knowing you, Abby, I can't imagine you not asking someone a million questions before you sleep with them."

"Well, yeah. I need to know who I'm dealing with. I'm not going to waste my time with anyone who's not a good person—even if I'm wildly attracted to them."

"Sometimes less is more," I mumbled.

"This from the man who interrogated me the first time he met me."

"Well, I need to know a bit more about someone who's going to be carrying my child than I would someone I'm merely going to..."

"Fuck?" She finished my sentence.

The word on her tongue gave me an unwanted thrill. I wouldn't have minded hearing her say it a few more times, which probably meant I needed my head checked.

"You wanna go?" she asked.

Somehow I'd forgotten my urgency to leave. I'd become pretty comfortable in this spot on the hay. It wasn't about the hay at all, though, was it?

"Well, now you've made me lazy. You're a bad influence, Knickerbocker."

She leaned her head on her hand. "Why don't you just sleep at the inn tonight? Lavinia loves your company."

"She'll be conked out by the time we get back there, but I suppose you have a point. At this hour, I might as well just drive into London with you in the morning."

"You keep work clothes at The Bainbridge, right?"

"Yes. I have everything I need in my room." I looked out through the barn door. It was now completely nightfall. "Now that it's dark, you need to be careful driving back."

"You'll be behind me anyway, in case I run into trouble, right?"

"Well, you won't find me driving in front of you ever again," I teased.

"Good one." She laughed as she stood and brushed off her dress. "Can you turn around for a minute?"

I narrowed my eyes but did as she asked. "Okay...why am I doing this?"

A few seconds passed. "All good now."

"What was that all about?" I asked.

"You promise not to make fun of me?"

"No. But tell me anyway."

"I had a piece of hay stuck in my underwear." She flashed a goofy smile.

And then...I laughed for what felt like the first time in years. "The road home is quite curvy and dark at night," I told her when I'd gotten myself back together. "I should drive in front of you to provide some light."

"You mean you trust me not to rear end you again?"

"Well, it's quite difficult to spot the sheep at this hour, so I trust you'll keep your eyes on the road."

"I will." She winked.

She followed me back to the inn that night and managed not to cause a collision. It was quite late by the time we got to The Bainbridge, and Abby headed straight to her room after grabbing a snack from the kitchen.

As expected, Lavinia was asleep. *Or so I thought.* As I walked down the hall, her head peeked out of her bedroom.

"What are you doing up?" I asked.

"I was concerned about Abby because it's late."

"We went to Leo's to pick up a car."

"I know. She sent me a text, but I was still worried about her driving on that dark road at night."

"I drove in front of her to provide some light."

"Well, that was nice of you." Her mouth curved into a smile as she stared at me oddly.

"What?"

"It doesn't take four hours to pick up a car," she whispered.

I swallowed. "She wanted to see the animals."

"Hmm..." Her look grew even more suspicious.

"Why are you looking at me like that?"

"You're not normally a stop-and-smell-the-flowers, see-the-animals type of person, Sigmund."

"What are you implying, crazy woman? Get to the point."

"I think Abby is a good influence on you." She shrugged. "And I think staying out late might have been about more than just the car."

"I know what you're thinking. And I want you to stop, alright? Because you're wrong."

"You can't blame me for wondering."

"Yes, I can." I lowered my voice. "Mind your business and go to sleep."

"Goodnight, Sigmund," she said in a sing-songy voice as I resumed walking down the hall. "Nice to see you here at the inn during the week. Another *unusual* thing."

"Bugger off." I turned and flashed her a look but stopped short of giving her the finger.

She smirked before disappearing into her room.

Nosy biddy.

CHAPTER 14

Abby

Track 14: "Naked" by Avril Lavigne

A week and a half had passed since I'd started working at Covington, and I was getting the hang of my new routine. I'd been on edge since yesterday, though, awaiting a call from my doctor after a blood draw to determine if I was pregnant.

I was getting ready for work when I realized my bathroom was out of toilet paper. I had no idea where Lavinia kept the spare rolls, so I ventured over to the other bathroom to get some from there.

I knocked on the door, and when no one answered, I assumed it was safe, turning the knob to enter. But I jumped as a flash of Sig met my eyes.

Not just Sig.

Sig's half-naked body.

Oh. My. God.

"What the...?" He quickly wrapped the white towel around his waist.

"Oh my gosh!" My eyes locked on his sculpted chest. "I'm so sorry."

Everything had happened so fast. I hadn't gotten a clear look at anything below the waist, but much to my surprise, not only was his body perfection, he had quite a bit of ink on his upper arm. Was he ever the perfect canvas... All I could think was *stunning*.

The vein at his temple looked like it was going to pop. "You don't know how to knock?"

That certainly snapped me out of it. "I *did* knock."

He removed his earbuds and tossed them, his expression softening when he seemed to realize this was *his* fault.

"Sorry," I repeated. "I, um, was just looking for toilet paper."

My eyes lowered again to his perfect, tanned torso, a stream of water dripping over the six-pack. *Holy shit.* I'd imagined what his body might look like, but the reality far exceeded my vision. Either this man worked out incessantly or he was insanely blessed.

He knelt, opening the door under the sink and offering a roll to me, his chest rising and falling.

"Thank you. Anyway, what are you doing here? I assumed you were in London."

"I came in last night. Leo and I had a late game of poker with some friends at his house. I decided to sleep here and drive into work with you this morning."

"Oh...okay. Well, thanks for the toilet paper." Feeling flushed, I returned to my room and sat on the bed, shaken by the whole thing.

I'd learned some things about Sig over the past few days. Number one, whenever we got a little close, he distanced himself. Aside from him driving me back to West-fordshire on work nights this week, I hadn't spent much quality time with him since we hung out in Leo and Felicity's barn.

Speaking of that night, it had taught me how protective he was. His insisting on driving in front of me proved that. Although, I had to wonder whether he was protective of *me* or the baby I was potentially carrying.

And unfortunately, I'd also learned I was incredibly attracted to him, as evidenced by the fact that I'd lost the ability to form a coherent sentence a minute ago. I'd found him attractive even before I saw him half-naked. Now? It was hopeless.

Thankfully, as we drove into London together that morning, Sig spared me any ridicule, not mentioning anything about me walking in on him. In fact, he was quiet almost the entire way. And I chose to leave well enough alone, enjoying the scenic view.

Once we got to work, I realized this wasn't going to be any ordinary training day. Sig followed me to my side of the office. "You're coming with me?" I asked.

He scowled. "HR notified me that Art is out again for the next several days. He has an ongoing personal issue he's been dealing with. As I mentioned before, Alistair isn't experienced enough to continue training you. So I'll be the one working with you today."

Tension built at the back of my neck. "Alistair seems experienced to me."

"He's experienced, alright. Just not in the right areas."

As Alistair approached my cubicle, I could see the moment he noticed Sig sitting next to me. I nervously turned on the computer.

"Everything alright?" Alistair asked. "You're not normally on this side of the building, boss."

"Someone has to train her with Art being out."

Alistair looked between Sig and me. "We did just fine that first day, didn't we, Abby? I've got it covered."

Sig stood, the look in his eyes almost murderous. "Come with me for a minute, Alistair."

I watched as they walked away, disappearing into a conference room. About five minutes later they emerged, and Alistair turned the other direction, rather than return to my cube.

"Everything okay?" I asked.

"Yep. Everything's fine." Sig sat next to me. "Open the database and navigate to the contact screen, please."

Alrighty, then.

For the next couple of hours, Sig sat with me, teaching me more about the ins and outs of their office database, which I'd be able to access via virtual private network on the days I worked remotely. As awkward as the start of our morning had been, I didn't exactly mind the smell of spicy masculinity as he leaned over me to type on my computer. Enjoying his nearness would have to be my little secret, but after what I'd walked in on this morning in the bathroom, it was hard not to let my mind fall right into the gutter. Now all I noticed was his physical presence—his big hands and long fingers as they pointed to the screen, that wrist tattoo that peeked out of his sleeve, the way a piece of black hair would occasionally fall over his forehead, the heat as his muscular thigh brushed against mine.

At one point, a woman approached us. "Sigmund, did you forget about the meeting at noon with Royer Investments?"

"Shit." He ran a hand through his hair. "Yes, I did. Thank you, Maxine. I'll be over there in five."

I rolled my seat away from the desk. "I messed up your day."

"It's my own fault." He stood. "You're good for a while anyway. Why don't you take lunch, and we can reconvene after my meeting. It should only take about an hour."

"Okay." I watched as he headed down the hall toward the elevators.

After a quick stop in the restroom, I took the elevator down and walked a block to the sandwich place I'd been frequenting. I ordered a pastrami on rye and an apple juice and took my lunch back to the office.

I went to the employee kitchen on my floor and took a seat at a small round table. At first I was alone, but a few minutes later, a couple of the administrative assistants walked in. While they smiled over at me, they didn't talk to me or ask me to join them.

Then Alistair entered the kitchen. He carried a paper bag that looked like it was from the same place I'd gone to. "Anyone sitting here?" he asked as he approached my table.

"No." I wiped the corner of my mouth. "Feel free to join me."

"Cool," he said as he took a seat. "Can I ask you something? You don't have to answer, if you don't want to."

"Sure." I took a long drink of my apple juice.

"Is there something going on between you and Benedictus?"

I nearly choked. "Why are you asking me that?"

"Because he seemed *very* adamant about me not training you, but also made it clear that I should, in his words, 'Stay the fuck away from you entirely'."

Oh my God. What? "He said that?"

"He did." Alistair took a bite of his sandwich. "He can be a right arse sometimes, but he's never done anything like that before."

I shook my head. "No, there's nothing going on between us romantically. He's a...friend of the family, though." I guessed the lying phase of my time here had begun.

"Ah, okay. That makes more sense, then. I couldn't imagine him being so protective of you for no reason."

"I suppose. But he doesn't have a right to dictate who I can talk to at work."

"Well, I won't tell him about this lunch, if you won't." Alistair winked and took another bite of his sandwich.

"He's in a meeting now, so you should be good."

"Oh, I know. I heard Maxine when she came to remind him. He doesn't normally come to this side of the office at all. It was a bit jarring to see him this morning, let alone be reprimanded for merely existing."

"I'm sorry he did that. You were very helpful to me on my first day before Art came back. I told Sig that."

Alistair popped open his drink and chuckled. "I don't think that's what he wanted to hear."

"How is he perceived around here?" I set down my sandwich. "Are people afraid of him or something?"

"He mostly keeps to himself, doesn't really socialize with us after hours or anything. We have a few tight-knit cliques that go out to the pubs after work. I know some of the women have invited him, but he never comes." Alistair shrugged. "Probably thinks he's too good for us."

"Hmm..." I said noncommittally.

Alistair sat with me for the remainder of lunch. I kept looking over my shoulder, unsure of what I wished more—that Sig would catch me with Alistair or that I could make it back to my cubicle without him seeing a thing.

CHAPTER 15

Abby

Track 15: "Pictures of You" by The Cure

I was already back at my desk, shortly after 1 PM, when Sig returned from his meeting. I'd either dodged a bullet or dodged the perfect opportunity to get him riled up.

He worked by my side the remainder of the afternoon, smelling like heaven and wearing a scowl on his face. And at the end of the day, he opted to drive me back to Westfordshire.

As we started our ride home, I decided to broach the subject of Alistair. I didn't want to get him in trouble, so I played dumb. "What did you say to Alistair when you pulled him aside this morning?"

"What does that matter?"

"Well, he basically disappeared after that. Plus, you were in that conference room long enough to say more than a sentence or two."

"It's none of your concern."

"If it involved me at all, it *is* my concern. Should I just ask him?"

Sig's jaw tensed. "I told him to stay away from you."

"Why would you do that?"

"Because he's bad news."

"You previously said that he wasn't qualified to train me. Now you're saying he's bad news?"

"He *is* bad news."

"How so?"

"He's a well-known womanizer who's only after one thing."

"It takes one to know one?"

Sig rolled his eyes. "Alistair is far worse than I ever was, even at his age."

"And that's saying a lot?"

"Well..." He paused. "Yes."

I crossed my arms and looked out at the London fog. "I can take care of myself, you know. I don't need you to decide who should stay away from me."

"I run the business. I have every right to decide what happens."

"You *don't* have a right to tell me who I can and cannot interact with."

"If it's at the business I run, I do have that right, actually."

I decided to mess with him—see where it would go. I liked him a little riled up.

"Okay, well, if I want to interact with him, I'll have to do it outside of work."

He adjusted his grip on the steering wheel, and he was grinding his teeth.

"You didn't think I'd have no social life here, did you?"

"You can have a social life without getting involved with a notorious philanderer."

"If you keep your distance from your staffers, as you seem to, how do you know so much about his reputation?"

He whipped his head toward me. "Who says I keep my distance?"

Shit. Alistair did. But I wasn't going to admit that. "Just a guess."

"Even if I don't join them for their little after-work outings, that doesn't mean I have my head in the sand. I listen to what they're talking about. I hear the whispers. He's bagged more than one woman from Covington."

"Good for him," I taunted.

Sig's eyes darted toward me.

Then I burst out laughing. "I love making you mad."

He sighed. "You're very good at it. One of your few talents."

I snorted. "In all seriousness, though, while I appreciate your opinion, I *don't* accept you telling me who I can and cannot associate with, at work or otherwise. I'm here in the UK for one reason, but that doesn't include you dictating who I date."

"Date?" His voice cracked. "You're going on a *date* with him now?"

"No. I didn't necessarily mean Alistair. But that's what this is about, isn't it? You're worried he's going to ask me out and I'm going to become the latest of his conquests? What would that matter to you?"

"Given the circumstances that brought you here, it should be clear why I have an interest in who you're associating with."

"Really... Well, that could be a problem, then. It's going to be a long nine months or more. I can't be expected to not date that whole time. You mean to tell me if I meet someone, I have to approve it through you? That's not what I signed up for." This had started as teasing, but now *I* was feeling a little riled up by his egotistical stance.

"You said you were ready for this, Abby. It doesn't sound like it, if your priority is dating."

"I didn't *say* dating was my priority. But this could take more than a year. That's a long time. I can't be expected to just be alone, not have a social life—at least during the time I'm not showing a lot. Do *you* plan to be celibate for nine months?"

Sig gnawed at his bottom lip and said nothing.

"I didn't think so," I muttered.

"Do what you want," he huffed.

"You don't sound like you mean that. Why does the idea of me having a life outside this situation anger you?"

"It doesn't," he said, keeping his eyes on the road.

"Now you're shutting down. I'm trying to have a serious conversation."

"And I've *seriously* told you to do what you want. You're right. It shouldn't be any of my concern." He expelled a long, frustrated breath. "You seem to have the hang of the database. You can work from home tomorrow."

"Oh!" Crossing my arms, I shook my head. "That's so passive aggressive."

"I'll have you know, I'd decided that before this ridiculous conversation. We're supposed to be getting heaps of rain tomorrow. It's not worth you having to travel ninety minutes in a tsunami when you can easily work from the inn."

"Oh," I muttered, feeling a bit dumb if that was the truth.

When we passed the onramp toward Westfordshire, rather than getting on the motorway, I asked, "Where are you going?"

"I have a spare work laptop at my flat. It already has the database installed. I'll set it up for you when we get to Lavinia's."

I picked some lint off my skirt. "Okay."

I'd been quite curious about his place. And while this wasn't a leisurely stop, I hadn't thought he'd have me over in any capacity. But what if he didn't plan to invite me in?

Sig pulled into his parking spot, and I looked up at the brick building. "Can I go in with you? I'd love to see your apartment."

He turned off the car. "If you insist..."

"You're so grumpy," I said as I followed him out of the car.

"Should I be excited about showing you my place? I haven't exactly prepared it for visitors."

"I'm sure it's fine."

Sig's one-level apartment on the third floor was spacious and modern, just as I might've imagined it. Large windows overlooked the street below, and it seemed immaculate.

He tossed his keys on a table by the door. "Make yourself at home. Laptop's in my bedroom. Just going to grab it."

After Sig left me alone, I wandered around the living room. I heard his phone ring and then the muffled sound of him talking to someone in the next room.

Since he was occupied, I wandered over to a corner of the living space. An amateurish painting of trees and mountains hung on the wall, and it had Leo's signature at the bottom. *Must be an inside joke?* I mean, it wasn't horrible, but not exactly the kind of art you'd display in your living room.

I then noticed a single framed photo on an otherwise empty bookshelf. My heart clenched. It was an image of Sig and Britney in front of Big Ben. It must've been taken shortly after they met because she didn't look sick. I knew they'd only had about six months together. According to her parents, the treatment she received had made her quite frail toward the end. She didn't look that way here at all, though. She was absolutely beautiful. I'd seen a couple of photos of her before, but never of her with Sig. Never of *them*.

And Sig? His beautiful dark blue eyes sparkled in the picture, filled with life, with hope. With *love*. He wore an expression I'd never seen. It broke my heart to discover his genuine smile, to know that at one point he'd been capable of such joy. I envied the love and connection they had. And though I couldn't see it here, there had to have been fear lurking within them as well. They'd known what they were faced with from day one. And yet...that didn't stop their love.

I focused on Sig's smile in the photo and wished I could experience that side of him, even if that wasn't meant to be *my* experience.

"What are you doing?" Sig's voice cut through me.

I shuddered. "This is a really nice photo."

He softened as he approached and took the frame from me. "That was taken the day before she started treatment. We wanted one day of normality. I took her around London, gave her the full tourist experience," he murmured. "It was a good day."

"It's beautiful, Sig." I watched as he continued to look down at the photo. "You were a good man to have stuck by her through all of that."

He finally took his eyes off the photo to turn to me. "It was my privilege. I didn't want to leave. It wasn't out of obligation that I stuck around."

"I know. I didn't mean to imply it was, just that it must've been difficult."

"There were many beautiful moments amidst the hard ones." His eyes returned to the image. "This day was wonderful."

My heart filled with sadness as I finally witnessed the unguarded and vulnerable Sig.

My phone began to ring, and I fished it out of my purse. When I saw the call was from the medical center, I put it in speaker mode. "Hello?"

"Is this Abby Knickerbocker?"

"Yes. This is she."

"It's Dr. Bonner. I wanted to call right away to let you know the results of your blood test were positive. You're pregnant."

CHAPTER 16

Sig

Track 16: "Panic Song" by Green Day

The second Leo opened the door, I rushed past him into his house. "We have a problem."

"Something happen with the Jenkles project?"

"No—God, who gives a shit about that right now?" Massaging my forehead, I paced. "It's Abby..."

"What's wrong?"

Sweat coated my forehead. I stopped and turned to him. "She's up the duff." I exhaled. "It happened."

"Whoa." His mouth fell open. "On the first try. Okay. Wasn't expecting that at all." He patted me on the back. "But congratulations, mate."

"No!"

"No?" His eyes widened.

"No!" I continued pacing.

"Wasn't that the idea of the insemination? To get her pregnant?"

"Yes, but...it wasn't supposed to happen *this* fast."

"Well, you must have super sperm, cousin."

"That's one accolade I *never* wished for. I've spent my entire life trying *not* to get women pregnant." I looked around. "Where's Felicity? I wanted her to know, too."

"She's at my mother's with Eloise."

"Oh," I muttered, still in a daze.

"When did you find out?"

"Just a couple of hours ago. The doctor called after work when I'd stopped with Abby at my apartment on our way home to pick up a laptop. I drove her back to the inn and came straight here."

"Do Britney's parents know?"

"We called them together on the way to Westford-shire. But that's it. No one else knows but you."

"It's normal to be in shock," he assured me. "It will set in eventually. You have a while to get used to it, thankfully. Nine whole months, to be exact." He led me into the kitchen. "Come have a drink. You could certainly use one, I'm sure."

"Something strong," I said as I took a seat on one of the stools.

He opened a bottle of whiskey and poured. "How is she doing?"

"Abby, you mean?" I blinked. "I've been in such a tizzy, I never really asked her."

"Well, that was pretty daft of you." He handed me the small glass.

"God, it was, wasn't it?" I downed the liquid in one shot and wiped my mouth with the back of my hand. "I barely said a word to her on the way home because I was in utter shock."

"Perhaps you should stop back at the inn on your way to London tonight and check on her."

"You're right." I tugged on my hair. "Not to mention, it hadn't been a good day for us before this."

"Why?"

I let out a long breath. "I tried to manipulate a situation. I wanted to protect her, but it backfired."

Leo leaned his elbows against the counter. "What did you do?"

"I told Alistair Jones to stay the fuck away from her."

Leo bent his head back in laughter.

"What's so funny?"

"Yeah. You don't like her. Not at *all*. That's very clear."

I ignored his comment. "She and I argued quite a bit about it. She doesn't like me controlling who she interacts with. But I did it for her own good. He's a prick."

"Actually, you're right. I know of him. He *is* a prick. But are you sure you didn't have an ulterior motive? Perhaps on a subconscious level you want to keep *all* guys away from her?"

"The woman is carrying my and Britney's child. Isn't that enough of a reason to protect her from opportunistic snakes?"

"I suppose. But she *is* your type. And you didn't know she was pregnant earlier when you acted out."

He had a point.

"Also...I saw you on the security camera leaving quite late the night you came to pick up the Fiat," he added. "You mean to tell me there's absolutely *nothing* there?"

"There isn't." I felt my eye twitch, as it sometimes did when I wasn't completely honest. "But it wouldn't matter if there were. She's the last person on Earth I would pursue. End of story."

"Obvious conflict of interest aside, what if she weren't the surrogate? How would you feel about her?"

"What's the point of even considering that?"

"I think it's relevant, actually."

I stared at him for a moment and decided to entertain his question. "She's funny. Witty. I'm comfortable around her. I like her as a person, and most of all, I respect her. Current situation aside, that's enough of a reason to spare her the misery of getting involved with a fucked-up man."

"You're not fucked up just because you're still a bit broken over losing your wife. You might never get over Britney. She's part of you. But that doesn't mean you can't move on and live. She'd want you to. You know that. She told you so."

My heart was full enough today without the direction this conversation was headed. "You can spare me the lecture. We've had this discussion many times."

He smacked me on the back. "You know what I think you should do?"

"What?"

"Stop talking to me and get the hell out of here. Go find out if Abby's alright. You think you're in shock? She's the one who has to carry a baby for the next nine months. Wrap your head around that."

I nodded. Despite the fact that it was getting late and I'd hoped to go back to London tonight, now was not the time to run again. It looked like I'd be spending the night at The Bainbridge. Sticking around and accompanying Abby to work tomorrow morning would be a nice gesture.

I bid my cousin goodbye and drove back to the inn.

CHAPTER 17

Sig

Track 17: "Tiny Bubbles" by Don Ho

Lavinia was sitting in the living room when I arrived.

"Sigmund!" She straightened in her seat. "I didn't know you were coming back tonight."

"Where's Abby?" I asked.

"She's up in her room, but I don't think she's asleep because I heard footsteps just a moment ago." Lavinia had a suspicious smile plastered across her face.

She knows. "Why are you looking at me like that?"

"Congratulations," she whispered.

"She told you..."

"She did. Don't be mad. She needed to tell someone." Her lip began to tremble.

"Don't cry, Lavinia."

"I can't help it." She sniffled before coming over to hug me. "Such a blessing."

I wrapped my arms around her, reluctantly accepting her embrace. "Christ, old woman, if you're crying *now,*

112

you'll have a heart attack when this baby comes. Save your energy."

She wiped her eyes. "Why did you come back?"

"I went to Leo's to tell him the news. I figured I'd just stay here since it's late."

"Ah."

"I also wanted to talk to Abby."

She smirked, and I chose to ignore it.

I headed upstairs and decided to stop in the bathroom before checking on Abby. When I opened the door, I flinched at the sight of her—in my bathroom. Abby was in her underwear and bra, her breasts spilling out of it.

She covered her chest. "Jesus!"

I turned around and stuttered, "I—I'm sorry. I thought you were in your room."

"Why are you here?"

"Well, it's technically *my* bathroom."

"I know. But I thought you returned to London."

"I ended up going to Leo's instead of home. It's too late to drive back now."

"I thought I had the upstairs to myself," she said. "I wanted to take a bath. My bathroom only has a shower."

"You don't need to explain," I said, keeping my back to her and feeling like a complete idiot. "You're welcome to use the tub anytime. You live here." I reached to pull the door closed again, but she stopped me.

"Don't leave, Sig."

I froze. *Don't leave? Is she mad? She's half-naked.*

"I'm about to slip under the suds," she said. "I'll be covered. I want to talk to you." She paused. "I'll tell you when it's safe to turn around."

I swallowed. *It will never be safe with you.* My pulse raced, and my dick struggled to comprehend this situation. It wasn't supposed to be incredibly excited by such a prospect.

"Okay. You can turn around," she finally said.

I turned to find her enveloped in the soapy water. Much to my relief, you could indeed see nothing below her neck.

"Hi." She smiled.

"Hi," I said, not moving from my spot near the door.

"You can come closer."

Against my better judgment, I relented, moving forward and sitting down on the ground a few feet from the bathtub. I tried my best to ignore what I imagined to be heaven hidden beneath those bubbles.

"You went to Leo's instead of back to London so you could tell him the news?"

"Yeah."

She nodded. "I told Lavinia—I had to—and my dad. But that's it." She lifted an arm and ran a hand along her smooth skin. "I'm surprised you came back here tonight."

"I wanted to see you," I admitted. "Talk to you."

Her eyes widened. "You did?"

"I need to apologize for shutting down earlier, for not acknowledging the impact the pregnancy news must have on you. You're the one most affected here. Leo asked me how you were doing, and I was ashamed to realize I hadn't asked."

"It's okay, Sig." She smiled. "There's no playbook for this situation."

"How *are* you doing?"

"It feels like I'm outside of myself, watching all this unfold." She moved around beneath the water, a stray bubble flying into the air. "Maybe I feel that way because this baby isn't mine. Not sure if I'd feel differently if it were. Then again, I don't really have any signs of pregnancy yet." She closed her eyes. "Well, there's one. But I'm embarrassed to admit it to you."

"What is it?"

"Not going to say right now."

"Alright."

"Anyway..." She sighed. "I also never asked how *you* felt after we got the news."

"I'm gobsmacked that it happened on the first try."

"Me, too." She nodded. "It's strange how we got the call right when you were talking about Britney, when we were looking at the photo. It makes me feel...like she was there."

My chest tightened. "Perhaps."

Silence hung in the air for a few moments.

"I know this is hard for you," Abby added. "I didn't expect you to be all that excited. You don't have to pretend to feel a certain way for my sake. You have a right to feel anything you need to, even if that's sadness right now."

Abby didn't give the impression she was saying things to appease me. I believed her words came from the heart. "You make it very difficult, you know."

"Make what difficult?" she asked.

"Disliking you."

"Have you been trying?"

"Maybe subconsciously. But there's nothing not to like. You're phenomenal. And I'm glad I made the right decision. I'm glad it's you."

Not sure what possessed me to be so honest, but she deserved it, especially after the way I'd handled things earlier.

"Well, thank you." She looked like she might cry. "I'd hug you right now but...well..." She blushed.

I felt my body temperature rise. I'd been aware of the fact that she was stark naked under those suds without her having to remind me.

Fuck.

My dick moved, reminding me just how complicated this situation was—how I could go from fear to sadness to horniness in a matter of seconds.

"We'll figure this out, Sig." She reached out a delicate, soapy hand.

I took it. "I suppose we have time." When I caught myself about to rub my thumb along her soft skin, I released her and stood. "I'd better let you get on with your bath." But I didn't move.

"I'm just going to be sitting here for a while. You don't have to leave." She scooped suds into the palm of her hand and blew, sending tiny bubbles in my direction.

Why is that so fucking hot? I didn't *want* to leave. That was a problem.

This was going to be a very *long* nine months.

CHAPTER 18

Sig

Track 18: "Hey Jealousy" by Gin Blossoms

Even after two weeks, it didn't feel any more real. Abby and I had immersed ourselves in our daily routines, the pregnancy not seeming to change much as of yet. In fact, it was fairly easy to pretend it wasn't happening.

Abby had told me she was bored on the days she worked from home and much preferred to work in London. She'd asked to work in the office four days a week and be remote on Fridays only. As much as the idea of her being there stressed me out, I wasn't going to stand in the way, if that's what she wanted. I had no good reason to ask her to work from the inn.

She'd been taking a car every morning, but rather than calling her a ride in the evenings, I offered to drive her back to the inn most nights before returning to London. Since that was nearly three hours round trip, it got me back to my flat close to 9 PM.

One Thursday afternoon, I was in my office, just about ready to log out for the day when Abby called from her end of the building.

"What's up?" I asked when I answered. "I was just about to go get the car."

"That's why I wanted to catch you. A bunch of people are going to the pub down the street after work."

"And you're telling me this because..."

"Well, I'm going. I wondered if maybe you wanted to join us."

"I'd rather not."

"Okay, then. Sean has offered to give me a ride back to Westfordshire, so I won't need to call a car."

Sean? Another fuckboy from the office. My blood pressure spiked. "He's going to be drinking and then driving you back?"

"I don't think so. I mean, we never discussed it. But I doubt he would—"

"I'll drive you home." I tugged on my hair. "Just call me when you're done."

"That makes no sense. You shouldn't have to wait around."

"I'll drive you," I snapped.

"If you insist, but that's really not necessary."

"Anything else?"

"Yeah. Why are you such a grump sometimes?"

"Any *serious* questions?"

"No."

"Okay."

We hung up, and I opted to stay at the office rather than going home. It seemed counterproductive to drive to my place on the other side of London, only to return here later. I certainly had no lack of work to keep me occupied.

But sitting at my desk after hours was quite a miserable experience. I'd worked late before, but I'd never stayed at the office this long after closing, until I was the only person here. A cleaning crew now made their way around the floor, the distant white noise of a vacuum the only sound aside from the muffled traffic outside my window.

My phone chimed with a text from Abby.

It was a photo of her sandwiched between Alistair and Sean at the pub. Somehow I knew she'd sent it to ruffle my feathers. It did more than that, though. A feeling of intense jealousy rose to the surface—an unpleasant realization that my feelings for this woman had officially crossed a line, even if *I* could never cross it.

Sig: Any reason you're sending me this photo?

Abby: We're at The Bend. There's still time to join us. We'll be here a little longer.

Christ. My concentration went to hell after that. If that had been her intention, mission accomplished. I relented, shutting off my computer and grabbing my jacket.

After walking the few blocks down to the pub, from the pavement I could see the office crew occupying a large table inside. I entered, and when they spotted me walking toward them, everyone's conversations seemed to cease at once, aside from a few whispers. I stood at the end of their table. "What's wrong with all of you? You act like you've never seen me outside of work before."

"We haven't," Kimberly from HR said.

"Who invited you?" someone asked.

"I did," Abby announced.

All of the heads at the table turned toward her.

"Something wrong with me being here?" I asked.

Emma from accounting cleared her throat. "It's just that you've never accepted an offer to come out with us before. We weren't expecting you."

"I'm aware of that." I pulled out a chair. "I figured I'd come out for once—see what all the fuss is about."

"Well, boss, nice to have you," Sean said.

I glared at him. But what I really wanted to do was deck him.

A waitress came by. "Fancy a bevvy?"

Knowing I was driving Abby back tonight, I'd opened my mouth to decline when Abby placed her hand on my forearm.

"Relax," she whispered. "I'll be your designated driver."

"There is nothing *relaxing* about the idea of you driving." Though I supposed one beer wouldn't hurt, in any case. "I'll have a pint, thanks," I said.

The waitress turned to Abby. "Are you sure you don't want anything to drink, miss?"

"I'm positive," she replied. "I still have my sparkling water with lime. Thank you."

"Do you not drink, in general, Abby?" Sean asked.

None of your bloody business.

"It just hasn't been agreeing with me lately." Abby glanced over at me, her cheeks reddening.

The table remained quiet.

Looking around, I crossed my arms and chided, "Nothing to talk about now that I'm here, eh?"

"Well, yeah, we talk about *you* half the time," a very drunk Melanie giggled.

Emma elbowed her.

As the minutes passed, everyone eventually went back to their normal mode of conversation. And after a while, I managed to forget my troubles for a bit, even talking shop with some of my employees, many of whom I was sure had hated my guts before tonight. My job wasn't to be their friend, but rather their boss, but I supposed it wouldn't have killed me to socialize with them from time to time, actually get to know them.

About an hour later, when everyone began readying to disperse, I realized I needed to make sure no one saw Abby and me leave together.

I texted her just before I left the pub.

Sig: I'm going to walk out ahead of you. I'll get my car and park around the corner on Devonshire.

Abby approached my car about five minutes later. Once she spotted me, she picked up her pace. Upon entering the car, she yawned. "Are you okay to take the wheel? My offer still stands."

"I am," I said as I pulled away. "I only had one pint. And any buzz I had has worn off."

"You didn't trust me to drive when I offered, did you?"

"Well, you're not the greatest driver when you're fully awake and alert." I looked over at her. "You seem tired."

It didn't make sense to go all the way back to the countryside at this hour. As uncomfortable as I felt, I knew what I should offer. "It's too late to go back to Westfordshire," I told her. "We should just stay here in London. My flat has a guest room."

CHAPTER 19

Sig

Track 19: "I'm on Fire" by Bruce Springsteen

"I don't have any spare clothes," Abby said as I parked.

"I'll give you a shirt to sleep in. You work from home tomorrow anyway. I'll just drive you back in the morning."

She sent a text to Lavinia as she followed me upstairs to my flat. I reminded myself again that a little discomfort with having her stay the night was better than driving all the way to Westfordshire right now.

She wriggled her brows. "I might just be the first woman who doesn't get kicked out before morning!"

"Very funny."

She yawned. "That was a good idea leaving the pub separately, too."

"I didn't want them to get any ideas."

"Any ideas they got would never top the truth." Abby chuckled. "If they only knew what the hell was really going on with me."

"It would make for an interesting watercooler discussion."

She tossed her purse on my sofa. "I'm glad you came out tonight. You surprised me—and them. I loved the looks on their faces when you arrived. They all shut up real fast."

"Yeah, that was pretty telling. I guess I should make more of an effort. I didn't realize what an ogre they thought I was."

"You *are* a bit of an ogre on the surface, but deep down you're a cinnamon roll."

"A what?"

"A cinnamon roll."

"What the hell does that mean?"

"It means you're, like, sweet...selfless."

"I've been called a lot of names in my life, but nothing as ridiculous as that." I chuckled. "I suppose there are worse things."

"Like *that prick*. That's what my dad calls you."

"Well, that's just brilliant."

She cackled. "Only because of the attitude you gave me when we first met. I've told him you're nicer now, but he hasn't quite gotten over it." She followed me into the kitchen and took a seat on one of the stools. "You're very intimidating. I don't know if you know that. The way they were all talking about you—before you got there—they're all afraid of you."

"I don't intimidate *you*, though."

She leaned her arms on the center island. "It's more like you don't *fool* me. I know you're not who you portray yourself to be. But you still make me nervous sometimes. I have this idea that you're judging me a little. Must be PTSD from the day we met. Although I sense you do actually like me now."

I took two glasses from my cupboard and filled them with water from the fridge. "You've got me all figured out. There's nothing more to say." I handed her one.

"Thanks." She took a sip and looked around my kitchen. "Got anything good to snack on? I ate so early tonight that I'm hungry again."

I'd nearly forgotten she was eating for two. "Why don't I make you something? What are you in the mood for?"

"No need to cook anything. I don't want much. Just something to satisfy my sweet tooth." She chuckled. "You don't happen to have Devil Dogs, do you? Do they even have those here?"

I squinted. "Devil Dogs? Like hot dogs?"

"No. Devil Dogs are these packaged devil's food cakes. They sort of look like..." She made an elongated gesture with her hands.

"Like wankers?"

"Never mind. Anyway, I keep them in the refrigerator. They're so good with an ice-cold glass of milk. I would kill for one of those right now."

I rummaged through my cupboard. "I have Cadbury chocolate. Will that do?"

"Sure!" She took the bar from me and removed the wrapper. "I guess I *am* having cravings, huh?"

She took a bite, closing her eyes and bending her head back for a moan my dick certainly didn't miss. I needed to get laid.

"Is that the symptom you were referring to in the tub—the one you were embarrassed to admit? Cravings for chocolate?"

"Oh…" She shook her head. "No."

"I'm pretty sure I know what it is," I teased.

"You do?"

"Yeah."

"What do you think it is?"

"There's only one thing you could possibly be embarrassed to admit, and I read about it."

"What's your guess?"

"Flatulence."

Her eyes widened. "Well, you're right, that would be embarrassing, but that's not it." She took another bite of chocolate. "Maybe I misled you. What I'm experiencing *shouldn't* be embarrassing, but somehow it would be embarrassing for me to admit it to *you*."

"Hmm…" I tapped my fingers against the counter. "Okay, well, I guess I'll have to continue to make educated guesses, then."

When she licked chocolate off her bottom lip, I had the sudden urge to do the same. That was my cue to leave the room. "Let me find you a shirt to sleep in," I said.

I rummaged around and found one of my largest T-shirts hanging in my wardrobe. I returned to the kitchen and handed it to her.

She held it out in front of her. "This will fit me like a dress. Awesome."

I pointed. "The guest room is the last door on the right down the hall."

"Thanks," Abby said before leaving the kitchen.

I put our water glasses in the dishwasher, unsure whether she was coming back out. But then I turned to find her standing in the kitchen again, wearing my shirt. I could see the form of her breasts clearly through it, as well as her nipples poking slightly at the cotton fabric. My dick stirred.

"Thanks for this." She looked down at herself. "Really sweet of you."

"Like the cinnamon roll I am." I winked. "I'm sure your coworkers would disagree, though."

"Do you want to know what they think of you? I've been holding back a bit."

"I don't need to—"

"The guys take issue with your attitude, mostly. But the women all think you're hot, so they cut you more slack." Her cheeks turned pink. "I can't say I blame them. As much of a dick as you can be sometimes, you are a very good-looking man, Sigmund. That can't be denied."

I said nothing, but managed to keep my mouth from falling open.

She cleared her throat. "They have a lot of sympathy for you because of your...circumstances. It makes you more appealing, you know? That's what I gathered tonight." She looked into my eyes. "I'm impressed that you never capitalized on your power and dated any of those women. A couple of them are very pretty."

"I don't date."

"That's right. I should say I'm surprised you've never *entertained* any of them and kicked them out of your apartment after."

"I have no trouble finding attractive women elsewhere," I assured her. "I don't need to be shagging my employees. I don't shit where I eat."

She nodded. "Makes sense."

"That would be inappropriate in any case."

"Inappropriate…" She tilted her head. "Sort of like dating two women at once, both who know about each other?"

I rolled my eyes. "There was nothing wrong with that as long as they were okay with it."

"I'm just kidding." She blushed.

"You bring up the Marias a lot. Sounds like you're still judging me for it."

"I'm absolutely *not* judging you. A harem is nice work, if you can get it. More power to you. I mean, I would *never* be okay with that—regardless of your self-proclaimed ability to make both women feel wanted. The idea of it is just…ick." She laughed. "Although, I might get down with a reverse-harem scenario."

"Oh yeah?"

"Maybe with Alistair and Sean." She winked, clearly trying to push my buttons.

It was working. *She-devil.*

Abby broke out into laughter. "Oh my God. I swear you have steam coming out of your ears right now. I'm totally kidding."

"Why would you do that?"

"Because getting you riled up takes your mind off of all the other things."

She had a point. With Abby, I never focused on my problems but rather was always immersed in our conversations, even when we were sparring.

"Reverse harem… It wouldn't happen for you, anyway," I said.

Her eyes narrowed. "Why? Because I'm a woman?"

"No. That's not what I'm getting at."

"What is it, then?"

"Someone would have to be out of their mind to want to share you." *Fuck.* Why did I say that? Because it was the truth. She was a ten. And for a moment, I'd lost my bloody mind, staring at her breasts pressed against my shirt.

She moved her hair behind her ear. "Oh...well, thanks." After an awkward silence, she shook her head. "I shouldn't have had that chocolate so late. I'll be up all night."

I snapped my fingers. "Heartburn. That's what it is, isn't it? Your symptom."

"I wouldn't be hesitant to tell you I had heartburn, no."

"Hmm..." I scratched my chin. "Nothing embarrassing about that, I suppose, yeah."

"Anyway..." She yawned. "I'm gonna hit the hay. Not the literal hay this time though," she added. "Although that was a fun night."

Good. If she stayed up much longer, Lord knew what other inappropriate things would come out of my mouth.

She started to exit, but then she turned around. "It's heightened arousal." She blushed. "My symptom. Increased libido is apparently common in the first and second trimester. It feels like I'm on fire." She shrugged and disappeared down the hall, leaving *me* in an unfortunate, heightened state of arousal.

Alright, then.

CHAPTER 20

Abby

Track 20: "Where Does My Heart Beat Now" by Celine Dion

Despite enjoying the cool countryside summer, I'd missed Sig over the past few weeks.

Ever since I'd slept at his apartment that Thursday night, he'd made himself pretty scarce. He seemed to be avoiding me—conveniently started working late. So now I took a car in the afternoons, too, rather than getting a ride to Westfordshire from him. He'd even stayed at his London apartment the past couple weekends, without visiting the inn at all. I had to wonder if I'd done something, or was he really just busy? He *had* taken a business trip to Scotland recently...

Anyway, whatever the reason, today would be the first time I'd spend any quality time with Sig since that night at his apartment. I'd worked from home, even though it was Thursday, and he was picking me up this afternoon to accompany me to my first ultrasound, which I was way, way beyond nervous about. More than anything, I was afraid they might find something wrong. That was the one thing I couldn't handle. *Please, God, let this baby be healthy.*

When Sig arrived at the inn, I nearly did a double take. He was dressed uncharacteristically youthfully—in a black hooded sweatshirt and black baseball cap worn backwards. The look was sexy as hell, and my desire to jump him hadn't waned in the time we'd been apart.

He looked me up and down. "You ready to go?"

I cleared my throat. "Yeah…" I followed him to his car and got in.

He started the engine and pulled out before he finally turned to me. "How have you been?"

"Good." I breathed in his masculine scent. "I've missed seeing you." When he didn't reciprocate the sentiment, I added, "How was Scotland?"

He shrugged. "The whiskey was good."

"Is that all?"

"I've been there plenty of times. Nothing too exciting. It was mostly business, not pleasure."

"Right. I figured."

"How are you feeling about today?" he asked.

"Nervous."

"Yeah, you're not the only one," he admitted.

"Kate and Phil were hoping to come for the first ultrasound," I told him. "But Phil's mother down in Florida isn't doing well. They've had to move there temporarily to be with her. Not sure if you knew that."

"They called and have been keeping me apprised of that situation, yeah."

"There'll be other opportunities for them to come."

He nodded.

We kept the conversation light for the remainder of our ride to the medical center in London.

When we arrived, we checked in and waited our turn. After a few minutes, the ultrasound tech called us into a dark room. Sig stayed in a corner, leaning up against the wall.

"You want to come sit here by your wife so you can see?" the tech asked.

I cringed, my stomach forming knots. *Ugh.* Why did she have to make that assumption?

Sig said nothing, stone faced.

"I'm not his wife," I explained. "I'm a surrogate." I glanced over at him. "We're not together."

"Oh. I'm sorry. I shouldn't have assumed."

"My wife is the biological mother. But she's deceased," Sig added. "Abby is carrying our baby."

The woman's mouth dropped open. "Wow. All these years doing this... I can't say I've ever had such a situation before." She smiled. "That's amazing." She shook her head and put on some gloves. "I'm gonna have to ask you to remove your trousers and knickers."

What? "Um, my underwear? Isn't this done on my stomach?"

"No, the earliest ultrasound is done transvaginally."

Oh boy.

"Would you be more comfortable if I left?" Sig asked, already walking toward the exit, ready to flee the premises.

"Don't be ridiculous," I said. "You can't see anything from behind me. Just look at the screen."

He swallowed. "Alright."

He kept his distance as she eased the wand inside of me. There was a bit of pressure as the probe went in. Once something appeared on the screen, I waved him over. "Come closer so you can see."

My heart raced as I waited for the tech to say something. I couldn't make much out within the snowy image myself.

"See that?" She finally pointed. "That's the baby's heartbeat."

I finally noticed it, a little rhythmic flickering of light—of *life*. I felt like a stranger in my own body, because how could I not have felt that? For the most part I still didn't feel any different, and yet this life was forming within me, growing by the day.

"I'm happy to tell you that everything looks good. You're about ten weeks along." She typed a few things into her computer. "Due date of February tenth."

I finally pried my eyes away from the little beating heart to look behind me at Sig. He stared at the screen, mesmerized and barely blinking. I imagined he was wishing Britney could've been here. Heck, I could barely hold it together, and it wasn't even my baby. That's what I had to keep telling myself—*this is not your baby. Don't get attached.* But I still felt emotional, seeing that little heartbeat.

When I looked over at the ultrasound tech, she was also looking at Sig, perhaps trying to gauge his reaction.

She cleared her throat. "I'll print a picture for you."

She then removed the wand, and the image disappeared. My chest remained heavy with emotion as I got dressed. After she handed me the printout, Sig and I went back to the waiting room. I stopped at the desk to make my next appointment as he waited by the exit.

We were quiet as we walked out together. I didn't want to say something dumb that would undermine how difficult it must have been for him to see his child for the first time without its mother being alive.

When we'd settled in the car, rather than start the engine, he laid his head back on the seat.

"That made it feel real, right?" I murmured.

"Yeah," he agreed.

"February tenth. Hope you don't have plans."

He turned to me. "That's Britney's birthday."

My stomach dropped to the floor. "Oh. That's... Wow. I didn't know."

He looked out the window. "Chances are it won't be born on the due date, but yeah..."

I placed my hand on his forearm. "Are you okay?"

He turned to me and forced a slight smile. "I'm fine."

I offered him the photo. "You want to keep this?"

"No." He shook his head. "You keep it."

"Alright." I slipped the printout into my purse. "What are your plans for the rest of the day?"

"After I drop you off, I have to head back to the office."

"I'm actually going to Felicity's, since I took the rest of the day off," I told him. "She invited me over. Leo has some event tonight, and she wanted company. You want to skip work and come along?"

"No. But thank you. I have far too much to do."

"Okay." I feigned a smile, disappointed that I probably wouldn't see him again for a while.

CHAPTER 21

Abby

"Oh my God. It looks like a little acorn." Felicity gushed over the ultrasound image I'd taken out to show her.

We'd just finished eating, and now she and I sat in the living room as Eloise played with her dolls on the floor. I looked at the photo for the first time since I'd placed it in my purse earlier, and tears filled my eyes.

"Oh no." Felicity's expression darkened. "Did I say something to upset you?"

"No. You're fine." I sniffled. "It's just... I've been emotional ever since I saw the heartbeat. But I didn't want to cry in front of Sig earlier. Didn't feel like I had a right to. So I guess it's coming out now."

She stood and grabbed me a tissue. "You have *every* right. You're just as much a part of this experience as anyone else—the biggest part, if you ask me."

I blew my nose. "I didn't expect to be so emotional about it."

"How was he during the appointment?"

"At first he seemed reluctant to be there, but when that little heartbeat was up on the screen, he was transfixed. He admitted in the car that it made everything seem real. Then he told me the due date is Britney's birthday."

Felicity covered her mouth. "Oh my."

"Yeah. So he opened up a bit in the car, but then true to form, he shut down after that." I stared blankly at Eloise playing by her mother's feet. "I get why he went quiet *today*. But he's been standoffish overall, even before this."

"That's strange. I thought things were going well?"

"We were getting along for a while. He even came out to a pub one night with the work crew last month. It was late by the time we got out, so I spent that night in the guest room at his apartment in London."

Surprise crossed her face. "Really?"

"I was shocked he offered that, too. He's so private about his personal space. But that night..." I sighed, unsure what I should be admitting right now.

Felicity searched my eyes eagerly. "Is there something you're not telling me?"

"Nothing crazy." I shrugged. "I just might have...divulged a little too much, and I think that's why he's been avoiding me."

She leaned in curiously, and I ended up telling her what I'd admitted to Sig about feeling more aroused since the pregnancy. I told her I feared he thought I'd been insinuating something.

She had a bit of a different theory. "Trust me, it wasn't what you said that freaked him out. It was probably his reaction to it."

"What do you mean?"

"I think, much to his chagrin, he likes you, and it's making things complicated."

"What do you mean *likes* me?"

"I think he likes you as a person, but I imagine he's attracted to you in other ways."

My heart fluttered, even if I didn't believe it. "What are you basing that on?"

"Several things. When people are scared, they retreat. And you mentioned him being protective toward you when it came to that guy at work. He wouldn't care about that unless it affected him personally."

"I think he's protecting his unborn child—not me. I'm just a...vessel for something that's important to him."

"Don't fool yourself, Abby. You're a beautiful woman. Sig is not blind. And I think he genuinely likes you as a person, too. You're the whole package. How could he not like you?"

Her opinion on the matter reminded me of what Sig had said about me not being the kind of woman a man would want to share. I hadn't confessed that part to her. Could she be right? Was he attracted to me? Was that the reason he'd been staying away?

"I do have a crush on him," I admitted, my cheeks tingling. "I don't want to. And it's a bit embarrassing for me to admit. It doesn't help this situation." I blew some air out. "I haven't told anyone, not even Lavinia."

"Well, thank you for confiding in me." Felicity smiled. "I can completely understand. He's a handsome, charismatic guy, albeit complex."

"Developing feelings for that man would be the most futile thing I've ever done. He'd never cross the line with me."

Felicity looked away as she seemed to ponder that. "I agree that he wouldn't come around to the idea very easily. But that doesn't mean he wouldn't want to, if things were different."

"This situation was a lot easier when I thought he was a jerk."

She laughed. "Let me tell you a secret about Sig. He comes across as almost heartless sometimes because he doesn't express his feelings. But he's just the opposite. He has the *biggest* heart out of everyone."

"I've definitely figured out there's more than meets the eye."

"He also doesn't always know what's good for him," she added. "He's convinced himself he's better off living the way he is, keeping everyone at a distance. But I know he's craving happiness. He didn't know what true happiness was until he met Britney. But now he *does* know. And I think you being here has made him feel things he hasn't in a long time. That's why he's taken a step back. He doesn't know what to do with it all." She sighed. "But don't let fear stop you from trying to connect with him. He's not a brick wall. He's more like..." Felicity paused. "An onion." She laughed. "You have to peel back the layers to get to what's inside."

Huh. "Yeah, well, onions will ultimately have you in tears. That's my fear. I didn't come to England to get hurt. I have *one* task, you know? I don't want to fuck anything up by getting emotionally attached to him—or worse, the baby. As you can see, that already happened today."

"I wouldn't be any different. You're not a machine, Abby. You're human." She began to braid Eloise's hair. "We can't help how we feel, can we? Feelings can't be controlled. When I first met Leo, I was certain we could never be together because we were from two different worlds. That didn't stop me from falling for him. We impose rules on ourselves that the heart doesn't recognize. You know?"

"I do," I murmured. Boy, was I grateful to have someone I could trust to confide in. "Thanks for letting me vent." I exhaled. "I feel like all I've done is talk about myself. How are you feeling? You don't have too much longer to go now."

Felicity rubbed her stomach. "I don't feel prepared to go from mother of one to mother of two. I've been trying to be a good mom, work, and juggle social responsibilities as it is. I don't know how much more I can handle. I won't know until she gets here."

Felicity was a lawyer. She worked part time in London teaching American law while balancing motherhood.

"Well, I have no doubt you'll handle it just fine. You make it look easy, but I'm sure juggling it all is not."

"It definitely isn't, but thanks for the vote of confidence." She wrapped an elastic around the bottom of Eloise's braid. "Do you think you'll find out what you're having?"

"That's gonna be their choice, right? The Alexanders and Sig? I have a feeling he won't want to know. He'll want to be in denial as much as possible until the last minute."

She nodded. "You're probably right."

Felicity made tea for us before I hit the road in her lime green Fiat, headed back to the inn. On my drive, I called my dad to catch up.

"Hey, Dad," I said when he answered.

"How's that prick treating you?"

I laughed. "He's not mean anymore. Just a bit...standoffish lately."

"I tell you this all the time, but the option is always there to come home."

"Well, as I get further into the pregnancy, leaving is only going to get harder." I slowed as I approached a car in the distance, still paranoid after rear-ending Sig. "Overall, I'm happy here. Happier than I thought I'd be. I just miss you."

"I miss you, too. But I'm glad you're having this adventure. The one thing I always regretted was not getting to see the world."

"Speaking of you seeing the world, do you think you could get some time off to visit me out here, sooner rather than later?"

My father worked in masonry for a construction company in Massachusetts, not too far from where we lived in Rhode Island.

"You read my mind," he said. "I'm gonna talk to Joe Silva about that time off and see what I can coordinate."

The prospect of getting to see my dad filled me with hope. He was already planning to come when I gave birth, but that was too long to wait to see him. "That would be amazing. You'll love it here. And there's plenty of room at the inn. You'll love Lavinia, too."

"Well, I love anyone who treats my girl nice."

We talked a few more minutes, and I hung up smiling. Talking to Dad had really boosted my mood.

When I walked into the inn, Lavinia seemed to be eagerly awaiting my return. I'd gone straight to Felicity's after Sig dropped me off from the ultrasound earlier, so I hadn't had a chance to talk to her about it. She stood up carefully from the couch. "Sigmund said you have a photo to show me."

"You spoke to him?"

"He came by briefly to drop something off on his way back to London. I asked him how the ultrasound went, and he told me you had a picture."

I reached into my purse and handed her the printout.

Her mouth curved into a smile. "Well, look at that. Looks like a little ink spot."

"Felicity said acorn, but ink spot might be an even better description."

"Have you eaten?" she asked.

"Oh, yes. Felicity prepared a nice charcuterie board for us. Then we had tea and cookies. I'm totally stuffed. Think I'm just gonna go upstairs to take a bath."

"Okay, lovely. Enjoy it."

After relaxing in the tub, I went to my room to get dressed. There was something sitting on my bedside table.

A box of Devil Dogs.

CHAPTER 22

Abby

Track 22: "I Love Onions" by Susan Christie

After at least an hour of debating whether or not I should call him, I decided to pick up the phone.

Sig answered on the second ring. "Everything alright?"

"Yes, but you shouldn't have." I bounced on my bed. "The gift you left me was perfect."

"Well, I didn't want your sweet tooth to keep you up tonight."

"That was really *sweet* of you." I stilled at the sound of a woman's voice in the background. Suddenly, I wanted to crawl into a hole. "Is...someone there with you?"

He hesitated. "She was...just leaving."

"Oh." A rush of jealousy caused me to perspire. "Gosh. I'll let you go, then."

"No," he insisted. "Hang on."

I heard some muffled talking, followed by a door slamming shut. He then returned to the phone. "Hi. Sorry."

"I didn't realize I was interrupting. Why did you answer the phone if you were hooking up with someone? I would've much preferred your voicemail."

"It was more like a *botched* hookup...all I seem to be having as of late."

"Botched because of my interruption?"

"No. I'd botched it all on my own before you called."

I had to ask. "Nothing...happened?"

"No."

"How did you botch it?"

"It's not the first time this has happened, particularly lately. When I reach out, I'm looking for an escape in the form of company. But by the time she gets here and is right in front of me, I..." He paused. "I don't know...lose interest."

His candor surprised me. Calming a bit, I lay on the bed and crossed one foot over the other. "Like when you have insomnia and order something online in the middle of the night? By the time it arrives days later, you're like 'What the heck is this? I must've been crazy to want it'?"

"Sort of like that, yeah."

"You're like an avocado, Sig."

"An avocado? First I'm a cinnamon roll. Now I'm an avocado?"

"Yes. An avocado is only ripe and ready for a very brief time. Many times, you open it and it's already brown. You miss the window if you so much as leave the room for too long."

"Any other foods you wish to compare me to?"

"An onion."

"Sorry I asked."

"Actually, Felicity came up with that one."

"Did she? Well, Ginger is just as mad as you are." He sighed. "So tell me, Abby, how am I like an onion?"

"You have many layers. And it takes a while to get through them to see the real you, not the one putting up walls."

"And you, Abby Knickerbocker, are a fruitcake."

I giggled like a fool. "I like fruitcake, actually—probably one of the few people in the world who does. I'll take that as a rare compliment from you." I fell silent for a moment, then couldn't help myself. "The last compliment you gave me really caught me off guard, though."

"What was that?"

"When you told me a man wouldn't want to share me."

"Ah... I did say that, didn't I?"

While I'd hoped he would elaborate on *why* he'd said it, he remained silent. "So..." I cleared my throat. "When was the last time you had a successful hookup?"

He sighed. "The rhinoceros. Well, I wouldn't call that *successful*. But it...went to completion."

My forehead wrinkled. "Rhinoceros?"

"She snored like one. Fell asleep, and I didn't have the heart to wake her. Big mistake. She kept me up all night. Then Phil and Kate knocked on my door the next morning and saw her here."

I snorted. "That must have been awkward."

"Indeed. So was Phil's yodeling."

"What?" I laughed. "I'm not even gonna ask, but that sounds like a circus." I slid between my sheets. "Why did they come over so early anyway?"

"That was the trip when they flew in to talk to me about the surrogacy. They surprised me that morning."

"You haven't been with anyone in *that* long?"

"You're taking a great interest in this topic, Abby."

"Well, I have nothing better to do right now than pry."

"Perhaps you should get a hobby," he teased.

"I don't need a hobby. I'm currently growing a human inside of me. What's your superpower?"

His deep laughter vibrated through the phone. "Touché, love." After a moment he added, "What else are you itching to ask me? I can hear the wheels turning in your head."

"Who was the woman at your apartment tonight?"

"Name's Rose. Someone I met on an app."

"And you just...what? Changed your mind and kicked her out?"

"Despite my reputation for kicking people out, generally they leave of their own accord."

"*She* decided to leave?"

"We were...in the middle of things, though we didn't get very far before I stopped it. She asked me why, and I blurted out that I was distracted because I was having a baby with my dead wife."

"Well, that'd do it." I covered my mouth with my hand to smother a laugh.

"It took her several seconds to wrap her head around it before she asked me what the hell I was talking about. I tried again to explain why I was preoccupied. I don't know if I made any more sense, but she finally got the picture that nothing was going to happen, despite my original intentions. And that's when you rang. It was rude of me to take the call. That made things worse. So she left."

"You are *quite* the romantic, Sig."

"I was for a brief time, about six months to be exact. Never before and probably never again. Now I'm just good at making women disappear."

"I think we found your superpower."

"Yeah." He exhaled. "Anyway, I'm glad you called."

"Why?"

"I wanted to apologize if I seemed a bit freaked out today. The ultrasound was...a lot. And once again, I neglected to ask how *you're* doing in all this. I'm sorry for that."

"There's no need to apologize. Your reaction was to be expected. I can't imagine what you were thinking." I settled deeper into the mattress.

"It was amazing to see that life inside of you." Sig paused. "These past few weeks, I'd fallen back into pretending it wasn't happening. I don't have to tell you how absent I've been. But after today, I know I can't pretend anymore. I can't pretend that little beating heart doesn't exist. And I won't react like that again. There's no excuse for my absence lately." He sighed. "But today after the appointment...I just needed some time to process."

"And you figured you'd do that by shagging some broad from the Internet?"

"I have a strange way of handling things sometimes."

"Don't worry. I get it. And I wasn't offended."

"Are you happy here, Abby?"

My eyes widened in surprise. "I am, actually. More than I thought I'd be."

"No thanks to me, though."

"Well, you did bring me Devil Dogs. That's a major point in your column."

"I'd been searching for them ever since you told me you were wanting them."

That gave me goose bumps. "Where did you find them?"

"I just happened to see them in the shop attached to the petrol station where I stopped to fill up tonight. Imagine that? Maybe the universe was telling me what an arse I was today and showing me a way to make it better. So I turned around and drove back to the inn to drop them off. You'd already left for Felicity's."

"Well, I'm gonna put them in the fridge and have them for breakfast tomorrow."

"Ah, breakfast of champions."

"Crap. I don't have milk, though."

"Yes, you do."

"I do?"

"Go look in the fridge."

"Really? You bought me milk, too?"

"You said you eat them with ice-cold milk. So I picked some up."

"Wow. I'm amazed that you remembered that."

"Onions have a good memory."

I smiled. "It's nice to talk to you again, Sig. I've missed your snark and your sense of humor. I thought I'd scared you away."

"Scared me away? Why?"

"The night I stayed at your apartment, you sort of went quiet after I told you about my *symptom*." My voice quivered. "I wondered if you thought I was insinuating something. You know, coming on to you."

"I didn't think that at all. But you disappeared into the bedroom so fast after you announced it, I'm not sure how you could gauge my reaction."

"I suppose I did disappear. I was referring to your disappearing act in the days after." I paused, trying to find the right words. "I also let it slip that I find you attractive that night. I wasn't sure if that made you uncomfortable, too."

A few seconds of silence passed.

"My absence has had nothing to do with any of that, Abby."

"If you say so."

He cleared his throat. "How's everything going in that regard, by the way? With your *symptom*?"

"It's still...going."

"Good to know."

"So, speaking of that, I have to tell you something," I said, bracing myself.

"Okay..."

Here we go. "Sean from work asked me out."

Dead silence followed.

"Are you still there?"

After a moment he said, "I'm here."

"I didn't give him an answer. He asked me about a week ago." I took a deep breath. "I know how you feel about the guys from work, and honestly, I don't want to do anything to upset you. But it's gonna be a long nine months here—and I'm only going to get more pregnant as time goes on. That will complicate my social life." I paused. "So I may take him up on his offer."

Sig said nothing.

"I think you were right about Alistair," I added. "But Sean seems like a nice guy."

He finally grunted. "Hmm..."

"Is that all you have to say?"

"I don't know what to say. You're an adult. You don't need my permission."

"Do you think Sean's a bad person?"

"I don't really know him."

"But you had opinions about Alistair. I just thought—"

"Alistair is a wanker. Stay away from him. End of story."

"Alright, since you have nothing bad to say about Sean, I'll assume no news is good news."

"Right," he muttered.

"Okay, then. Glad to see you're back to talking in monosyllables." I shook my head. "Good talk."

CHAPTER 23

Sig

Track 23: "I Heard it Through the Grapevine" by Marvin Gaye

The weeks continued, and I realized I'd somehow managed to make it through the entire month of August without involving myself in Abby's business. That was for the best. But when I heard her name as I passed the employee kitchen one morning, I had to pretend to be casually interested in the conversation. "Some good gossip, I take it?" I asked, stirring cream into a paper cup of coffee.

Emma's face reddened. "Oh, you weren't meant to hear, boss."

"I know that. But you were talking about two of my employees, so I'm curious."

"Abby from customer relations and Sean from accounting went out on a date. Kim ran into them this past Friday night. I was just telling Camille." She glanced at her coworker. "I think they make a cute couple. But please don't say you heard anything from me."

I pretended to zip my mouth. "My lips are sealed." Putting on my acting hat, I did my best to seem genuinely curious and not as miserable as I felt. "So, do we think there's something going on between them?"

Emma's eyes darted around the room, likely freaked out by my sudden interest in the personal lives of my employees. "Not sure." She shifted uncomfortably. "Too early to tell, I suppose."

Not wanting to seem any more inappropriate than I already did, I chose not to pry for additional information. I hadn't asked Abby if she'd taken Sean up on his offer, but now I had my answer, and that was all I needed to know.

But *why* was I so perturbed by this? I had no right to be. In fact, the more I thought about it, the more I realized Abby getting involved with anyone besides me during her time here was probably the safest option. I should've welcomed this development. But alas, the idea of her going out with Sean turned my stomach and made it impossible for me to concentrate on anything else for the rest of the morning.

Leo came into London to join one of our board meetings that afternoon, and he and I went for drinks at the pub down the road after.

He took a sip of his beer. "How's Abby?"

I massaged my forehead. "Just splendid."

"That was sarcastic, I take it. Is something wrong with her?"

"Oh, no. She's doing better than any of us. Next thing I know, she'll be joining the cast of *Love Island*."

"What are you talking about?"

"She's dating blokes from work now," I said, mutilating my napkin.

His eyes widened. "Blokes plural?"

"One bloke."

He smirked. "And that bothers you."

"Why would it bother me?"

"For the umpteenth time, because you clearly fancy her, even if you'll never admit it."

"What good would admitting it do? It wouldn't change anything if I developed feelings for her."

"There are no rules, Sigmund, aside from the ones you've self-imposed. No one ever said you couldn't fall for her."

"Do you not understand that she is literally the last woman on Earth I could get involved with at this point in time? Imagine the complications of her feeling obligated by this situation somehow. Imagine me fucking things up and having to tell this child I broke the heart of the woman who gave birth to it." I took a sip of my beer. "Not to mention, she's too young for me."

"And yet you seem pretty affected by the fact that she's dating someone." Leo leaned back in his seat and scratched his chin. "I'm going to tell you something, and I'm probably going to go to hell for it..."

I stopped shredding the napkin for a moment. "What?"

"Felicity told me Abby confessed to having a crush on you but that she believes any hope is futile." He paused. "She likes you."

My chest constricted. That confirmed what I'd already suspected. But it didn't change anything. I couldn't let it—even if I couldn't forget it. I swallowed. "I didn't need to know that."

"Do not ever let it be known that you heard it from me. I'll kill you, if Felicity doesn't kill me first."

"Well, wouldn't that be an interesting headline? The Duke of Westfordshire locked away for killing his own cousin..." I sighed. "Of course I won't say anything to her."

"Maybe she's getting involved with this guy as a distraction from her feelings for you, because she believes they won't go anywhere."

"Probably for the best, then." I grabbed another napkin and began the process of destroying it.

"You're torn because this is the first woman you've felt something for since Britney," he declared.

"Well, aren't you just a genius," I scoffed.

"Doesn't take a genius to see what's going on here, mate. It's quite clear."

I tossed the napkin aside. "Is she beautiful? Yes. Do I like her as a person? Yes. None of that matters, Leo. Okay? It doesn't matter. The best thing I could possibly do to thank that girl for sacrificing her body for nine months is to stay the fuck away from her, let her return to her life in the US unscathed, and not turn both our lives into a fucking soap opera."

CHAPTER 24

Sig

Track 24: "A Sky Full of Stars" by Coldplay

That weekend, my better angels told me to stay in London, but I'd gone too long without checking on Abby personally. I'd vowed not to pull a disappearing act again, so I needed to catch myself. Not to mention, it wasn't fair to Lavinia that I was now ignoring her, too, anytime I distanced myself from Abby. I owed them both a visit. Or that's what I told myself as I pulled into The Bainbridge Saturday evening.

I used my key to open the door and made my way into the kitchen, where I could hear them talking. "Hello, ladies," I announced from the doorway.

Abby turned, looking like she'd seen a ghost. "Hey!"

Lavinia's face lit up. "Sigmund! I thought I might croak before you came back."

"I'm glad you didn't. Nice to see you, crazy woman."

"We've missed you around here," Lavinia said.

I walked over to where Abby was stirring something on the stove. "Hi, Abby," I spoke softly over her shoulder.

She smiled. "It's good to see you."

Her breathing seemed to quicken, or maybe I was imagining that now that I was hyperaware of her crush on me.

"Abby is making potato and leek soup," Lavinia announced. "You're just in time to join us."

"That sounds like a bit of a risk," I mocked. "Since when does Abby cook?"

"You're a wiseass." Abby elbowed me.

"You missed me, though." I winked.

Why did every word exiting my mouth sound like I was flirting with her? *Am I? Fuck if I know.*

"I did miss you." Her face reddened as she tapped the spoon against the pot.

Knowing our attraction was mutual made me unsettled, but also a bit energized, though I couldn't do anything about it.

About ten minutes later, Abby ladled soup into bowls she'd set out, and the three of us sat down to dinner.

"You used fresh chives," I remarked. "Nice addition."

"You noticed."

"I notice everything." I licked the corner of my mouth. "Coriander, too, yes?"

"You're good."

"I have to say, this is quite delish, Abby."

"Why, thank you. Coming from such a temperamental chef, I take that as a huge compliment."

Lavinia stayed silent, but looked between us, amused. She was likely just as aware of the sexual tension between Abby and me as we were.

After we finished eating, I got up to take my bowl over to the sink. Abby cleared the rest of the table while

I handled the dishes. When she started wiping down the counter near me, I felt my body stir. She looked up, and when her eyes met mine, I knew I'd been kidding myself thinking I was the one doing *her* a favor with this visit. I'd missed seeing her, and I'd been off balance ever since I'd discovered she'd gone out with that bloke from work. *I* had needed to see her tonight, and *that*'s why I was here.

"Are you sleeping here tonight?" she asked.

"I was debating it."

"It's mild out. Since you don't have to go back to London, want to take a walk?"

I closed the dishwasher. "Sure. Yeah."

"You want to come, Lavinia?" Abby asked.

"Oh, no. You two have fun. You don't need me slowing you down."

"We can walk slowly," Abby insisted.

"No. I'd prefer to relax and watch something on the telly, but thanks for the offer." Lavinia flashed me a knowing look, which made me suspect she wasn't coming along specifically so Abby and I could be alone.

I glared at her as Abby and I got our jackets and headed outside. It was indeed a beautiful night—just a slight breeze, but not too cold. The leaves rustled as we made our way down the street before turning right onto the first side road.

"So, to what do we owe the honor of your presence tonight, Sig?"

"I just thought it was time I came and said hello."

"I'm glad you did. Lavinia was beginning to get concerned."

"Just Lavinia?"

Even in the darkness, I could see her blush.

"Well, I wondered if you were avoiding me again."

My mind went to war with itself. *Don't do it. Don't ask.* "I heard you went on a date with Sean."

Her eyes widened. "How did you know about that?"

"I overheard one of the gossipmongers at work talking about it."

"Really? I never told anyone, but come to think of it, Kim from HR saw us out. That's probably how they know." We walked in silence for a few moments. "Aren't you going to ask me how it went?"

"It's none of my business."

"You used to think I was your business. Just ask Alistair. What changed?"

"That was to protect you from *him* specifically. I have no business interfering if I don't have a good reason."

"I kind of liked it when you interfered, when you showed interest. It's not fun when you go MIA. You disappeared again, even though you promised not to."

"I know. But I caught myself this time. Why do you want me around anyway? Isn't it better for everyone if I give you occasional space?"

She looked around us. "Who's everyone? It's just you and me in this equation. We're the only two people sharing this experience. Phil and Kate are in the States. So yeah, I like having you around. It would be nice if you didn't disappear again."

When she put it that way, I felt like crap for continuing to distance myself. She needed my support. The fact that I no longer trusted myself shouldn't have gotten in the way of being here for her. She was carrying my child, for heaven's sake.

"Sometimes I think it's better for you when I disappear."

She slowed her pace. "Better for me, why?"

"Nothing good can come from us spending too much time together, Abby. Even if we don't intend to grow close, that's bound to happen if we're constantly around each other."

"So you think us getting close is a bad idea..." She walked a few steps in silence. "I understand. I might even agree."

"Right." I slipped my hands into my pockets. "It wouldn't be good for you to get close to me."

"I see where you're coming from." She knocked into me playfully. "But you're like...a black and white cookie."

"Christ, here we go!" I yelled up toward the sky. "You and the food references again. Black and white cookie? What the hell does that mean?"

"You know those cookies that are split down the middle? One side is white and the other is black—or chocolate. Everything is black or white to you. You only want to view me the way you think you should: as someone you need to have a boundary with because I'm the surrogate. But being a surrogate doesn't change the essence of who I am. I'm *also* a woman in a new place looking for a pleasurable time and to make memories. I'm both of those things, a surrogate *and* a woman." She paused. "And similarly, you can also know it's not a good idea to get close to me and *like* me at the same time. Life is complicated that way."

I kicked some dirt. "Why do your stupid analogies always make sense in the end?"

"I'm brilliant like that."

We shared a smile.

"Who said I like you anyway?" I teased.

"It could be just a delusion of mine. But you did say men wouldn't want to share me. And then you disappeared after that night I spent at your apartment. I feel like you're keeping your distance to ensure no lines are crossed."

"If I *did* like you, you realize that would be dangerous, right? The success of this entire endeavor depends on neither one of us getting emotionally involved. You need to be able to go back to the US and resume your life. And I need the ability to let go, if that's what's best for this child."

She stopped walking and faced me. "You think what's best for this child is a life away from its father?"

Her question cut like a knife. I didn't have the answer, except to say, "I have no business raising another human alone, so yes. Phil and Kate are perfectly capable and still young enough."

"So you're firm in your decision to let them raise it? I wasn't sure if seeing the ultrasound changed anything for you."

My chest tightened as I thought about that little beating heart. I only wanted what was best for it, never wanted to disappoint it. There was so much fear inside of me when it came to that tiny soul.

"I can't tell you how I'm going to feel once the baby is here," I said as we resumed walking. "But as of now? My original decision stands. Phil and Kate made it clear they're happy with that."

"I hear you," she muttered, disappointment in her tone.

Our conversation ceased for a while, replaced by the sound of crickets. Eventually I couldn't stand the silence any longer. "So...how *did* your date go?"

"Oh, now he asks." She flashed an impish grin.

"Just changing the topic off of the deeper stuff."

"It went well, actually. But I'm not sure it's worth pursuing anything. I don't love the idea of dating a coworker. And it feels sort of deceptive going out with someone and not divulging the very important fact that I'm pregnant." She expelled a long breath. "So I'm not sure how to handle things."

"He hasn't asked you out again?"

"Oh, he has. More than once. I've just been putting him off."

Grinding my teeth, I nodded, feeling selfish relief about her hesitation.

Then she changed the subject. "I told my sister today—about the pregnancy."

"You never talk about your sister."

"We're not that close. She's older by five years, very judgmental, and doesn't always understand me. As expected, she had a lot to say about my decision to be a surrogate."

I didn't like that at all. "What did she say?"

"She doesn't understand why I wanted to do this—sort of like you in the beginning. Except it's already happened. So her judging me at this point is not helpful."

"Well, I'm sorry your decision is causing strife between you and her."

"There would be strife anyway, no matter the situation. That's the kind of relationship we have." She paused. "Things got worse when my mother was sick."

"How so?"

"To make a long story short, she and I disagreed on many things toward the end. Mom was already doing poorly and didn't want to try this last-ditch experimental treatment the doctors suggested. I supported my mother's wishes. Claire didn't. She felt I was encouraging my mother to give up. And she continued to say nasty things to me after my mother passed, blaming me for not convincing her to take those drugs."

That struck a chord with me. There was nothing worse than having to make difficult decisions toward the end of a loved one's life. "I'm very sorry, Abby. That's horrible of your sister to make you feel guilty about something that's not your fault."

"Things were bad between us before then, but they've never really recovered."

"Ultimately, it was your mother's right to decide how she wanted to live her last days. You were merely supporting her."

"That's how I felt. And I also had to follow my gut, which told me everything they'd tried up until that point had only made her sicker and sicker. I couldn't stand by and let them take away the last quality of life she had."

That gave me déjà vu. As much as I avoided talking about Britney with Abby, I couldn't stop myself. "We went through a similar thing—turning down a last-ditch offering of more chemicals." I shuddered at the memory. "Britney, her parents, and I thankfully were in agreement that she'd had enough. I can't imagine how much more difficult it would've been if there had been discord among us."

She nodded. "I'm glad you didn't have to go through that."

After a minute, Abby pointed to a large stone at the side of the road. "Want to sit here?"

"Are you getting tired?"

"Not really," she said. "I just think it would be nice to sit for a bit."

I held out my hand, and after she sat, I took the spot next to her on the rock.

"Our house is on the water back home," she explained. "I love sitting out and listening to the sounds of the bay and looking up at the sky like this."

The sky was littered with stars tonight. We both gazed upward.

"Are you thinking about her right now?" she asked, intuitive as ever.

"It's hard to look up at a sky full of stars and not think about her." My throat felt heavy as I exhaled, my emotional walls slowly melting away. "I often wonder *what* she is now. What form. Whether she can see me. Whether she's an angel, or perhaps a star in the sky. It's hard not knowing whether she's okay. That's all I really need to know. I feel like if I knew that, I'd be able to breathe again."

Abby rested her hand on my knee. "We're forced into blind faith. But it's hard to maintain it when you've been let down in life. Everyone says people who die are in a better place. It's what we *want* to believe, what we *have* to believe. But the only certain thing is that we aren't meant to know."

"Well, thank you for not bullshitting me like everyone else."

She chuckled. "That said, I'm choosing to believe Britney's in a good place and still with you. The same with my mom. I feel her with me."

As she continued to look up at the sky, my gaze moved from the stars to her beautiful profile. Abby didn't ask for much, just my company and my honesty. I felt compelled to deliver, even if I might regret it later. "I like you more than I should," I admitted.

She turned, her eyes wide. "I like you, too."

I returned my attention to the sky. "I nearly fired Sean the other day, by the way."

"What?" She laughed. "Why?"

"He made an error balancing the books. I *really* wanted to fire him."

"Because of the books."

I turned to her, feigning innocence. "What else?"

CHAPTER 25

Abby

Track 25: "Secrets" by OneRepublic

A few days after I'd last seen Sig at the inn, Sean arrived at my cubicle so we could go to lunch together. I still hadn't taken him up on his offer of another evening date. A platonic work lunch seemed like a much safer option while I sorted out my weird feelings for Sig and tried to figure out whether getting any closer to Sean was a good idea.

Just as I looped my purse over my shoulder, it somehow slipped from my arm, the contents emptying onto the floor. Sean bent to help me pick up the items.

"Oh no. You don't have to," I insisted. I knelt and scurried to get what I could, not wanting him to pick up a tampon stashed away in there from long before I was pregnant—or worse.

But it was too late. I panicked as I saw him lift the ultrasound photo I'd continued to carry in my bag. "What's this?" he asked, staring down at it.

"It's a..." I had no clue what to say.

"It says OBGYN and has your name on it." He looked up at me. "Are you pregnant?"

I froze. I couldn't deny I was pregnant. It was all there in black and white.

"Excuse me one moment." I held up my index finger. "Stay right there."

I rushed down the hall and disappeared into the bathroom to dial Sig as fast as I could.

After a couple of rings, he picked up. "Everything okay?"

"You're gonna kill me," I said.

"Don't tell me you—"

"Whatever you're guessing, it's worse," I said.

"What's wrong, Abby?"

"I was just headed out to lunch with Sean. My purse slipped off of my arm and everything fell out. He was helping me pick it up, and he saw it. The ultrasound photo."

"Shit."

"He saw my name on it and the name of the OBGYN place. I can't deny it."

"Well, that's just brilliant. What did you tell him?"

"Nothing yet. I excused myself to the bathroom. I don't know what you want me to divulge. I can't deny that I'm pregnant. Not sure if I should make up a story or—"

"Bloody hell." He sighed into the phone. "Okay. I'm heading to your side of the office. Just keep him with you and try not to say anything until I get there."

How the heck do I do that? "Okay."

Thankfully, by the time I garnered the courage to exit the bathroom, Sig was already coming toward where Sean still stood at my cubicle. At least I wouldn't have to stall.

Sig greeted him with an authoritarian tone. "Hello, Sean. Can you follow us into the conference room, please?"

Oh my God.

"What's going on?" Sean asked as he took a seat across from Sig. "Are you firing me or something?"

"Not yet," Sig muttered.

Sean squinted in confusion as I took a seat as well.

Sig locked his hands together as he bounced his knees. "Abby told me you saw the ultrasound photo in her purse."

Sean looked over at me. "I did."

"You weren't supposed to see that," Sig said.

"I figured as much." Sean nodded.

I swallowed, waiting.

"Abby is a surrogate for my biological child, conceived using my deceased wife's egg," Sig explained. "Abby is working here while she's in the UK for the surrogacy."

Sean's jaw dropped as he looked over at me again. "Holy shit."

I forced some words out. "We hadn't come up with a plan for how to handle things or what to tell people once I couldn't hide it anymore. We were trying to keep it private for now, especially since it's so early. I've been trying to live my life in the meantime."

"I would appreciate it if you didn't tell anyone until we're ready to figure that out," Sig told him.

"Of course," Sean assured us.

"I'm sorry for not being up front about this," I said. "I didn't feel like it was fully my right to divulge."

Sean shook his head. "No apologies, but I mean, I'm blown away. I can understand why you didn't say anything."

Sig's mood was hard to read. He stood suddenly. "I don't have much more to say here, except that I appreciate your discretion."

Sean nodded. "You got it, boss."

"Cheers, then." Sig's eyes moved to mine. "Have a good lunch."

He'd started to walk out when I lifted my finger toward Sean. "One second." Leaving him sitting there, I followed Sig out of the conference room. "Sig," I called after him.

He turned. "Yeah?"

"I'm sorry that happened."

He pursed his lips. "It is what it is."

"I—"

"We shouldn't talk about it here, okay?" He looked over his shoulder and lowered his voice.

I looked down at my shoes. "Of course."

He made his way swiftly down the hall toward the elevators, and I returned to the conference room where Sean was waiting.

He smacked his hands together. "Well, file that under things I didn't expect to hear today." He smiled, but I could tell he was uncomfortable.

"I know. I can't imagine what you're thinking right now."

"How did this come about? I mean...why you?"

I took a seat across from him. "I'm a friend of Sig's wife Britney's family. I volunteered to be the surrogate after her parents indicated they wanted to use her eggs to conceive a grandchild. It's the only reason I'm here in the UK. I know I told you I'd moved here to be closer to a friend. I'm sorry I wasn't completely honest, but I didn't want to say anything until Sig was ready. You know how people talk around here."

"Makes sense."

I fidgeted with my purse strap. "I'll understand if you want to skip lunch."

"Of course not. We still need to eat, right? And now that I know you're eating for two, lunch is even more important." He winked.

My stomach growled. "I *am* pretty famished."

"Let's get out of here," he said, flashing a megawatt smile.

Sean and I headed to the deli down the street and took a seat in the corner. Throughout lunch, the mood became gradually more relaxed as we talked more about the surrogacy. His initial shock turned into curiosity.

"That's really awesome of you to have volunteered, you know." He stood to collect our trash.

"I felt like I was meant to from the moment Kate and Phil told me about it."

"Is it weird carrying a baby that's not your own?"

"It's weird carrying a baby period." I laughed. "But yeah, it's a challenge to keep my natural feelings in check. I constantly remind myself not to get too attached, since I'm going to have to let the baby go."

He nodded.

All in all, Sean and I ended up having a nice lunch together. I couldn't imagine having been in his shoes today, though he continued to insist he wasn't freaked out by the revelation. It almost seemed like he was relieved to have discovered this as the reason I'd been hesitant to go on a second date with him. He didn't realize, of course, that it was much more complicated than that.

As we got on to take the elevator back upstairs to our office, Sean turned to me. "Just for the record, Abby, in case I haven't made it clear, I'd still like to go out again. I'm eagerly awaiting your response to my most-recent invitation."

"Yeah." I nodded. "Okay. Maybe next weekend."

"I understand why you might be hesitant," he said. "But this doesn't change how much I fancy you." Then, before I could blink, Sean leaned in and planted a kiss on my lips.

The elevator doors slid open shortly before he pulled back. And when I turned? My heart fell to my stomach.

Sig was standing there.

Adrenaline coursed through my veins as I exited the elevator, Sean following me. I expected Sig to say something—anything, maybe chastise me—but instead he got into the elevator and pushed the button to close the doors without making eye contact.

CHAPTER 26

Abby

Track 26: "The Reason" by Hoobastank

I couldn't concentrate for the rest of the afternoon.

This had been my most stressful day since I'd arrived in England. Between Sean finding out about the pregnancy and Sig catching me and Sean in that unexpected kiss—today had been *a lot*.

But I knew the latter was bothering me more than anything. It had consumed me, in fact. That evening, at the end of my day, I'd tried to call Sig, but he didn't answer. Rather than call my usual car back to the countryside, I'd taken a couple of the girls up on their offer to go to the pub. That had been a much-needed distraction.

After I left the pub, my driver was supposed to take me home, but instead of the ninety-minute ride back to Westfordshire, I requested that he drop me off at a different location: Sig's London apartment. Sig seemed to be avoiding me, but for my own sanity, I needed to talk to him about what had transpired earlier.

When I arrived at his place, another resident let me in the front entrance. Once upstairs, I paused at Sig's door to find my bearings before I finally knocked.

A few seconds later, he opened. He was shirtless, the sight of his carved, tanned chest causing me to gulp hard. He blinked, seeming shocked to find me standing there. He ran a hand through his messy hair. "What are you doing here?"

"Is that how you greet me?"

In that moment, I looked beyond his shoulders. My heart sank as I spotted a redhead who looked like she was rushing to put on her blouse.

What the fuck? I just interrupted a booty call? "I'm sorry." A rush of jealousy tore through me. "I didn't know you weren't alone."

"Don't worry," she called from behind him. "I was leaving either way. Hope you have better luck than I did." She grabbed her purse and rushed past me, leaving a cloud of perfume in her wake.

I watched as she disappeared down the stairwell before turning to face him. "I wouldn't have come by if I'd known you had someone here."

"Why are you still in London this late?"

"Am I supposed to be safely tucked in bed at this time?" I placed my hands on my hips. "Aren't you going to invite me in?"

He moved aside.

"I went out with the girls from work," I said, dropping my purse on his couch. "I was going to have the car take me to Westfordshire, but I wanted to talk to you, so I had him drop me here. You didn't answer your phone earlier. I thought you were mad. But now I realize you were...busy."

He looked at his feet. "Nothing happened with her."

"You don't owe me an explanation," I said bitterly.

"I know I don't." His eyes met mine. "But since you seem to have assumed I was busy shagging her when you called earlier, I thought I'd clarify."

"She was buttoning her shirt, Sig. What am I supposed to assume?"

"Yeah, well, that's because it started but didn't go anywhere."

"You really didn't sleep with her?"

He shook his head.

"I guess that's your MO. You used to kick them out after sex. Now you kick them out before."

"Actually, once again, there was no kicking out. She decided to leave on her own. That's what I do, remember? Make women disappear."

"You have mad skills where that's concerned." I tilted my head. "You're a magician."

"Not really. Just a right prick. Or as your father would say, *that* prick."

I narrowed my eyes. "There's got to be more to this, why you can't get it up."

"Whoa!" His eyes widened. "That's not the problem at all, Abby. Trust me, there's *nothing* wrong in that arena." He cleared his throat. "Anyway, what did you want to talk to me about?"

"You don't know?"

He fidgeted with his hands and cracked his knuckles. "If you mean that awkward kiss I witnessed, there's nothing to say."

"Awkward because you had to watch the tail end of it?"

"No, awkward because your body language *clearly* showed you weren't into it."

"That's interesting. How so?"

"You were stiff as a board. He was doing all the work."

"I'm surprised you were able to analyze so much in the short time you caught it."

"Well, it was right there, in my face."

"What were you doing on my floor anyway?" I asked.

"I'd realized I'd come across a bit harsh earlier and went to see if you were okay."

My heart fluttered. I cleared my throat. "Well, there's some truth to your assessment—what you said about my body language." I bit my bottom lip. "I was preoccupied, still worrying about whether I'd upset you, when he sprung that kiss on me. I still can't believe I let the ultrasound photo slip out of my bag."

"You're not at fault for your clumsiness. It's who you are."

"Okay, you're busting my balls right now, so I guess that means you're not mad anymore?"

"I never said I was mad. Getting angry would do no good. What's done is done. At least it's only Sean who knows for now, unless you managed to let the cat out of the bag again tonight?"

"Of course not."

He gave me a once-over. "So what now? Are you staying here?"

"That doesn't sound like an invitation."

"It's late. You should stay in the guest room."

"Why, thank you for asking." I chuckled. "I think I will." I looked down at myself. "Of course I'll have to wear these same clothes to work tomorrow. I suppose I can wear the tank top I have under this blouse as a shirt to make it look different." I looked down. "Maybe no one will notice the skirt. I randomly have a clean pair of underwear in my purse, so I'm good there." I shook my head. "But you didn't need to know that."

"Thanks for sharing. It seems you carry the whole world in that purse of yours, including my biggest secret."

"I thought you said you weren't mad."

"I'm not, but I like giving you a hard time...a little too much."

"Just like you like me *a little too much*—in your words."

He glared. "Why did you really come here, Abby? You could've called me again if you needed to speak to me."

"You didn't pick up the first time. I assumed you would continue to ignore me."

"My phone was dead. I would never have ignored your call."

"Because of the baby."

"No." He grimaced. "Not just because of the baby." He looked me straight in the eyes. "I wouldn't have ignored you."

As his stare lingered on me, I felt the energy shift in the room. I couldn't put my finger on it, but something felt *different* tonight. It didn't help that he was shirtless in front of me looking hot as hell. Maybe that was it.

"So..." he asked. "Where did you leave things with Sean after he mauled you in the lift?"

"I haven't given him an answer about going out on a date again." *Here it comes*. The words barreled out of me, and I couldn't stop them. "Part of that hesitation is *you*."

He rolled his eyes. "You care too much what I think."

"It's not that."

"What are you referring to, then?"

"I think you know."

"Tell me anyway."

Here goes. "I have these weird feelings for you that I can't shake." I moved a bit closer. "After this baby comes, I'll be gone. You've made it clear to me and half the women in Britain that you don't want much. You might never. You had your one great love, and no one should expect more from you. I don't plan on sticking around or complicating your life. Once I'm back in the US, all of this will be out of sight, out of mind." I took a few more steps forward until we were only inches apart. "But as long as I'm here...I don't want to be alone. And if you continue sticking your head in the sand, I'm going to go out with Sean—especially now that he knows the truth."

"Is that a threat?"

I put the ball back in his court. "Is it? Does the idea of him threaten you? Because your attitude today certainly gave me that impression—that you were jealous. I'm gonna be honest and tell you that when I walked in tonight and saw what's her name—Rose—*I* was very jealous." I blew out a breath. "You say you appreciate my honesty, but it would be nice to get a little in return."

Sig stared at me for a long while. "The reason is you, actually."

"What do you mean?"

"The reason I can't take anything to completion with anyone." He leaned in. "You're the reason. *You're* distracting me. I don't want them. I only seem to want you. And it's a problem."

My body buzzed. "You look at me a lot, when you don't think I notice. Then I catch you, and you look away. I was never certain it meant much—until now."

"I'm extremely attracted to you. That's never been up for debate. All my life, I've had this problem of wanting things I can't have." He shook his head. "But that's just it. I *can't* have you, Abby."

"I get it." I nodded, feeling ready to burst. "But I need to let you know, if you really don't think anything can happen between us, I'm going to move on with Sean."

His gaze lifted. "You're gonna fuck him? Is that what you're trying to say?"

"Well, I wouldn't say it as crudely as that..."

"How *would* you say it?" I felt his breath on my face.

"I would say if I can't have a true relationship while I'm here, since I'll be leaving anyway, at the very least I need someone to...keep me company." I licked my lips. "I may be your surrogate, but I'm also a woman with needs." *What the hell has gotten into me tonight?* It was like I had no filter. *Is this what they're referring to when they say pregnancy brain?* I needed to escape before saying something I'd regret. "Can I take a shower?" I asked.

"Of course."

"Thanks. I'm just gonna do that and go straight to the guest room."

I practically ran away, disappearing into the bathroom. I ripped off my clothes and turned on the water. As I got in and let the water rain down on me, I swore at myself for being so candid.

But he'd admitted *I* was the reason he couldn't be with anyone else. *Holy shit.* He wanted me, too. I'd always known there was something between us, but I never imagined he felt the way I did about him.

After the shower, I wrapped myself in a towel and went into the guest room. He'd placed one of his T-shirts on the bed. I'd been so worked up that I'd forgotten to ask for one. But he had me covered. I slipped it over my head, intoxicated by the masculine smell. Had he worn this recently? My body buzzed with arousal. Did he give this one to me on purpose to drive me mad? I didn't want to go out there and say goodnight, afraid of what I might say or do that I would regret tomorrow.

Instead, I lay down on the bed, debating whether to take things into my own hands and relieve the tension that had been building from the moment I arrived here tonight. A knock on the door startled me.

His voice was low. "May I come in?"

"Yes." I got up from the bed and cleared my throat.

He'd put on a fitted white T-shirt with the gray sweatpants from earlier that hugged his bottom half so damn nicely. He stood there in all his gorgeous glory, not saying a word.

"Can I help you?" I swallowed.

His eyes held a certain playfulness I hadn't witnessed before.

"One thing about you, Abby. You know *exactly* what to say to push my buttons."

"What are you talking about?"

He walked toward me and didn't stop when our bodies met. Instead, he pushed me up against the wall. My knees grew weak as his hard chest pressed against my breasts. My nipples stiffened.

His eyes burned into mine. "No one is going to fuck you while you're pregnant with my baby but me."

My breathing sped up.

"*I* want to satisfy you." His chest heaved. "If you'll let me." Before I could answer, his lips crashed against mine.

Never in my life had I seen stars the moment someone kissed me, and it felt like I was transported somewhere else for a few seconds. Sig groaned, and the vibration activated every nerve ending in my body. He wrapped his hands around my face, the possessiveness in that act such an incredible turn-on. I threaded my fingers through his hair, and he kissed me harder as his tongue explored my mouth.

What the hell is happening? It was like a switch had flipped inside of him. But I was totally here for it, losing myself in it.

Placing one of his hands behind my head, he rasped, "You tell *me* what you need. Do you understand?"

"Uh-huh," I panted into his mouth, feeling ready to collapse.

He spoke against my throat. "You have to promise, if we do this, you won't fall for me."

As painfully aroused as I was, his words gave me pause, causing me to push back. "You don't think I know falling for you would be a losing game?" As much as I wanted him, I wasn't sure this man would ever be ready for love again. And I certainly didn't want to be second fiddle to his dead wife. I deserved better than that.

Yet even knowing Sig's limitations, I wanted to experience being with him. It was a dead end that would be one hell of a ride.

But one thing still held me back.

CHAPTER 27

Sig

Track 27: "I Want You to Want Me" by Cheap Trick

I'd spiraled completely out of control tonight. When Abby pushed back, I thought she'd come to her senses. But what came out of her mouth confused me.

"I want you to want me," she said. "You've made it clear that you don't want me with anyone else. If this is some egotistical way of keeping me from other men, just because I'm carrying your child, I don't want any part of it."

Had she not looked down to notice exactly *how* much I wanted her? "Haven't I made it clear that I'm struggling with my feelings for you?"

"Exactly. I don't want it to be a struggle. I don't want you to have regrets. I want you to feel *good* about every moment. As much as I'm a horny, hormonal mess lately, I couldn't live with myself if I felt you were wanting this for the wrong reason."

She can't be serious. She has it all wrong. "You don't think I want you? I've been doing everything in my power *not* to want you. And yes, I used the word *struggle*, but there's nothing painful about it. It's only a struggle because of how powerful it is, how hard to fight, how natural my desire for you feels. I merely have to look at you, and I get hard. It's not like that with anyone else. From the day we met, I knew I was in trouble. I've wanted you from the moment you first told me to fuck off. And you are very right. I *do* like to look at you, because you're exquisitely beautiful. Every other woman pales in comparison." He cupped my cheek. "My attraction to you is one-hundred-percent *easy*, Abby. Not wanting you *enough* is not the problem. I just don't want to hurt you. That's it. My one and only hesitation."

I should've excused myself and walked away at that point, ended things right there. But instead, my hand had a mind of its own, deciding to gently rub along the length of her upper thigh. My conscience was still hanging on by a thread, yet my body had no fucks left to give. It was ready to take her without a second thought.

Abby shuddered as she closed her eyes. My hand moving down her leg seemed to put her in a trance. I couldn't imagine what all the other things I wanted to do to her might elicit. Placing my mouth at her neck, I gently glided my teeth along her skin. "What do you need, Abby? Because whatever it is, trust me, I *want* to do it." I pressed my body against hers. "Can't you feel me right now?"

She bent her head back against the wall as my hand inched closer to where her upper thigh met her groin.

"I just..." she breathed. "I need..."

"This?" I slid my hand toward her center and applied pressure to her clit with my fingertips. "Seeing him kiss you today, even for those few seconds, made me insane. I lost my mind for the rest of the day. I thought I could invite someone over to forget, but it didn't work. That hasn't worked from the moment you came into my life."

She panted as I circled slowly over the material of her knickers, pressing more firmly against her clit. "I've never been jealous in my entire life before today."

I moved two of my fingers under the material, slowly inserting them into her hot, wet pussy. *Fuck.* My dick stiffened as it yearned to replace my fingers, to bury itself in the depths of what I knew would be sexual napalm. But that couldn't happen tonight. Despite my apparent loss of control, I needed to take this slow. "I want to pleasure you, Abby. Let me."

She nodded between breaths.

I tugged at my shirt she was wearing. "Take this off and lie down for me."

She did as I said, lying on the bed. I hovered over her, stopping for a moment to take in the sheer beauty of her naked and swollen breasts, not even knowing where to begin. There was so much I wanted to do. Do to her. I lowered my mouth, taking her mauve nipple gently between my teeth, careful not to pull too hard.

"Hold on to the bed," I demanded. "Or better yet, hold on to me. You're gonna need it."

I lifted myself up long enough to tear my shirt off before sliding my body down, unable to slip her thong off fast enough. Her beautiful pussy was so close to my lips, I could practically taste it. I'd dreamed about this moment but never imagined I'd actually *be able* to taste her. Never imagined I'd let myself lose all control.

I positioned my face between her legs, hardly able to believe she'd opened them for me, inviting me to do whatever I wanted. It had been a long while since I'd had the desire to pleasure a woman like this. I'd lost interest in this particular act in recent years, merely wanting to get the job done with the women I'd been with. Now? In this moment? I was practically shaking, foaming at the mouth to devour her, not only for the pleasure it would give her, but to satisfy my own selfish need.

The first taste was like a drug as I flicked my tongue over her clit, alternating between licking and sucking. My pace slowed as I willed myself to savor the soft feel and flavor of her flesh. But soon I couldn't take it anymore. The movements of my tongue became more rapid with each moment as I lost control, unable to hold back the unintelligible sounds escaping me.

Her hands gripped the sheets for leverage, and I slipped my tongue deep inside. In and out—using everything in me not to come from the sheer ecstasy of her taste. I looked up curiously, expecting to find her eyes closed. Instead, she was watching me intently. I knew I was absolutely fucked if I thought this was a one-off deal. Her impish—almost challenging—grin prompted me to devour her with even more intensity.

She reached for my hair and pulled on it. "God, Sig. You sure as hell know what you're doing. This feels so good. Better than anything."

"Trust me, the pleasure is all mine," I rasped as I reached up to cup her breast.

I was about to lose my mind with the urge to fuck her, and I prayed she came soon before I gave in. "Let go anytime you need to, love. Come all over my mouth. Give it all to me."

To my surprise, her body began to tremble, practically on cue after my command.

Fuck. So responsive.

So. Fucking. Amazing.

Abby pulled my hair as her scream echoed through my bedroom. I pressed my tongue into her even harder as she came against my mouth. I savored every last pulse, every last moan...every last second.

CHAPTER 28

Sig

Track 28: "Big Ten Inch Record" by Aerosmith

Two days later, I was still drunk off the high of that night.

I hadn't seen much of Abby the morning after I'd pleasured her in my guest room, since we'd been late getting to the office. Then she'd gone straight to the inn that evening after work, and she'd worked from home on Friday. True to form, I'd kept my distance on Friday evening as I pondered how to handle things moving forward now that I'd royally fucked up the plan.

But now it was Saturday, and I couldn't wait any longer to see her. I called my cousin as I drove out to Westfordshire on this brisk September afternoon to fill him in on the latest...*happenings*.

"What's up, Sigmund?" he said when he answered.

"We have a problem."

"Actually, I can guarantee you my problem is bigger. I was just about to call you."

Alarmed, I slowed my car. "Everything okay, mate?"

"No. Not in the least." He let out a long breath into the phone. "I mean, everyone is healthy. Nothing like that. But my biggest nightmare just happened."

"Don't scare me. What the hell is going on?"

"Remember the little baby girl Felicity is carrying that we're naming Britney?"

My stomach dropped. "Yeah?"

"Well, apparently, she is a *he*. They made an error during the earlier ultrasound. We just had a follow-up, and it clearly showed a little knob this time."

Holy shit. "A son? Congratulations! Why are you upset? This is monumental news. Now your family name will continue."

"I was hoping my child could avoid the stressors I had growing up. This poor little guy is the next Duke of West-fordshire, and he doesn't even know it."

"I doubt you're going to put the same pressure on him as your father did you."

He sighed. "True, but there are some pressures inherent to the title. They're unavoidable."

I couldn't help but laugh. "Your mother must be over the moon. All she's ever wanted was an heir."

"I haven't told her yet. I'm not in the mood to experience her satisfaction. Let her think it's a girl for a few more days."

"How is Felicity taking it?"

"She's handling it better than I am."

"You'll get used to the idea. How many more weeks do you have to go?"

"Just two. I truly don't understand how this happened. He was breech, in a weird position, for the last ultrasound, so they couldn't see clearly. He finally turned around this time, and there was his willy."

"I feel for you, mate, but this was meant to be. And it's kind of nice knowing the Covington name will live on."

"Well, thank you. I'll admit, I'm excited to have a son despite my fears." He sighed again. "Anyway...what was the problem you called about?"

My lack of self-control seemed trite now. "We don't have to talk about it."

"Sigmund, what's going on?"

"Something went down between Abby and me."

"*Something*..."

"Well, more specifically *I* went down."

"Ah, you devil. Wow. I wasn't sure you'd go there."

"My face between her legs, you mean?" I shook my head. "I should be shot for that."

"Don't tell me you're beating yourself up for something that was bound to happen?"

"You act like I couldn't have stopped it. I have free will."

"It was pretty much inevitable. It shouldn't be a surprise to you."

"I don't know how to feel. On one hand, I'm a prick for taking advantage of the situation. On the other...I don't plan on stopping anytime soon."

"Well, now that you've gone there, why would you?"

"I have many good reasons to stop before things get even more complicated. But the truth is, I can't expect her to be celibate for nine months any more than I could expect myself to be. Since I don't like the idea of her being with another man while she's here, this was the best solution."

"Ah, so this is about finding a solution for *her* and not about your intense attraction to her that's been obvious from day one..." he mocked.

"It's all of the above, alright? But mostly about my lack of self-control."

"Am I allowed to tell Felicity?"

"I'd prefer she not know right now—unless Abby decides to tell her. The fewer people who know, the better."

"Alright, then."

I pulled into the driveway. "I'll let you go. I'm just arriving at the inn."

"Ah... A trip to the inn in the middle of the day. Whatever could *that* be for?"

"Lavinia is making her stew I can't pass up."

"Better not let the *stew* get cold, then."

I chuckled. "Goodbye, cousin."

Abby and I spent a G-rated afternoon hanging out with Lavinia, and now I was counting the minutes until our sweet innkeeper went to bed. Lavinia had insisted on playing cards after dinner, which was like torture, really. All I wanted to do as I looked at Abby across the table was touch her. Kiss her. Smell her. Taste her. None of which I could do with Lavinia here.

I still wasn't sure how I was going to handle things this evening—whether I'd sneak into Abby's room or ask her to come to mine. Or maybe I'd opt to do nothing at all. I didn't want to be presumptuous. But based on the way she'd screamed in pleasure the other night, it seemed safe to assume she might want a repeat. Ever since the night she'd spent at my apartment, *I'd* been craving a repeat. I'd actually been craving much more, and I was unable to concentrate on anything else.

When Lavinia finally went to bed, Abby also went upstairs—without saying anything to me. I got the impression she was intentionally making me sweat. After I shut off the lights on the ground level, I followed them upstairs, still not knowing what to do. When I passed Abby's room, I knocked lightly. There was no answer. I slowly opened the door to find she wasn't inside. Down the hall, I could see light under the door of the main bathroom.

She must've been taking a bath. I decided to wait in her room, kicking my shoes off and lying back in her bed. About ten minutes later, I straightened as the door opened. Abby appeared, wrapped in a towel, her long, brown hair drenched. One look at her, and my cock began to strain against my trousers.

Her eyes widened. "What are you doing in here?"

"I thought I'd wait for you."

She lowered her voice. "What if Lavinia sees you?"

I had to chuckle at that, although I understood. "We're not fourteen, Abby."

"I know. But..."

"I'd tell her I was giving you a massage."

"You do give good massages." Her neck turned pink.

"I'd like to massage you with my mouth again. I've been dying for it actually."

Her skin turned redder.

"Are you not comfortable with me being here?" I asked.

She looked down at her feet. "It's not that..."

"What is it, then?"

"Since the other night, I haven't been able to think about anything else." She licked her lips. "I wonder if maybe we need to slow things down."

"Oh..." I wasn't sure of what to say to that, considering slowing down was the last thing on my mind, even if she was bloody right.

Her breath was shaky. "It's not that I don't want an encore. But I feel more consumed than I'd anticipated."

Her chest rose and fell as I approached her. "I might've given you the impression that what happened the other night was about me pleasuring you. But I needed it just as much—if not more—than you did. I can't stop thinking about it, either. This is all me. Me needing you."

"You came all the way out here today, suffered through stew and cards with Lavinia and me, just to come up to my room later?"

I lifted a brow. "Dodgy, right?"

"Very dodgy, Sigmund." She wrapped her arms around my neck. "Very."

I leaned in and took her mouth, my dick now hard as a rock.

"We don't have to do anything you don't want to," I mumbled against her lips.

"I want to do *everything*. That's the problem."

"We're on the same page, then." I kissed down the length of her slender neck.

She pulled back. "I don't think we should have sex, though."

"Whatever you want," I panted. "I'm not sure sex is a good idea anyway. I'm sort of afraid to...disrupt things."

"Hurt the baby, you mean?"

I nodded. "Yeah."

"You know that's not likely, right?"

"You haven't seen my cock." I winked.

"Well, excuse me." She snorted as she threaded her fingers through my hair.

"It's potentially dangerous."

"I don't believe you," she teased.

"Are you daring me to show you?"

"Well, you did keep it meticulously under wraps the other night. I didn't have a chance to see it."

I showered her neck with kisses again. "Is there a reason you'd like to see it? Something you plan to do with it?"

"I want to give *you* pleasure, too..." she murmured.

I groaned. "What did you have in mind?"

Rather than answer, Abby opened her towel, letting it fall to the floor as she dropped to her knees.

Good God. I held my hands up, signaling my surrender as I looked down at her.

Abby unzipped my trousers, lowering them to my thighs before sliding my boxer briefs down. My wet, throbbing cock sprung forward to greet her, practically smacking her in the face.

"You weren't kidding." She looked up at me, her eyes hazy. "No wonder you've been getting away with murder all this time."

I flashed a devilish grin. "You don't have to do this if you—" *Ah!* My words failed when she took me into her hot, wet mouth. *Fuck, yes.* I looked down, transfixed at the way she let me fuck her mouth. In and out. In and out. In and out. *Going to hell. Going to hell. Going to hell.*

And loving every minute of it.

Abby going down on me was the highest level of ecstasy I'd experienced in years. Fisting her hair, I bent my head back, allowing myself to escape into the nirvana I desperately needed. I wanted to be a gentleman, to let her take control, but I couldn't help bucking my hips once or twice until my cock was at the base of her throat.

When I felt ready to explode, I tugged on her hair to stop her. "I want to taste you while we come together."

She stood, seeming almost drunk. I kicked off my trousers and followed her beautiful, naked body as she sauntered over to the bed. The sight of her lying there, legs open, ready for anything, was almost too much to bear.

"How does this work?" she asked.

"I'll handle the logistics," I said, inching toward her on all fours before taking her mouth.

I moved her body to straddle my face as my tongue slid out eagerly to worship her.

Ass on my mouth, she bent forward, finding her way to my cock. I let out an unintelligible sound as she took me down her throat, sucking while I ate her out. Sixty-nine with Abby might have been my favorite thing I'd done in all of my thirty-seven years. And I'd forgotten all the reasons this was a very bad idea. Right now it was the best fucking idea I'd ever had.

I lapped against her clit faster with every movement of her mouth over my shaft. I wished I could see her sucking me off, but with her grinding against my face, that was nearly impossible. And anyway, seeing it might have pushed me over the edge too quickly. It was already nearly too much to handle as it was—her taste, the feel of her hot mouth around my cock as she went to work on me. *I don't fucking deserve this.* Not a single bit.

Wrapping my hands around her beautiful backside, I guided her hips as she rode my face harder.

When she slowed down, I knew she was close. My balls tightened as I tried to control my orgasm and avoid ending this ecstasy abruptly.

"I want to finish in your mouth," I panted. "Can I?"

She nodded as she took me deeper.

That did it. My body shook as I lost control, cum shooting shamelessly down her throat. She rocked her hips and pressed her clit harder against my mouth as her muscles contracted. She moaned, almost too loudly to avoid being heard by Lavinia.

But I didn't care. I wanted to hear Abby as she came. I wanted *all* of it.

When we'd come down from our mutual high, Abby turned to face me. It seemed she'd swallowed everything, leaving no evidence of me on her mouth. That was enough to make me ready for round two almost immediately. I still felt her wet arousal on my face. I already planned to wank myself off again later as I licked away the remnants. I was officially addicted. I wouldn't be able to resist her as long as we were around each other.

Moving to sit on the edge of the bed, I grabbed my trousers to slip them back on.

She pulled at my shirt. "Stay."

I froze. I wanted to. I *really* did. But that felt too... intimate.

Too intimate might have been a ridiculous excuse after what we'd just done, though. "I should go to my room."

Her smile dimmed. "Okay."

I had myself convinced that if I kept things purely sexual, it would be less complicated—even if I knew better. I caressed her face. "Why don't I make us a grand breakfast tomorrow?"

Her expression perked up a bit. "Sounds good."

"Any requests? I'll get up before you and go to the supermarket. And don't say Devil Dogs and cold milk."

She rested her cheek on her hand. "What are my options?"

"I could do a full English or something sweet like pancakes."

"Mmm..." She licked her lips, causing my dick to stand at attention again. "Pancakes sound great."

"Have you had pancakes here yet?"

She shook her head.

"They're different than in the States. They're thinner and bigger. We don't make them as fluffy. And we roll them."

"Kind of like a crepe?"

I brushed my thumb along her cheek. "Kind of like that, yeah."

She shut her eyes briefly.

I want to stay. But instead of giving into the need to climb into her bed and wrap my arms around her, I stood. "See you in the morning."

"Okay," she muttered. "See ya."

As I stepped out of the room, I stopped to compose myself. Then I tiptoed down the hallway. Unfortunately, my giant feet failed me, because just as I passed Lavinia's room, her door opened.

I froze. "Can I help you?"

"Oh no. I don't need anything." She smirked. "From what I can hear, your cup is full enough already."

Shit. "You *heard* nothing, crazy woman. Got it?"

"Your secret's safe with me." She winked before closing the door.

Great.

Once in bed, I tossed and turned, unable to stop thinking about what Abby and I had done, what we *didn't* do, and what I still *wanted* to do. I attempted to shift my focus by considering the pancakes I planned to make for breakfast tomorrow. I imagined all sorts of toppings as I made a virtual shopping list in my head.

But as life would have it, that breakfast would never end up happening.

CHAPTER 29

Abby

Track 29: "Goodbye for Now" by P.O.D.

My nipples were stiff when I woke this morning, and I had an uncontrollable ache between my legs. While the orgasm Sig had given me last night was even better than the first, it wasn't nearly enough to satisfy the need that only grew within me with each bit of contact we had. I longed for Sig as if he were an ocean away instead of just down the hall.

It hadn't surprised me that he didn't want to spend the night in my room. He probably knew we wouldn't be able to stop ourselves from taking things further. I also suspected spending the night in my bed might've been too much for him. It would've crossed the line he'd drawn when he made it clear I couldn't fall for him—which was the same as admitting he could never love me.

I looked over at my phone to find a text from him.

Sig: Heading to the supermarket. Didn't want you to wake and forget I was making breakfast and instead assume I'd escaped to London without saying goodbye. I know I sometimes do that. But I'm not running this time. Well, except to buy stuff to make you pancakes. See you soon. P.S. Lavinia heard us last night. So if you get up before I get back, she might give you a look or something. That woman couldn't keep her nose where it belongs if her life depended on it. P.P.S. Last night was fun.

Smiling from ear to ear, I put the phone back on my bedside table. I could hear downstairs that Sig was already back. Just as I was about to get dressed and head down, my phone rang.

When I saw that it was a Rhode Island number I didn't recognize, I rushed to answer. "Hello?"

"Abby? It's Doris Gray."

Doris Gray was my dad's neighbor. My stomach dropped.

"Your dad was just rushed to the hospital. I think he might've had a heart attack. He gave me your number in case of an emergency."

My hands started to shake. "He's alive, though?"

"Yes. He was alive when they took him to Newport Hospital. He was able to call nine-one-one himself."

I couldn't breathe.

"Are you there?" she said.

"Yeah." I looked around my room. "I need to... I need to come home."

"Can I do anything to help?"

"No. Just keep me posted if you hear anything more."

After calling to book the next flight out of London, I grabbed my suitcase from the corner of the room and threw some clothes into it as fast as I could.

I ran downstairs to find Sig unloading items from a paper bag onto the counter.

"There's the sleepyhead now," he announced before catching the expression on my face. His smile faded. "Abby? What's wrong?"

"It's not the baby. Um...it's my dad. He had a heart attack." My lip trembled. "I have to go back."

"Oh God." Sig dropped what he'd been holding to come over and hug me. "I'm so sorry."

"I just booked a flight. It leaves London in three hours. It was the first one I could get direct to Boston."

He nodded. "Let's leave for the city right now."

"Thank you."

Lavinia came around the corner. "Everything will be okay, dear. I'll say some special prayers for your sweet dad."

"Thanks, Lavinia. I'll need them. I can't lose him." My voice cracked. "He's all I have."

"Don't worry about the food, Sigmund," she said. "I'll put everything away."

"Thank you." He placed his hand on her shoulder, then turned to me. "Ready?"

"Yes." I hugged Lavinia one last time, unsure when I'd be seeing her again. "Goodbye for now."

On the way to the airport, I spent a half hour trying to get through to someone at the hospital to no avail, and my father was not answering his cell phone. I called my sister, Claire, to make sure she knew what was going on, and Dad's neighbor had contacted her as well. Claire was also on her way to the airport.

Sig offered his hand to me. "You okay?"

I took it. "Trying."

He let go to reach into the center console, where he took out a granola bar. "Here. I know you probably don't have an appetite, but you need to eat something."

"Thank you." I reluctantly opened the package.

"Your sister is booking a flight?"

"Yeah. She'll get there before me, most likely."

"Don't let her upset you," he said.

"I'll try. I know it's not good for the baby."

"It's not the baby I'm worried about right now, Abby." He took my hand again, his warm touch calming me for just a moment.

Sig parked when we got to the airport and insisted on walking me in.

My hands shook as I used the kiosk to check in. Sig excused himself for a moment to talk to the woman at the ticket counter. It seemed to be taking forever, but it wasn't like we were in a rush. We'd made it here in good time, so there was still more than an hour before my flight.

When he finally returned, I noticed him holding something.

"What's that?"

"It's my ticket." He waved it. "I'm going with you."

CHAPTER 30

Abby

Track 30: "Daddy's Girl" by Red Sovine

Feeling frantic as I entered the hospital, I was grateful to have Sig by my side. I still couldn't believe he'd made that spur-of-the-moment decision. By some stroke of luck, he kept his passport in his glove compartment. I hadn't even noticed as he'd reached over me and grabbed it before we'd exited the car at the London airport.

When we got to my dad's floor, I told the woman at the desk I was his daughter, and she directed me to his room. Relief flooded through me when I found him sitting up in bed and talking to a nurse. "Dad!"

"Oh my God!" He looked like he might have another heart attack. "Abby!"

I rushed to embrace him. "What happened?"

"It was just a mild heart attack. Luckily, I recognized the symptoms and called when I did. The paramedics were able to stop it from getting worse. You didn't have to come."

"Of course I did. I didn't know what condition you'd be in when I got here. I had no information other than you'd been taken to the hospital. I couldn't get through to anyone before my flight. I was so scared."

His eyes finally moved to the tall man standing in the corner. "Who's this?" he asked.

"It's Sig, Dad. He came with me because he didn't want me to be alone." I turned to Sig. "This is my dad, Roland Knickerbocker."

Sig nodded. "Good to meet you, Mr. Knickerbocker."

"Well, if it isn't *that prick* himself."

Sig's face turned uncharacteristically red. "I've been told that's my nickname."

"Yeah, for being an arrogant jerk to my daughter when she showed up there. But she told me you've since mellowed out. She even likes you now, it seems." He looked to me for confirmation, and I nodded. "So I'll agree to like you, too. But just a warning, once you get a nickname from me, it usually sticks. Don't take it to heart."

Sig grinned. "Well, I didn't fly all the way here to get my arse beat, so I'm glad to hear you no longer despise me. I'll happily accept the nickname, which is probably deserved."

"Is Claire here?" I asked.

Dad nodded. "She went to the house to bring me some things, since I'll be here a few days. How long are *you* staying?"

"As long as you need me," I assured him.

"I don't need you, honey. I'm fine."

I pushed a chair up next to the bed. "Well, as good as you seem, I'm still gonna need to talk to your doctors and make sure you're okay before I feel comfortable heading back."

"I'm not going to complain about having you around." He reached for my hand. "I've missed you so much."

I took his hand and kissed it. "I missed you, too, Daddy. I'd rather see you under different circumstances, though."

"Oh, you're here." A voice came from the doorway.

I turned to find my sister Claire holding a couple of bags. Standing, I let go of my father's hand. "Hey."

Her eyes moved to Sig. "Who's this?"

"This is Sig. He flew from England with me."

She gave him a once-over. "You're the sperm donor..."

Sig's eyes went wide before he glared at her. "And you're the rude older sister."

I cleared my throat. "Yes. This is my sister, Claire."

He nodded.

"It's nice to meet you, despite the fact that you just insulted me," she told him.

"Same," he said as he flashed me a sympathetic look.

Claire walked over and set a bag on the chair next to Dad. "Got you some pajamas and snacks." She turned to me. "How long are you here?"

"I haven't gotten that far."

"Well, I need to get back to work in California tomorrow. Now that I know he's fine, I booked my return ticket. But it would be nice if you could stay a few days."

My sister was a lawyer, trying to work her way up the ranks at her firm. She believed everything revolved around her and her job.

"*Is* he okay?" I challenged. "Have the doctors confirmed that?"

"We haven't gotten the results of every test they ran, but he seems fine enough to me. I'm comfortable going back. Work is really busy."

"I have a job, too."

"It's not the same," she said.

I gritted my teeth. "Well, I didn't come all the way here just to head right back anyway." I turned to my father. "I'm not leaving until you're settled and back home again, Dad."

Sig put a hand at the small of my back. That simple touch brought me such comfort. He literally had my back. "You need to eat," he said. "Why don't I get you something and bring it back here?"

"That'd be great. Thank you."

When he left, I immediately yearned for his return, once again so thankful he was here with me. It felt good to have someone looking out for *my* well-being while I focused on my father's.

"Is something going on between you two?" my sister asked.

"He just accompanied me for support."

"Claire," my dad interrupted. "Aren't you going to ask Abby how she's feeling?"

She scoffed. "I'm still in denial about the rash decision she made. Asking her how she's feeling would force me to acknowledge it. So, no."

God, the nerve of her.

"Well, that's your problem," Dad said. "You should still have the courtesy to ask, regardless of your feelings."

"Save your energy, Dad." I shook my head. "It's a lost cause."

He ignored me, turning to her again. "And I'll have you know it wasn't a rash decision. Abby knows what she's doing, thought long and hard about it. Her choice is selfless. And I admire her for it."

"Thanks, Dad."

"I'm sorry." Claire sighed. "You know my thoughts on the matter. I do hope you're feeling well, though."

I forced a smile. *Too little, too late.*

Twenty minutes later, my sister was gone by the time Sig returned with takeout. I had no idea whether she'd returned to a hotel or taken off for California.

Sig and I ate while hanging out with my dad, and then my father announced that he was going to try to get some sleep. I promised to come right back to the hospital in the morning. Hopefully we'd receive the remaining test results by then, which would help determine when I'd be able to return to England.

"What's the plan?" Sig asked as we left the hospital.

"I don't really have one. I wasn't prepared for this."

"I just meant for tonight," he said. "I can get a hotel for myself or book rooms somewhere for both of us."

"Oh no." I shook my head. "We'll both sleep at my house, where I live with Dad. You can sleep in his room."

"Are you sure? I don't want to impose."

"There's no one to impose upon. It'll just be you and me."

"I thought maybe you'd want to decompress tonight and not have to deal with anyone—including me." He opened the passenger door to the rental car for me before getting in on the driver's side. "Your sister is...a lot. I'm sorry you have to deal with her."

"Yeah, well, there are worse things in life." I sighed. "Actually, I'd kind of like you to see where I live. You know, since we're here anyway. Definitely never thought I'd have the opportunity to show you around."

"Alright." He nodded. "Considering I hadn't made the decision to fly here until I got to the airport, I obviously have no spare clothes."

"I'd offer you some of Dad's, but you're way too tall." I chuckled.

"There must be a department store nearby?"

Then a lightbulb flashed in my brain. "Actually, I have an idea..."

CHAPTER 31

Abby

Track 31: "My House" by Flo Rida

The beach was choppy tonight, the wind fierce. But just the sight of the sign reading *Little Rhody* made me smile. Sig pulled up in front of my family's store, a small structure, purple on the outside with a whole lot of history and heart on the inside. I used the key I always carried in my purse to open the door before turning on the lights.

Sig entered behind me. "So this is the famous shop, eh?"

"It sure is. I figured I could show it to you and we could steal some extra clothes for you at the same time."

"Brilliant."

Everything was as we'd left it, fully stocked, when we'd had to close. I walked over to a shelf of men's sweatpants. "These say Rhode Island down the leg."

"Ah." He took them. "I'll wear these tonight and on the way home, enjoying the stares of people wondering whether I'm a lunatic."

Laughing, I grabbed a T-shirt and held it against my chest. "And what do you think of this?"

Sig read the words on the front aloud. "Someone from Rhode Island Thinks I'm Cute. Shouldn't that be for an infant and not in size extra-large?"

"You can be big and still cute."

"I suppose I'm evidence of that." He winked. "Although *cute* has never been a word used to describe me."

"Well, it looks like it'll fit you." I giggled. "I think it's coming home with us."

"You don't happen to have men's boxers, do you?"

I snapped my fingers. "Believe it or not, we do."

I walked over and held up two pairs. "You have your choice: lobsters or the Rhode Island state logo over the crotch."

Sig scratched his chin. "How does one choose?"

"You're right." I laughed. "We'll take them both."

"You spoil me, Abby." He looked around. "This place is sort of magical. I hope you can get it up and running again."

"What am I gonna do with all this overstock if not, right?"

"I'm sure the market for State of Rhode Island-crotch boxer shorts is hotter than you think." Sig wandered over to a stand. "This is saltwater taffy?"

"Yeah." I laughed. "Are you a taffy guy?"

"No, but I'd like to buy some for Leo, if you don't mind. He grew a taste for it when we spent the summer here. It's sort of a running joke. He can't find it very easily back home." He grabbed a stack of four boxes.

"You didn't even bring a suitcase. You're gonna have to get something just to trek all of that taffy back home."

He lifted a tote bag off the rack. "I suppose this *Rhode Island Slut* tote bag will do?"

"Go for it!" I cackled. "You know, I would've loved to meet you and Leo when you spent that wild summer here." I paused to calculate. "Although I was probably in middle school then."

"Ouch."

"Not sure I could've gotten in on the fun." I chuckled.

"You wouldn't have liked me at all."

"I barely like you now," I teased. "Actually, you're right. I might not have gotten along with Mr. Threesome."

He rolled his eyes. "Here we go again, bringing up the Marias."

"I wonder whatever became of them. Hopefully they didn't marry the same man and kill each other. What were their last names? I'll look them up." I laughed.

"I have no idea."

I rolled my eyes. "Of course you don't."

I could hear the waves through the shop windows. I paused and closed my eyes for a moment. "Listen to that. I love that sound. I forgot how happy it makes me to be here, especially this store."

He looked around. "It suits you—whimsical and a little corny. But *very* fucking adorable."

We got to the house, and Sig changed into his Rhode Island sweatpants and T-shirt. Everything fit him like a glove, and I was digging it—especially the snug sweatpants, which left little to the imagination below the belt.

I put on a tank top and some soft leggings; I still had a good amount of clothes here. We walked out to the back deck, which overlooked the water. While the store was right near the ocean, our house overlooked a small inlet.

It was late, but I wanted to show Sig the view from our backyard.

"Beautiful," he said as we looked out toward the water.

"Thank you. I was hoping you'd like it here."

"I was referring to you, love, not the water. You've had one hell of a day, yet you still managed to make me smile, make your father smile."

"I try..."

"No, you don't even have to try. That's just it. It's who you are. I see that now. I was wrong to ever judge you in the beginning. Your intentions have always been pure."

"Well, thank you."

"No need to thank me. Just stating a fact." He rolled his eyes. "Your sister, on the other hand... She deserves a wedgie. She's the opposite of you, nothing but self-serving."

"I'm glad you got to see her in action."

"I did, and I didn't like it one bit."

I sighed and closed my eyes, listening to the sound of crickets. "You said now you see my intentions are pure. Time has taught me that you were never the judgmental prick I thought you were. You were just scared and protecting everyone involved from getting in over their head."

"All that, only to get in over our heads anyway, right?" He winked.

"Everything is going to turn out okay. I don't know how I know that. I just do." I looked up at the night sky. "I'm glad I got to show you the store today."

"Me, too."

"Being back there reminded me of my childhood. It always does. Warm summer days, people strolling in smelling like salt and coconut sunscreen. And of course, it reminded me of my mother." I turned to him. "Lately, though, I've been having doubts about whether reopening it is the right decision."

"You hadn't mentioned that. How do you mean?"

"I have to wonder if I'm doing it out of nostalgia and guilt or because it's a good business decision. The bulk of the business is seasonal, but we have to pay rent year-round. I'm not sure it makes financial sense long term. Back when my grandmother opened it, there was less competition. Since then, so many other stores like it have popped up around here. And it would also bind me to Rhode Island. Being in England has helped me see that there's a whole world out there I'd be missing if I committed to running the store. I have a lot to think about."

He put his hand on my shoulder and squeezed. "You want my advice?"

"Well, you *are* an *old* and wise man," I teased.

"You're young. I think you should experience life and not be tied down. I don't think your mother or grandmother would want that. The only reason you should be running that store is if it's your passion."

A hard truth rose to the surface in that moment. "I don't think it is."

"Well, that's your answer."

"I couldn't tell you what my passion is, though. How do we even know?"

"I suppose a passion is something you'd rather do with your free time than anything else. And when we can somehow turn it into our life's work, even better."

"I don't suppose being operations manager at Covington is your passion?"

"You're right, but why would you think that?"

"Oh, I don't know. Because you're kind of grumpy at work. I don't get the impression you're overly passionate about managing everything, even though you're good at your job."

"Well, you're correct. My job is not my passion, although, yes, I am excellent at it and grateful for it. I acknowledge the fact that pure nepotism got me there, but it wouldn't keep me there if I fucked things up. Revenue has quadrupled since I took over. I'm very proud of that." He looked out at the water. "But as far as a passion? I don't think I have one."

"Maybe it's yet to come." I smiled. *Maybe it's your son or daughter.*

"There are small things I enjoy, like cooking, getting lost in that process." He leaned in to whisper in my ear. "And don't tell her this, but I like lazy weekends at the inn with Lavinia far more than partying in London. Helping her keep the inn up and running was definitely a highlight of the past few otherwise miserable years for me. It was a good distraction."

"Maybe the small things are enough." I smiled. "And I can totally relate to loving the inn. There's a certain peace there that I don't find anywhere else. I know I can't stay forever, but I'll always cherish my time in Westfordshire with her."

He scratched his chin. "You should see more of Europe while you're there, though." His eyes seemed to shine. "You know what? We should travel before you're too far along."

We? Of everything he'd ever said to me, that suggestion came as the biggest surprise. "You want to travel with me?"

His smile nearly melted me. "Call me crazy, but I do."

"Had you thought about this before now?"

"No. The idea just came like an epiphany. It would be fun to show you more of Europe. Must be the Rhode Island joggers I'm wearing. They're magical, transforming me from a miserable prick into a ball of fun."

"Well..." I tugged at his shirt playfully. "What if I can't get time off from work?"

"Considering I'm your boss's boss, I'd say you stand a good chance."

"Then I would love that." Excitement filled me. "Now you're making me *really* not regret this surrogacy decision."

"I'm glad you don't regret it, love."

"I regret nothing so far, even things I probably should." I reached up to rub the scruff on his chin, wanting so badly for him to kiss me.

"Speaking of things you probably should regret, I'm going to stay far away from you so you can actually sleep," he said as we walked back into the house. "You need your rest, even though right now I feel like keeping you up all night."

"You say that while sporting a stiffy in those sweat-pants and expect me to resist you?"

He looked down. "Yeah. I'm sorry. I can't help it. Your tits in that shirt have me wanting to tear it off you with my teeth."

I batted my lashes. "You can, if you want."

"Don't tempt me."

"You should go to my father's room before I *do* tempt you."

He pulled his brows together. "That sounds bizarre—going to your father's room when all I want to do is fuck you right now."

"It does sound kind of wrong." I laughed.

After we walked up the stairs, Sig stopped in front of Dad's door. "Goodnight, Abby."

"Goodnight, Sig. Thank you for coming with me. I'll never forget it."

"You're welcome, gorgeous."

That night I went to sleep feeling relaxed, cared for, and remarkably content, despite the fact that the future was still uncertain.

Maybe it was being near the ocean again, back at the store, being home.

Or maybe it was *him*.

But tonight held the last peace I'd feel for a while.

CHAPTER 32

Sig

Track 32: "(Sittin' On) The Dock of the Bay" by Otis Redding

If life had taught me one thing, it was never to be surprised when the other shoe drops.

That first day in Rhode Island, everything had appeared relatively stable. Abby had hoped her father would be released with some heart medication and instructions to make some lifestyle changes, and it would be safe for her to return to England within a week or so of getting him resettled at home.

But when we'd returned to the hospital the second day, Abby's father's doctor told us there'd been an incidental finding on one of his cardiac scans: a lung nodule that looked suspicious. It was a blow no one saw coming; in fact, Abby's sister had already flown back to California, believing there was no need to stay.

For the next week, we'd held off on booking return tickets until we had the results of Roland's biopsy. Abby's dad had come home, so I'd spent the nights on the

Knickerbockers' living room couch and cooked dinners for them, trying to distract from their worries. And I was at the house with Abby and her dad when they got the call that the nodule was cancerous.

Now, nine days after we arrived, I was leaving tomorrow for England without her. Abby would stay in Rhode Island for the foreseeable future while her father underwent treatment for stage-two lung cancer. There was never any question about how to proceed. She'd see an OBGYN here. And the controlling manner in which I'd handled the logistics of the surrogacy thus far would have to change.

The last thing I wanted to do was leave her. But I couldn't stay indefinitely. I had a company to run and had already taken more than a week off with no warning, rescheduling several important client meetings. So, I'd finally booked my ticket for tomorrow.

Before I left, though, I wanted to do something nice for Abby, get her mind off of things for just one night. Since her father wouldn't be starting treatments until next week, I asked her if she would take twenty-four hours and spend them with me. Roland was insistent that she do so even if she was reluctant to leave him.

Once we left for our mini trip, I could see the stress lifting from her a bit. We'd rolled the windows down, and she closed her eyes as the wind blew her hair around. I hadn't told her where we were going, but when we passed the signs for Narragansett, she figured it out.

Her mouth fell open. "You're taking me to your old stomping grounds?"

"Well, you said you wished you'd known me the summer I stayed here. I thought I'd give you a bit of that experience retroactively."

"Oh my goodness!" She bounced in her seat. "Am I about to enter a time warp?"

A little while later, when I pulled up at the massive house on the bay, Abby's eyes widened. "This is where we're staying?"

Instead of answering, I walked around to the passenger side and got the door for her. "Welcome to the very house where Leo and I stayed that summer."

"Are you kidding?" She looked up. "It's stunning."

"It looks the same, honestly."

"It's still for rent?"

"Apparently. I couldn't believe it, either. The owners have rented it out all these years."

"And it was available on short notice?"

I smiled. "No, actually. Someone had rented it for three weeks. But I pulled some strings and gave them an offer they couldn't refuse to disappear for one night so we could have it."

"I can't believe you did that."

I used the code the management company had given me to open the door. When we stepped inside, the smell of cleaning chemicals registered. They must have scrambled to have it tidied between guests.

"Oh my God." She looked around. "This place is amazing."

I smiled. "Hope you're ready for the full experience."

Abby laughed. "Don't tell me you invited the Marias. I'm *not* having a foursome."

"No, wiseass. But we *are* having a clam bake. And the weather is perfect. I've rented a boat so we can take a ride out on the bay."

"Do you have to pick it up?"

"Someone's delivering it, actually."

"Ohhh. Fancy." She wrapped her arms around my neck. "I just... I can't thank you enough. I needed this so much, Sig."

"I know that, beautiful," I said, cradling her face. "I know you're scared. The next several weeks aren't going to be easy. And I hate that I can't be here." I kissed her forehead. "This is the least I can do to get your mind off things. I'm not gonna let you worry about a thing today."

"Thank you," she whispered.

Narragansett was even nicer than I remembered, but maybe that was because of the present company. Thankfully, it was warm for late September, and Abby and I made the most of our precious last hours together. We swam in the heated pool, took the boat out, went shopping at the gourmet market, and cooked together. Or, well, *I* cooked while she leaned against the counter invading my space, which I secretly loved.

After a long, action-packed day, we cleaned up the mess we'd made in the kitchen. We'd devoured the lobster, crab legs, clams, and corn on the cob, so there was no food to put away, just dishes to clean.

We eventually took our drinks out to the back deck—beer for me and lemonade for her. I pointed my bottle toward a house in the distance. "See that property over there across the bay?"

"Yeah?"

"That's where Felicity lived."

"Oh yeah! That's right. I forgot she said she was right across the bay when you guys met her."

"She still owns the house, but the same people have been renting it for years."

We stared across the bay for a while before she turned to me. "Has anything that's happened with my father been triggering for you?"

"Because of the cancer, you mean?"

"Yeah."

I pondered that. Strangely, it hadn't. I'd been too concerned about Abby's mental health and her father's condition. "No. It's mainly made me feel sorry for *you*. I imagine you wouldn't have signed up for the surrogacy if you'd known how this year was going to play out."

"There's still nothing I would change so far," she insisted, looking up at the stars. "It's so beautiful here."

"It is," I said, looking straight at her and not at all at the stars. I cleared my throat. "I can appreciate more about this place now than I did when I was younger."

"You had ants in your pants, then." She smirked.

"Go ahead. What else do you want to say?"

"Ants in your pants and two Marias in your pants." She snorted.

Her laughter was like music to my ears. I couldn't believe that come tomorrow, I wouldn't hear it in person again for a while. An unidentifiable feeling gnawed at me. A mix of happiness and guilt, perhaps—guilt over being happy. "I'm relieved you met the person I am now and not then," I told her. "Parts of him are still here, I suppose, but mostly the good ones."

"I'm glad I met this version of you, too."

Abby's long brown locks blew in the evening breeze. She looked more beautiful than ever. I wanted nothing more than to take her upstairs and worship her body tonight. It was the first time I'd yearned to be inside of someone for reasons other than escapism in as long as I could remember. But I vowed not to go there. I was leaving. But God, did I want it, did I crave her.

She shivered.

"Are you cold?" I asked.

"A little." Her teeth chattered.

I thought about grabbing a sweater from inside but instead—despite the vow I'd just made to myself—I prompted her to sit on my lap. "Come here." Abby settled in as I wrapped my arms around her.

"I wish I had more time here with you," she said, resting the back of her head on my chest. "Actually, I wish I could freeze time right now."

"Me, too." I rubbed her arms. "But I have one thing to look forward to when I get back."

"What's that?"

"Not needing to kill every man at work for making a move on you."

She turned to look at me. "Were you really jealous?"

"Unfortunately, I was."

"Is it because I'm carrying your baby? Or something more?"

"Well, considering I started feeling this way before I knew you were pregnant, pretty sure you have your answer."

"You like me, Sig, but you don't know what to do with it."

I squeezed her. "I have some ideas tonight."

"You won't go there, though."

"Is that a dare?"

"No, it's not. I think you're too scared to fuck something up, especially before you leave tomorrow. And I get it."

"You're underestimating my weakness." I nuzzled her neck, feeling my dick stir. "Have you looked at yourself lately?"

"Not really..."

"You're blossoming into kryptonite. I can't stop looking at you."

"I've noticed."

"I've never been good at hiding it, have I?"

"Is it just physical attraction or something more?"

"It's definitely *not just* physical attraction, Abby."

After a long moment of silence, she muttered, "Britney was lucky."

I blinked, taken aback. "Because she's dead?" I quipped, immediately regretting my sarcasm.

"No, of course not." She squeezed my arm. "I'm sorry if that sounded insensitive."

"I know you didn't mean it that way. I was being a sarcastic arse."

"I meant because you loved her so strongly. I think we all have to learn to love ourselves, so it doesn't matter whether anyone feels as strongly about us as we do about ourselves. But finding someone who loves you that deeply is really rare and special. Of course she wasn't lucky to have passed. I didn't mean to imply that. But she *was* lucky to have found you before she did."

I swallowed. "I didn't know I was capable of love until I met her. Didn't even know what it felt like."

"It takes a special person to bring it out in someone so resistant to it."

I sucked in some air, anxious to change the subject. "Were you in love with that boyfriend—the one who hurt you?"

"I definitely *thought* I loved Asher. But in retrospect, I couldn't have possibly loved someone who didn't love me back. One-sided love is a delusion. Because how could you love someone who doesn't return it? Him hurting me took away any love I thought I had for him, if that makes sense. It was erased."

"Of course."

"But you know, in the end, the breakup didn't hurt me as much as it should've. It wasn't like I couldn't eat or anything. I would think losing your great love would nearly paralyze you."

Boy, did I understand that. "Yeah."

"So I don't think he was ever the one. Which means it wasn't that great of a loss."

"Probably not, if you got over it fairly quickly."

She sighed. "Lucky me. That probably means my greatest heartbreak is yet to come."

"I hope not." What I wanted to say was, *I hope it's not me.*

She hopped off my lap. "As much as I don't want this day to end, I think we should go upstairs."

I stood. "I never properly showed you the upstairs, did I?"

"Lead the way."

I took her hand as we reentered the house and headed up to tour each room. Abby would be sleeping in the bedroom Leo had stayed in all those years ago, while I took my old room for nostalgia's sake.

We were standing in her room when she said, "Thank you for an amazing day." Abby placed a firm kiss on my lips, and that was all it took. When she pulled back, her eyes fell to my crotch. "Are you saluting me?"

My dick was completely hard and clearly not ready to bid her adieu yet. "It's saying goodnight."

"Ah."

My eyes went to her breasts. She hadn't been wearing a bra all day, which was torture. At nearly five months along, Abby was showing only slightly, but her swollen breasts were another story altogether.

"Do you want to touch them?" she asked, her voice barely audible.

I nodded slowly, still unwilling to *actually* touch her for fear of what I might do next.

Abby lowered her shirt, causing her gorgeous tits to pop out the top.

I dragged my tongue along my bottom lip. "Who knew pregnancy could be so damn sexy?"

"I *feel* sexy, which I never expected to."

My mouth watered as I stood there taking her in.

She looked up at me. "Are you afraid or something?"

"It's not that I don't want to touch them. It's that I want to do too much more."

"Like what?"

I finally reached out, succumbing to the need. Cupping her breast in my palm, I murmured, "I want to slide my dick between them and watch my cum drip down your skin." My cock strained against my trousers as her breath hitched. "You're exquisite," I said before snapping out of my stupor and forcing my hand away. "Goodnight."

I dashed out and made my way down the hall. Once in my room, I paced, unable to think straight. Still hard as a rock, I felt as though I might die from blue balls for the first time in my life. *You fucking idiot. Leaving her standing there after telling her you wanted to titty fuck her? What the hell is wrong with you?*

CHAPTER 33

Sig

Track 33: "Rocket" by Beyonce

I must've stared out at the bay for a full thirty minutes before I realized I'd be getting no sleep tonight in this state. I burst out of my room and headed back to Abby's.

Before I could say anything, she opened the door. "It took you long enough," she panted.

I gripped her tank top, pulling her toward me and crashing my mouth into hers. "I'm a big fucking idiot," I groaned through our kiss.

She spoke over my lips. "I already knew that, Sigmund."

Abby practically tore my shirt off, lifting it over my head and tossing it into the air. I did the same to her tank top. There was no chance she'd be putting it back on anytime soon. I took a moment to marvel at her utterly perfect tits, begging to be sucked. My dick throbbed.

She slipped out of her knickers before falling back onto the bed, spreading her legs to invite me in. Ravenous, I reached for my belt buckle, undoing it at warp speed before whipping the leather strap out and tossing it. I unbuttoned my jeans and lowered them.

I hovered over her, soaking in her eager eyes. Unable to wait any longer, I took my cock out and rubbed the tip against her beautifully slick opening. So hot, so inviting. I bent to take her nipple in my mouth as I rocked my body back and forth, my shaft sliding repeatedly over her clit. I devoured her supple breasts one by one, knowing in my bones there was no turning back.

Our kiss grew deeper as I ached to enter her. I explored her body with the palm of my hand as my tongue continued to ravage her mouth. Stopping the frenzy for a moment, I looked into her eyes. "I told myself I wouldn't let this happen. But you're too fucking beautiful, Abby. And I'm too fucking weak. I want you more than I've wanted anything in a very long time. I need to be inside you."

"Don't think about the consequences right now. I need you, too."

I nodded, sliding my hand down to her warm opening, cupping her gorgeous pussy before I moved on top of her and positioned my crown at her entrance.

Not wanting to hurt her, I slowly pushed inside. *Holy fuck.* I nearly lost my breath. Abby was so tight as her beautifully wet pussy began to envelop my cock. Still being cautious, I sank inside her much more gradually than I wanted. I barely fit. As amazing as that felt for *me*, I didn't want to hurt her. "You okay?" I asked.

She smiled up at me. "I'm good."

"Take a deep breath and relax." I wouldn't be able to move freely inside of her if she didn't loosen her muscles.

"Don't be afraid. I can take it."

"It doesn't feel like you're taking it," I muttered as I pushed deeper, struggling to contain my need to come, which would've happened at any moment if I let it. The last thing I needed was her encouragement, because all I wanted was to fuck her hard. "I don't want to hurt you. But I'm so fucking weak," I rasped before thrusting into her again, this time with a little more force.

With each movement in and out, her pussy opened for me until she seemed to fit me like a glove. In fact, in a minute's time, it felt like she was made for me. I'd thought I'd be afraid to go balls deep, afraid to hurt the baby, but the pleasure was too intense to hold back. I pushed deeper until there was nowhere left to go. While some part of me was still conscious of the fear of physically hurting her, that paled in comparison to my need for the intense pleasure of being fully inside of her—over and over again.

I felt things I never thought I'd experience again—and they weren't merely sexual. This woman had enraptured every part of me, mind and body. But I fought the need to analyze that right now.

Abby tugged on my hair. "You feel so good, Sig."

Suddenly my only goal in the world was to continue making her feel good. "Tell me what you need."

"Go faster. Harder."

With her permission, I did just that, growling in pleasure with every thrust as I tried not to imagine that I was crushing her with my weight and injuring my unborn child all at once. But in truth, I couldn't have stopped. At this point, the baby could've verbally told me to knock it off, and I might've told it to hush.

I squeezed her breast as I continued pumping in and out of her, Abby's fingernails digging into my back. When she grabbed my backside, I could've come instantly if I'd released the hold I had on myself. I stopped for a moment before slowly pulling out, then thrusting back into her as a guttural sound escaped me. She tightened around me, and again I had to resist the urge to explode.

There were many things I would never forget about this—the way she looked up at me while I fucked her, the bounce of her breasts with each thrust, the way she writhed under me, the sounds she made, the peace of knowing I could fuck her bare and not have to worry about getting her pregnant. That was certainly a first for me. In fact, I couldn't imagine having a barrier between us right now.

"You're perfect, Abby. So fucking perfect." I searched her eyes. "I want to come inside you."

"Please." She bit my shoulder. "I need to let go."

With that, my body spasmed as an orgasm tore through me like a rocket, my balls tightening as I bottomed out, emptying into her as I groaned loudly. Ripples of pleasure warped my vision as I yelled again. Her muscles clamped around me, further amplifying the absolute ecstasy of this moment.

And after we'd both come down from it, I stayed inside of her, appreciating the feel of moving my cum in and out. It was rare that I still felt aroused after an orgasm, but with her, there was no end. I wanted to do it again and again. But I didn't want to wear her out. Though I could've stayed inside her all night, I slowly pulled out. I moved to her side and brought her in closer, placing a firm kiss on her lips.

"Don't tell me you're going back to your room tonight," she said.

I felt her soft breath on my face. "I have no plans to, love."

"Good."

She searched my eyes. "I was afraid you'd want to run again."

"Believe me, that's the last thing I want to do right now."

"What do you want to do?"

"That again, as soon as you're ready," I said.

"I'll be ready sooner than you think."

"We may not be getting any sleep tonight, then."

She brushed her fingers along the scruff on my jaw. "You can sleep on the plane."

"That's true."

Abby sneezed suddenly.

"Did I give you a virus?" I chuckled.

"If so, I'm willing to risk another inoculation." She sniffled as she laughed.

"Do you need a tissue?" I reached into the side-table drawer to see if there was anything there. Tissues were nowhere to be found. But—*holy shit, what?* I couldn't believe my eyes. My mouth dropped as I looked back over at her. "You're never going to believe this."

Abby seemed alarmed. "What? Is there a body part in there or something?"

I shook my head.

"What's wrong? You look like you saw a ghost."

"I basically *have* seen a ghost. Or an artifact." I lifted the gargantuan box of condoms out of the drawer. "How is this possible?"

"What?" She laughed. "Don't tell me those were yours."

I shook the container. "If they'd been mine, the box would be empty." I winked. "But this box of condoms is a decade old. I bought them as a joke for Leo. I remember distinctly what the box looked like. It's this one. And look at the expiration date." I pointed the box toward her.

"Oh my gosh. They expired years ago!"

I looked inside. "There are only a few left. I'm not sure how they haven't disintegrated at this point."

"I guess no one ever thought to throw them out? Maybe every person who looked in that drawer figured someone else could use them. Probably never checked the expiration date."

"I'm totally gobsmacked. I'm taking them home for Leo."

She laughed. "You're bringing him taffy and an old box of condoms as souvenirs. What a lucky guy."

"Well, he's good to me," I joked. "He deserves it." As I tossed the box aside, I turned to Abby, pulling her close again, so her naked body was flush against mine. "I'm gonna tell you a secret."

"I love secrets." She beamed. "What is it?"

"You're the first woman I've ever come inside."

Her eyes widened. "How is that possible?"

"Well, one of my biggest fears was always getting someone pregnant. I was always careful and never trusted anyone, even if they said they were on the pill. So..."

Abby blinked rapidly, seeming genuinely confused. "Yeah, but not even with your wife?"

I realized how strangely impossible that seemed, but the circumstances with Britney were unique. "We were scared she'd get pregnant in the midst of her treatments. That would've been bad. And she couldn't tolerate birth control." I shrugged. "So we used condoms."

"Wow. So I'm really your first, since you knew you couldn't get me pregnant."

"Because you already are, yeah." I chuckled.

She cackled. "That's crazy."

"It *is* a bit crazy. The first person I ever had unprotected sex with is already pregnant with my child, even though we'd never had sex before. Wrap your head around that one."

"I feel like that's a story. Like...it would lead the news if someone found out about it."

I squeezed her ass cheeks. "It's definitely something."

We lay there for a bit, just being together. But as the minutes passed, reality began creeping in, a distant voice in my head trying to ruin the moment. *What have you done?*

Abby apparently sensed the change in my demeanor. "What's wrong?" she asked.

"I hope I haven't fucked things up with you," I admitted.

She forced a smile. "Don't worry. I won't be stupid and fall in love with you or anything." She poked me with her finger. "Your dick is not *that* powerful, Sigmund Benedictus." She winked. "Close, though."

Relieved that she was making light of my very real fear, I kissed her, knowing full well that if anyone was in danger of falling too far here, it was me.

CHAPTER 34

Sig

Track 34: "Detached" by Lyn Lapid

"Everything okay?"

Lavinia interrupted my thoughts as I sat at the kitchen table with her after dinner. I'd come on Friday evening to stay the weekend at the inn, and we'd just poured some tea.

"Yeah," I said. "Why?"

"You were staring off into space."

I'd just been thinking about Abby. It had been a long couple of months since I'd left her in Rhode Island, and she'd had an ultrasound today. She was now a little over seven months along.

It felt like I hadn't seen her in forever. Felicity and Leo's son, Eli, had arrived the day after I returned from the States. The baby looked like a giant now, compared to when he was born two months ago. I kept using his size as a gauge to measure how long I'd been away from Abby. Not a day went by that I didn't miss her like mad.

Ever intuitive, Lavinia, as usual, decided to stick her nose where it didn't belong. "Are you thinking about her?" she asked.

"Even if I were, why would that be any of your business?" I took a sip of my tea.

"*You* are my business, Sigmund. What other business do I have?"

I immediately felt like an arse. Without children of her own, Lavinia looked at me like a son.

"I'm sorry. I suppose that's true." I sighed. "Yes, I was thinking of her."

"Anything you want to share?"

"Not particularly."

Lavinia obviously knew Abby and I had some sort of physical relationship before Abby left, but she'd never asked me for specifics, nor did I divulge anything. She knew nothing about what had happened between Abby and me in Rhode Island, specifically that we'd had the most amazing sex of my life right before I'd come back here.

"Anything you're *willing* to share?" she prodded.

Sighing, I rubbed my temples. "I miss her, alright? Is that what you want to hear?"

She smiled. "I miss her, too. She really brightened things up around here."

"Indeed, she did." I paused. "But we're better off being apart."

Lavinia tilted her head. "Why would you say that?"

"I took things too far with her. You already know that—I don't need to spell it out. This situation was complicated from the beginning, and I made it worse by crossing the line. This distance is probably a blessing in disguise."

"A blessing? Except you're not happy. And I doubt she is, either. How does *that* make sense?" She leaned in. "Why can't you two be together, anyway?"

My chest constricted. "Are you seriously asking that?"

"Yes. I want you to tell me the reasons."

"How much time do you have?"

She crossed her arms. "Plenty."

"I forgot who I was talking to. You don't have anything better to do."

"So, tell me."

"The very reason surrogacy works is the separation, the boundaries that go along with it. This baby doesn't have a mother. I *know* Abby. I know she would want to be involved in its life if she were around long enough. And I can't do that to her. She'd be stuck. She has her whole life ahead of her and didn't sign up for that."

Lavinia pursed her lips. "Hmm..."

"What now?"

"I have a theory here."

I rolled my eyes. "Alright..."

"Are you also afraid that if she's around and becomes invested, it will bind *you* to the child as well? Is this about more than just you and her?"

My stomach churned as a mixture of guilt and fear crept in. I hadn't thought of it that way, but it made sense. There were many layers to this situation. It was like...an onion, I suppose. *Christ, Abby has me thinking like her now. Froot Loops.* "There could be an element of that fear, too, yes," I conceded. "I've already decided Kate and Phil should raise the baby. I'm not suitable. If Abby's heart got involved, mine would surely follow. And that would bind me to the situation in a way I'm not prepared for. I don't want Abby sticking around out of obligation, either. She's far too young and needs to experience life before settling down in such a way." I exhaled. "What's best for both of us is to remain detached from the situation."

"*Detached* is a strong word, given the circumstance."

"It is. But it's the only way to make it work."

"Trying to remain detached seems like a lot of effort if your heart is not moving in that direction." She sighed. "Anyway, not everyone needs to travel the world or experience adventurous things in order to want to settle down, Sigmund. I certainly never cared about the number of worldly experiences I had. I just wanted to find the right person from a very young age. But unfortunately, I never did. That wasn't in the cards for me. Thus, I'm an old maid."

"You never fell in love?"

She shook her head. "I didn't say that. I fell in love many times—or thought I did. But most turned out to be bad apples in the end."

"How is it possible we've never talked about this?"

"There's no one worth talking about anymore."

"I'm sorry, Lavinia. You deserve better. Anyone whose arse I need to beat?"

"No one who's still alive." She laughed. "Anyway, God sent me a consolation prize—a young, strapping man to look after me in my eighties." She winked. "Can't get much better than that at this point."

"Are you kidding? You're the one looking after *me*, old woman."

She smiled, the wrinkles around her eyes creasing. "How is Abby's father doing?" she asked after a moment.

"He's still undergoing chemo, has been for the past couple of months. Then he'll need to have surgery to remove a portion of the lung. But the prognosis is good."

"It must be so hard for her."

"I'm worried about her." I rubbed my thumb along the teacup. "If things don't go well for some reason, she doesn't really have other family."

"She has a sister, doesn't she? They don't get along very well, though, from what she told me."

I nodded. "I met the sister—Claire—in Rhode Island. She's even worse than I expected. She's a selfish, judgmental bitch."

"Speaking of judgmental, have you told your mother about the pregnancy yet?" Lavinia could apparently surmise the answer by the look on my face. "Sigmund! You haven't told her?"

"I haven't." I took a long gulp of tea.

"You *have* to tell her."

I practically slammed my cup down. "Why?"

"She can't find out she has a grandchild *after* it's born."

"Why not?"

"I'm not going to dignify that with a response."

Though I knew she had a point, I attempted to justify my actions. "My mother is very conservative. You know that. She wasn't supportive of me being with Britney or my marriage. She surely wouldn't approve of this situation."

Mum had never understood my relationship with my wife, or how I could get attached to someone I'd just met so quickly. I think she was trying to protect me from getting hurt, but her criticism of my decisions at the time was the last thing I needed, given everything Britney and I were going through. Just like my mother's criticism would be the last thing I needed now.

Lavinia stirred more sugar into her tea. "Her opinions are merely her opinions. They don't need to matter. But she's your mother. She has a right to know what's going on." She looked up at me again. "And what about your father?"

"He's much easier to deal with. Stays quiet for the most part—just goes along with whatever she says and tends to agree with her, or at least he pretends to just to keep the peace."

"What do you think her problem would be with this situation? I can't imagine anyone finding fault with such a beautiful thing."

"You don't know my mother. What *wouldn't* she have a problem with is the appropriate question. She would have a problem with me fathering a child whose mother is dead. She would have a problem with the choice of an American to carry it. She would have a problem with my choice not to raise it and the possibility of the child growing up in the US. It's not that I give a shit what she thinks—I don't. But I don't need the stress, the added noise, of her criticism right now."

Lavinia softened as my words seemed to resonate. "Fair enough." She nodded. "We all do what we must for our mental health."

My phone chimed with a text. It was Abby. A photo. And not just any photo—the first ultrasound image

I'd seen since the original one. The baby now had a well-formed head and looked like an actual human. I could even make out a little upturned nose, like Britney's. My chest constricted as I tried to fight the emotions building inside of me with every ounce of my being. It was a mixture of torment and a love I couldn't allow myself to feel.

"What is it?" Lavinia asked. "What has you so transfixed?"

"Abby just sent a photo."

"It's not topless, is it?"

Rather than answer, I turned the phone screen toward her.

Her mouth slowly opened. "Oh my." Her eyes began to water. "You can really see everything now. Look at that giant head." She laughed. "It's definitely your child, Sigmund."

I rolled my eyes and chuckled.

"Did she find out the gender?" she asked.

"I don't think we're finding out."

"Why not?"

"I left that up to Phil and Kate. They decided on leaving it as a surprise. So, unless they change their mind, we'll have to wait."

"I might keel over and die before then. Bloody hell, I want to know."

"I'll whisper it to your grave."

Lavinia reached over to slap my head playfully.

After she handed the phone back, I got lost in the image, staring for a long while. While seeing the beating heart in the first ultrasound had made things seem real, nothing had hit like this—seeing its actual form. Seeing it as a human.

This was *my child.* My son or daughter.

God.

My eyes began to water.

Fuck.

"You're looking awfully *detached* right now, Sigmund."

I wiped my eyes. "Fuck you, Lavinia."

"Fuck you more, dear." She laughed.

CHAPTER 35

Sig

Track 35: "What Happens After You" by Weezer

That evening, I eventually went upstairs to FaceTime Abby, which had become our ritual every night before I went to bed. Due to the time difference, we spoke around her dinnertime. Our chats had become my favorite part of every day.

I'd responded with a *Wow* earlier to the ultrasound picture, but I hadn't said anything else, mainly because I'd have a hard time summarizing in a text what I was feeling.

"Hey," she said as she popped up on the screen.

Abby's hair was unruly, looking a bit knotted. Her cheeks were flushed. It reminded me of what she'd looked like the night we had sex and made me yearn to be with her right now.

"What are you up to?" I asked.

"I just vacuumed."

"Ah." I laughed. "Looks like it took a lot out of you."

"Are you saying I look bad?"

"No. Just the opposite. Beautifully flustered."

"Thank you...I think."

I kicked my feet up. "How was your day?"

"Busy. After the ultrasound, I had to take my dad to his chemo appointment. It's been nonstop."

"Are you eating when you should?"

"I'm trying."

"Abby..." I scolded.

"What?" She flashed a guilty smile.

"Are you going to make me get on a plane right now? Come to Rhode Island and force feed you?"

"Don't tempt me. If I starve myself, does that mean I get to see you? I might be onto something."

Every weekend I considered flying in to surprise her, even if just for a couple of days. But when I got close to booking a ticket, my common sense always kicked in. I'd remind myself that the separation we'd been dealt was for her own good, that the sooner she became *detached* from me, the better. *Detached.* There was that word again.

She'd also been busy with her father—another one of my excuses. I'd convinced myself that my presence would distract her from being there for him. But whatever I told myself, it didn't change the fact that I missed her every day, and more today than ever.

"The only thing I feel like lately are those pancakes you never had a chance to make me. I've been telling Dad how the British make pancakes differently. He felt bad that you were going to make them for me the morning I got the call about his heart attack. He wants to try them, too." She laughed. "He's a big pancake man."

"I should've made them when I was in Rhode Island. I wish I could make them for you both right now."

She blew a piece of hair toward her forehead. "You didn't say much when I sent you the photo today."

I picked at some lint on my bed. "I know. But I haven't been able to stop staring at him—or her. You don't know the gender, right?"

"No, I haven't cheated and asked. If Kate and Phil want it to be a surprise, a surprise it shall be." She lay back on her bed. "I don't think I could keep that from you anyway. It's better that I don't know. I'm not very good at keeping secrets."

"I have a secret," I said.

"Yeah?"

"I missed you something terrible today. But don't tell anyone."

"I won't tell the surrogacy police. But missing me isn't part of the protocol, Sigmund."

"I'm a terrible rule follower when it comes to you."

"First rule of Surrogacy Club, don't fuck the surrogate. And certainly don't miss her."

I raised my hand. "Guilty on both counts."

She smiled and moved the phone away from her face. "You want to see something?" Abby lifted her shirt, displaying her now visibly round stomach. Her pregnancy could no longer be denied from a physical perspective. I stared at her, wishing I could run my hand along that taut skin. I'd yet to feel her bump in person, since she hadn't had much of one when I'd left her.

"Is it twisted that I'm even more attracted to you now?"

"A little," she said as she covered her stomach again.

"This is exactly why it's a good thing I'm not there. That would be fucking dangerous."

"What would you do to me if you were here now?"

"Is this a lead-in to phone sex, Ms. Knickerbocker?"

"It can be." She smiled mischievously.

"Where's your father?"

"He's watching *Wheel of Fortune*."

"Is the volume up loud?"

She giggled. "Yeah, he's all the way downstairs, and I'm upstairs."

"If I were there, I would be trying with all my might not to fuck you hard like I want to. The bigger your stomach gets, the more freaked out I would be, but at the same time, the more turned on I am. So you see the conundrum."

"*You* are one big conundrum, Benedictus."

"That doesn't sound like a compliment."

"It's not. But it's who you are. One confused, complex man."

"There's no confusion when it comes to how much I desire you, Abby. That's not where the uncertainty lies."

"It's nice to be wanted physically." Her expression turned serious. "But that only gets me so far."

"As I've told you before, I don't *just* desire you physically. As an example, I can't have you physically right now, yet I've been looking forward to talking to you all day."

She stared at me quietly, then asked, "If you had met me under different circumstances, do you think we would've clicked?"

"You mean, if I had just met you in a pub or something?"

"Yeah."

"Let's put it this way… I most definitely wouldn't have kicked you out of my flat."

"God, you're romantic."

I laughed.

"I often wonder what it would've been like if you and I had met in another time," she said. "If there was no surrogacy in the mix, would we have stood a chance we don't have now? That thought makes me kind of sad."

"If we had met in a pub and got on well, I'd still want better for you than me, love. I'd still not want to tie you down—not figuratively, at least."

Ignoring my stupid innuendo, she remained serious. "So it wouldn't have worked out anyway. Is that what you're saying? Because I deserve someone who's capable of loving me as much as you loved Britney?"

You could've heard a pin drop as the conversation took a turn I wasn't prepared for. I'd specifically tried not to think about Britney as I considered my growing feelings for Abby. I was holding on to a lot of guilt in that regard. As for my ability to love again, if you'd asked me a year ago whether it would be possible, I would've said absolutely not. As of late? I couldn't be sure of anything. But the subject wasn't one I was ready for tonight.

"You deserve someone without any emotional baggage," I finally said.

"What someone deserves isn't always what they want," she countered. "Sometimes the things that make us the happiest aren't the things that are perfect for us." She shook her head. "Anyway, it's all a moot point, I suppose. We met the way we met. And the situation is the complicated situation it is."

I didn't like the troubled look in her eyes. What had started as a light and flirtatious phone call had turned into anything but. "Talk to me. What are you thinking right now?"

"Will we even see each other again, Sig? Or is your plan to just disappear from my life?"

I didn't have a quick answer to that. "I don't have a plan." I couldn't emphasize that enough. "But never seeing you again doesn't sit right with me at all. I couldn't imagine that, Abby."

"Well, I think it would be too painful for me to see you—if we're not together."

I blinked in surprise. "What are you saying?"

"I'm saying... I'm afraid I've already fallen too far. Despite trying to downplay my feelings, I *am* falling for you. Something you warned me not to do. And the distance between us isn't changing how I feel. All that does is prevent the physical part. What's been getting me through my days is knowing I get to talk to you every night. And I realize now how dangerous that is, if it's going to go away."

"Yeah..." I muttered, realizing how ill-prepared I was for the "after" of this surrogacy situation. It was foolish to think either one of us could turn off our feelings just because that's what we were *supposed* to do once the baby came and we went our separate ways. I'd not been allowing myself to ponder the after because I'd been having too good of a time living in the moment. I never wanted these days to end, and yet they *would*, whether I liked it or not.

"Your flaws, your hang-ups, your emotional fucked-upness—none of that scares me. Your complexities draw me to you more. They make you real. Vulnerable."

She shook her head slowly. "And your love for Britney? The fact that I know you were at one time capable of giving someone your whole heart? Loving her so much it broke you for all others? Ironically, it's one of the most attractive things about you."

I wanted to say so much, yet my throat felt like it was closing.

"I can't imagine what you went through, what you're still going through," she continued. "It's hard to lose a parent, but I imagine there's a special kind of pain that comes with losing your soulmate. And I'm not going to undermine that by expecting you to have the same kinds of feelings for me." She exhaled. "So the bottom line is, I need to get over you, get over whatever this is that we've built, because we'll have to tear it down when the time is up. I need to start protecting my heart. I miss you terribly right now, but I think I have to figure out how to walk away after the baby comes."

Protecting her heart made a lot of sense, of course. But I couldn't imagine her disappearing from my life. *How can I fix this?* My stomach felt uneasy as I finally mustered the words. "I wouldn't be okay with never seeing you again."

"Maybe you're stronger than me, if you think you could handle that." Her eyes glistened. "Every day we're closer to the end of this journey. And every day I'm trying harder not to fall for you. Those two things contradict each other. It can't continue like this." She looked like she was about to cry.

Fuck. "This is all my fault, Abby. All my fucking fault. I told myself I wasn't going to hurt you, and it seems I've already gone and done it."

"Don't apologize. I'm just as much at fault here. You told me not to fall for you. It doesn't get any clearer than that. I shouldn't have played with fire." She wiped her eyes. "I'd better go, okay?"

A wave of panic hit. "I don't want to say goodbye if you're upset."

"I'll be better tomorrow. I think it's just the hormones or something."

Bullshit.

"I have to go." She sniffled. "I'm sorry."

Then she hung up.

A hollow feeling developed in my chest as I lay in bed, staring at the dark screen. I was a bit frozen for a moment, but then that changed.

I knew exactly what I needed to do.

CHAPTER 36

Abby

Track 36: "Come to Me" by Goo Goo Dolls

I wasn't sure how tonight's call with Sig was going to go. After the mess I'd made last night, blurting out all my feelings and then essentially hanging up, I wouldn't have blamed him if he preferred to skip it.

But I hadn't been able to help my reaction. I'd needed to let him know where my head was—that I was *in over* my head with him. But I'd handled things poorly. I'd been too emotional and had shut down the conversation, even though I'd started it.

When I agreed to be the surrogate, I'd promised myself I wouldn't get attached to the baby. But I hadn't been counting on the possibility of falling for its father. This baby was now more to me than an infant I was carrying for "someone else." It was the child of the man I was falling in love with. That didn't change the job I had to do, though. I knew that. And it didn't change the boundaries I needed to set. It just made things harder.

"Going upstairs for your call?" my father asked, looking over at the clock.

"In a few."

My dad knew the drill—this was the time of day, about an hour before dinnertime, when I always went upstairs to talk to Sig. While I'd admitted to Dad that Sig and I had crossed the line, he didn't know specifics and didn't care to know too much. I couldn't blame him. But he understood that I'd developed feelings for the man. I always spoke of Sig in a positive light now, so my father didn't have any reason to dislike him anymore. He worried about me getting my heart broken, though. *Join the club.*

About five minutes later, I left my father downstairs to watch his nightly game show. As I entered my room, butterflies swarmed in my belly, a mix of nervousness about tonight's mood and the usual anticipation of hearing Sig's voice.

Ten minutes passed, though, and the phone didn't ring.

Then another ten minutes went by.

I had too much pride to pick up the phone and call him myself after last night. Though maybe I was overthinking things. It was always possible he'd gotten tied up with something. Although, it was nearly ten at night there and too late for him to still be working. A jolt of jealousy hit at the thought of him out and about at a pub, flirting with some woman he might take home only to kick out. Or maybe he wouldn't send her home this time. Had I driven him to that by being so forthcoming last night? He did have a tendency to seek out random women when he was trying to forget his problems.

That question continued to plague me for a full half hour. Once I determined Sig wasn't going to call, I forced myself to go back downstairs.

My father's expression darkened when he saw my face. "What's the matter?"

"He didn't call tonight. I'm not sure what happened."

"That's not good." His brows furrowed. "Why don't you give that prick a call?"

"I could, but...it's a long story. I feel like the ball is in his court right now."

Dad's eyes followed me as I went to the fridge and poured some orange juice. I hated having to drag him into my problems. He couldn't afford to be stressed out on my behalf. I was slowly sipping my juice and looking at a postcard Dad's sister, my aunt Maureen, had sent from France, when the doorbell rang.

My father went to open it, and I heard that undeniable British accent.

"The rumor is someone here wants to try British pancakes?"

My heart skipped a beat as I put my orange juice down.

"You're damn right we do." Dad stepped aside.

And there he was: Sig, holding a paper bag of groceries.

Our eyes locked as I stood, too stunned to speak. I placed my hand over my heart. "How...did this happen?"

He took a few steps inside. "I booked a ticket and got on a plane."

"But you didn't tell me you were coming."

"I know. I wanted to surprise you. I hope it's a good surprise and not a bad one." His eyes fell to my round belly. He mouthed, "Wow."

"I'll give you two a minute..." Dad turned and headed upstairs.

After my father's bedroom door closed, Sig set down the bag he was holding and reached for me.

I could feel his heart beating as he wrapped his arms around my body, his amazing scent as intoxicating as ever. It felt so damn good to be held by him. Despite my pronouncement about protecting my heart, my reaction right now was proof of my weakness—proof that I was nowhere near ready to rip the Band-Aid off.

"I couldn't leave things the way they were last night," he whispered as he caressed my hair. "I needed to see you. I hope this is okay." He looked down at me. "I know we can figure this out."

"I'm sorry if I—"

He pressed his lips against mine, stopping me mid-sentence and devouring the remainder of what I'd planned to say.

"God, I missed you," he mumbled over my lips.

My body felt ready to melt. "I missed you, too."

He pulled back. "We'll talk later, alright? I promise. After your father goes to bed. Right now, I'd like to make you both breakfast for dinner—the pancakes you were craving. Unless you've already eaten."

My heart felt ready to leap out of my chest. "We haven't. And that sounds amazing."

He kissed my forehead and lifted the bag to the counter.

"Dad, you can come out now!" I hollered up the stairwell as Sig followed me to the kitchen.

My father came back downstairs and patted Sig on the back. "What can I do to help, TP?"

"TP?" Sig raised a brow as he unloaded the groceries he'd bought.

"That Prick."

"Oh, that's right. Good to know the nickname has stuck."

"It has." Dad winked.

"Better than toilet paper, I suppose." He shooed my father away. "Go rest, Roland. I've got dinner."

"You'd think I was a cancer patient or something..." My father shrugged before retreating to the living room.

I lingered by Sig's side as he began preparing the food. "I know you hate it when people lean over you while you're cooking, but I want to watch anyway."

Sig turned around to make sure my father's back was toward us, then planted a firm kiss on my lips. "I'd prefer you near me every second of tonight, actually."

That sentence lit up my entire body. I watched as he whipped the batter and poured it into the pan, preparing perfectly thin pancake after pancake.

He made a huge batch and set them on the dining room table with lemon, sugar, and a chocolate spread. He'd also cut up tons of fresh fruit. It was quite the feast.

After the three of us demolished the entire batch and all the accoutrements, my father rubbed his stomach. "You know, I haven't had much of an appetite lately, but it seems I just wasn't interested in anything other than these delicious pancakes. Thank you for making them, son."

"My pleasure, sir. I'm happy you were able to eat them."

"Whether I can keep them down is another thing..." Dad chuckled.

Sig nodded. "My wife, Britney, never had much of an appetite during her treatments. We'd celebrate any time she ate something and kept it down. But it was really the lack of eating that made her weaker. I'm happy you were able to enjoy the pancakes."

My stomach dipped as it hit me—how concerned Sig always was about whether or not I'd eaten. I wondered if it was triggering for him when I told him I hadn't, whether it made him think back to those days.

My dad cleared his throat. "Britney was lucky to have you by her side through it all, just like I'm lucky to have my daughter. I'm sorry Abby had to leave England to come take care of me."

"She's exactly where she's meant to be right now," Sig said.

Dad offered me a sympathetic smile. "I know she wishes she was back there, though."

Sig grinned over at me. "We miss her, too."

Dad cocked his head. "We?"

"Lavinia and me."

"Ah." My father nodded. "The old lady. I heard she's a hoot. When I get through this, I'm personally delivering her a bottle of Fireball, since you told me that's her favorite." Dad stood. "Well, if you'll excuse me, I think I'm gonna head upstairs for the night." He turned to Sig. "You'll still be here in the morning, right?"

"Yes. I was planning to stay for a few days, if that's alright with you."

"You can stay as long as you like if you keep making those pancakes." Dad chuckled.

"That can be arranged."

Shortly after my father went upstairs, Sig went to take a shower while I cleaned up the kitchen. We needed to talk, yet all I could think about was getting him alone tonight. How were we supposed to have sex in this small house, though? My father was a light sleeper.

But where there's a will, there's a way.

CHAPTER 37

Abby

Track 37: "Light On" by Maggie Rogers

Sig crept up behind me in the kitchen after his shower. The heat of his body felt like an electrical current against my skin. And whatever cologne he'd just applied smelled incredibly good. I turned, and his eyes locked on my mouth. Rubbing my index finger along his bottom lip, I whispered, "I know we need to talk about serious issues, but I don't feel like keeping my hands off you long enough to have a conversation right now."

His eyes shimmered. "We need to chat, but having my knob inside you is more important for the moment? Is that what you're saying?"

I looked down at his prominent hard-on. "From the looks of things, talking is not exactly at the forefront of your mind either, Benedictus. Unless you plan on chatting with that missile in your pants..."

"You're right. I want you more than my next breath right now." He pressed his body against mine. "But tell me...how exactly is that supposed to work with your father upstairs? I'm going to explode if I don't get to have you tonight. Any good hiding places? I'm not picky."

Biting my bottom lip, I gestured toward the side door. "Have I ever showed you Dad's big tool shed out back?"

"No, but I have a sudden need for a screw...driver."

I smacked his chest. "That was terrible."

"I'm not very creative when my mind has been hijacked by my cock."

"Come with me," I said, leading him by the hand.

"That's the plan." He chuckled.

Leaves crunched beneath our feet as we crossed the yard. I opened the shed door and turned on the single interior light. There was also a switch to activate the heat, which I was grateful for in the middle of November. I closed the door behind us, and Sig and I fell into a passionate kiss.

Then he flipped me around to face the wall. "I want to fuck you from behind. We've never done that before. And we don't have room for much else in here. That okay?"

"Yes," I breathed, lifting my T-shirt dress over my head and hanging it on the handlebar of a lawnmower.

"I love how eager you are," he said.

I heard the clank of his belt buckle and then his zipper lowering, which sent a bolt of excitement through me.

"And you're *not* eager?" I taunted.

"*Eager* is not strong enough of a word," he answered, lowering my underwear and placing his hot, throbbing cock against my butt crack. "Feel how fucking eager I am."

I leaned my hands against the shingled wall to balance myself.

"God, your ass is beautiful. So fucking perfect." His erratic breaths tickled my neck. "Arch your back. Just like that. Fuck, yes."

I closed my eyes, incredibly turned on by the feel of his hard cock rubbing against me. My clit throbbed with anticipation.

Two of his fingers entered me. "Look how wet you are for me. I want to go easy, but I'm not sure I can."

"Don't." In the next instant, I felt the burn of his cock filling me. The muscles between my legs instantly squeezed around him.

"I nearly forgot how damn tight you are." He groaned, his cock twitching inside me. "Don't move for a second," he hissed. "I nearly lost it." He paused to regain his composure, then wrapped his hands around my waist as he pumped in and out, grunting with the rhythm. "Do you have any idea how good your pussy feels swallowing my cock?"

I whimpered, barely able to speak.

"The way your beautiful ass jiggles every time I thrust into you?" He sped up his movements and reached around to cup my swollen breasts, massaging them as he moved in and out. "I simply can't get enough of you." He squeezed.

I lowered my hand to massage my clit, feeling my orgasm at the surface. "I can't hold back anymore. It's too soon, but I'm gonna come."

"Come, baby. Come all over my cock."

The second those words exited his mouth, the heat of my climax tore through me. He let go, too, groaning in pleasure. The warmth of his cum filled me—that amazing feeling of receiving all of him, or at least as much as he was willing to give.

After, I practically collapsed against the wall, limp from the magnitude of that orgasm. He slowly pulled out, drops of his cum gathering at the top of my inner thighs.

He turned me around and enveloped my mouth in his, kissing me as if what we'd just done had barely scratched the surface of satisfying him. I knew it had barely satisfied me.

"I fucking missed you. Have I told you that?" Sig stared down at my swollen belly as his eyes glistened. He knelt for a moment and kissed my taut skin. "Look at you."

My body tightened, willing away all the emotions that simple act elicited.

He stood. "It's surreal."

"I know. Twenty-nine weeks. It's hard to believe, isn't it?"

"Hard to believe someone could be so beautiful, yes." He shook his head. "It's one thing to see a picture of you pregnant and another entirely to see it in person. This time is going by too fast."

I raked my fingers through his messy black hair. "Why did you come here, Sigmund? Was it for what we just did? I know it wasn't to make pancakes."

"You think I flew all the way here to fuck you?"

I shrugged. "I honestly don't know."

"Maybe that had a bit to do with my motivation, but no, that's not the *only* reason." He leaned his forehead against mine. "I didn't have a chance to address your concerns about what happens after the baby is born. Telling you I couldn't imagine not seeing you anymore wasn't a solution. It was just an opinion that only made things more confusing. I'm sorry for not having all the answers."

"None of this is your fault, Sig. Neither of us planned for this."

"I certainly didn't plan to fall for you, Abby." He held my face in his hands. "That's right—I warned you not to fall for *me*, but *I'm* the one who's falling. What we're doing...this isn't about biding time. This is about you and me, this undeniable connection we have. And as much as I might want to ignore it, my feelings aren't going to magically expire when you give birth." He swallowed. "I used to wake up in the morning and wish I weren't alive. Now I wake up and think of you—some funny thing you said or wondering when I get to see you next. And I think of you before I fall asleep. Our nightly phone call is the thing I look forward to most every day. You've taken over the dark places that used to exist in my mind." His eyes were piercing. "You saved me, Abby. You really have."

I moved his hair off his forehead. "Wow."

"But," he continued. "I can't in good conscience pull you into a situation you didn't sign up for. Part of the problem is that I don't know how I'm going to feel when this baby is born. I wish I did. All I feel right now is utterly unprepared."

"You think there's a chance you might change your mind?" I asked. "You might want to raise it?"

He caressed my hair. "I can't rule it out, even if I think the child would be better off with Phil and Kate."

My brain worked to piece together his insecurities. "And if you end up raising it, you're worried that if we're together I'll feel obligated to be its mother."

"Wouldn't you?" He searched my eyes.

That was the million-dollar question. And like him, I wasn't sure I had an answer. My heart said yes, but it wasn't a decision I could make overnight. It was life changing. "The funny thing is..." I paused. "I don't know how I'm going to feel, either. So we have that in common. I can tell you I feel more for this little baby inside of me than I'd anticipated. I can't imagine giving birth, pretending like nothing ever happened, and just returning to my life here. I know that was the plan. But it seems so...unnatural now."

He took my hands in his. "Here's the bottom line, Abby... I can't promise how I'm going to feel about becoming a father, but I *can* promise that it won't change how I feel about you. I'll never abandon you, unless you tell me that's what you want. I only want what's best for you. If you tell me that's to not see me anymore, then I will have to live with that. But know that's not what I want. After what you said last night about us never seeing each other again, it became very clear to me. I don't want to lose you."

Still mostly half-naked, we fell into a long embrace. My heart thundered against his as I said, "I think we need to wait until this baby gets here to know how we're gonna feel. Maybe the answer will come to us. Maybe we need to not force any decisions right now."

He kissed my nose. "If you're okay with that, so am I, love."

I nodded, though I still felt uneasy with all the uncertainty. I knew in my heart that things wouldn't magically fall into place after nine months, yet I couldn't help feeling a bloom of hope. We just had to keep moving forward. Quite frankly, I probably should have known better, but I was having too much fun to stop. "We should go back inside." I reached for my T-shirt dress.

"Ah, yes. My comfy couch awaits."

"You could always sneak into my room. My father knows there's something going on between us. He wouldn't be totally shocked if he caught you in there. But I understand if you're not comfortable with that."

He shrugged. "I'm not. I guess you could say I'm old fashioned that way."

"Such the conservative, yeah," I teased.

"Well, around parents, I suppose. Not really otherwise."

"You're right." I sighed. "It would be awkward. As much as I want you in my bed, I wouldn't feel fully comfortable with that, either."

We snuck back into the house as quietly as possible. I fetched Sig a blanket and pillow and gave him a long kiss goodnight. I could easily have gone for round two, but instead, I forced myself upstairs to my room.

A few minutes after I'd settled into bed, I received a text from my father.

Dad: You left the light on in the shed.

CHAPTER 38

Sig

Track 38: "Sledgehammer" by Peter Gabriel

My eyes blinked open the following morning, and I woke to find Abby sitting across from me in the living room. "Well, hello there," I said groggily.

She uncrossed her legs. "Hi."

"Waiting for something?"

"For you to wake up. How did you sleep?"

"Amazingly well, after the workout you gave me last night."

She climbed onto the couch and straddled me.

My dick immediately grew to full mast. "What are you doing?" I whispered. "What if your father comes down?"

"I just checked a couple of minutes ago. He was snoring. And the stairs are creaky. We'll hear him." She rubbed her pussy along my rigid dick.

"You know this is torture," I rasped. "I'm suddenly in great need of a sledgehammer. We might have to go out to the shed."

She stopped grinding, a guilty look on her face. "About that..."

"Don't tell me you're done letting me get you from behind," I teased.

"Not at all. But I don't think we can use the shed anymore."

I narrowed my eyes. "Why is that?"

"He's on to us."

My eyes widened. "Your father?"

She nodded. "He texted last night that I'd left the light on in the shed. He must have gotten up to use the bathroom and noticed it from the window."

Fuck. "Well, that's just bloody great. It'll be a miracle if he doesn't kill me before the end of this trip."

She shrugged. "What are you gonna do? Get his daughter pregnant?"

I pinched her playfully. "You're lucky you already are, or I might have."

After glancing toward the stairwell, I wrapped my hands around her bottom and pushed her down onto me for one shameless feel of her soft flesh over my starving dick.

That prompted her to begin grinding again.

"You definitely need to stop that if you don't want me inside of you in two seconds," I warned.

"What if I don't want to stop?" she teased. "How quickly can you finish?"

A few seconds later, the sound of a door closing upstairs registered. Then footsteps. Given that I was currently hard as a rock, this was not good.

Abby jumped off of me.

"Fuck!" I shot up off the couch and covered my crotch. Heading straight for my shoes, I put them on as quickly as possible.

Abby's face was crimson. "Where are you going?"

"I can't greet him like this. I'm going for a morning walk." I practically flew out the door, awkwardly waving to the old-man neighbor who was letting his dog out. Thank God I was wearing a shirt. Otherwise, I might not have had time to put one on before Roland came downstairs.

Strolling the neighborhood aimlessly, I kept thinking about how hot last night had been in the shed. Our situation was serious, yet Abby had a way of making me forget my problems—even if she was part of my biggest problem lately. Not a bad problem to have, though. When I was with her, nothing else seemed to matter—even if it needed to start mattering.

My phone rang a couple of minutes into my walk.

"Abby! However are you?" I answered. "Long time no speak."

"How's your situation?" she asked.

"My *situation* is not going down. What the hell did you do to me? It's like you slipped me some of your father's Viagra."

"Oh no." She giggled.

"Stop laughing. This is serious. Your neighbors are going to think I'm a pervert."

"You *are*."

"Only with you, love." I looked up at the sun, still feeling like a dog in heat. "We need to go somewhere. Take care of this. Fancy a quick car ride? We can figure it out. As long as you're on top of me, I don't care where we go. I'll fuck you in the car, if I have to."

"Your romantic side is so on point right now."

"You have a better option?"

"Actually, that sounds like a great idea. I'll tell my dad we're headed out to get coffee...and donuts."

"Donuts? Is that our new code word?"

"Sure. They have holes, I suppose."

"There's only one hole I want. Well, maybe three. And damn it, I'm hard as a rock once more. I may never be able to see your father again."

"Hurry." She laughed. "I'll be waiting for you outside. You won't even have to come in."

I picked up my pace. "Heading around the block to your house now."

The minute I spotted her, it was like seeing her for the first time. My heart sped up, and I simply couldn't wait to kiss her.

"There you are." She opened her arms and ran to me, beaming from ear to ear. I lifted her up as she wrapped her legs around my waist, our lips smashing together. Worst case, her father might've been watching from the window, but he was apparently on to us anyway. There were worse things than him catching us. *And I mean that quite literally.*

There *were* worse things. Because just as we broke our kiss, a car pulled into the driveway. Whoever it was had seen our public spectacle. And when I got a look at who it was, I just about died.

Phil and Kate.

CHAPTER 39

Sig

Track 39: "Secret Lovers" by Atlantic Starr

A rush of adrenaline shot through me. *What are they doing here?*

Abby and I froze the moment her feet landed on the ground again.

Britney's parents had been down in Florida for the past several months, taking care of Phil's mother. While we'd kept in touch regularly over the phone, neither I nor Abby had told them anything about what had happened between the two of us. I hadn't planned to hide it from them, but I would've appreciated them finding out any other way than this.

"You devil, you," Phil said as he exited the driver's side.

"Phil..." I swallowed before turning to his wife. "Kate..." My heart had never pounded so hard.

"It's so good to see you," Abby said, trying to remain casual, running a hand through her hair.

I wanted to laugh. *Good to see you?* I would've rather had a root canal.

Kate smiled hesitantly. "I guess there's a lot to catch up on, huh?"

You could cut the awkwardness with a knife. I had a lot of explaining to do. Needless to say, any plans to disappear with Abby for car sex were off the table. "A lot to catch up on indeed," I told them. "I didn't realize you were back in the northeast."

"We just got back after settling Marjorie in her new place down in Naples," Kate explained. "We figured before we went home to Massachusetts, we'd stop here to check on Roland. We booked a hotel down the road for a few days so we could relieve Abby. We certainly didn't know you were here, Sig."

"I flew over on a whim yesterday."

"It's clear why." Phil snickered.

My father-in-law looked for any opportunity to bust balls, and I couldn't blame him for putting me through the wringer. I deserved every second of it. I was just glad they didn't seem angry.

"Oh, stop, Phil." Kate smacked him. "It's none of our business."

I looked over at Abby, who was quiet but noticeably blushing. I suspected I might also be red in the face—or maybe green, based on how my stomach felt.

Kate looked down at Abby's baby bump and reached out. "May I?"

Abby rubbed her stomach and breathed out, likely relieved at the distraction. "Of course."

"How are you feeling?" Kate asked as she settled her hand on the bump.

"Really good, actually."

"Glad to see Sig's taking care of you," Phil cracked.

Kate stepped back and smacked her husband's arm again. "I know this has been hard for you with everything going on with your father, Abby. We've felt terribly guilty being down in Florida tending to Marjorie, but things should be easier now that she's in a good home. We'll be able to help."

"Were you headed out somewhere?" Phil asked.

Abby looked at me guiltily. "Just going to get donuts."

Phil clapped his hands together. "I could go for a good cup of Dunkin' coffee and a glazed donut. We haven't had breakfast yet."

"Why don't the three of us go and bring back breakfast for Abby and Roland?" I suggested. "I'd like to talk to them alone, if you don't mind," I added softly.

"Of course." Abby nodded.

It wasn't like I had anything to say to my in-laws that Abby shouldn't have heard, but I didn't want her to be uncomfortable as I explained myself. I needed to do that in private. And I blamed myself for this entire predicament. Abby shouldn't have to explain anything. It wasn't good for her to be stressed in her condition.

Phil threw his keys into the air and caught them. "I'll drive."

I got into the backseat of their car, feeling almost like a child about to be punished—or at least one who deserved to be.

"Do you secretly want to wring my neck?" I asked as we drove away.

"Not at all." Kate turned to face me from the passenger seat. "I'm a little shocked, maybe, but perhaps I shouldn't be."

Phil chimed in, "I'm not."

"As much as you think you have me pegged, Phil, this is *not* like any other situation I've gotten myself into." I cleared my throat. "Abby is special, and we've connected in a way I hadn't anticipated. There's been no one else since the day I met her, if you're wondering about that. This isn't a game to me."

"How long has it been going on?" Kate asked.

"It started shortly before she came out here when Roland had the heart attack. We'd been slowly growing closer before that." I rubbed my temples. "Neither of us knows what the future holds. I've told her I think she's better off without me, and I don't want to tie her down in any way. She needs to be able to walk away from this situation after the baby comes, but..."

"But you care about her." She completed my sentence.

I nodded. "I have no desire to end things right now. We're both a bit confused by this turn of events and what it's going to mean for the future." I sighed. "I really don't know much more than I'm telling you now, except to say I'm a better person when I'm around her. I feel alive. And I haven't been able to say that in a very long time."

"Well, no need for further explanation, then. Obviously, we don't want to see Abby get hurt, but we care about you just as much." Kate shrugged. "You're adults. That's the bottom line. And we want you both to be happy."

"But clearly I've screwed up the plan."

"We'll figure it out," she said.

Exhaling, I sat back in my seat. "I'm strangely relieved that you ran into us today. Because I had no idea how to tell you. I might have continued putting it off."

"I'm not sure why I didn't foresee this," Kate said.

"*I* certainly didn't. Abby and I didn't get along very well in the beginning. It was never my intention to fall for her, to complicate things."

Phil eyed me through the rearview mirror. "Some of the best things in life are complicated. Complicated makes life interesting."

I put my hands on the backs of their seats and leaned in. "Anyway, all this to say...don't hate me, alright?"

Kate reached back to pat me on the shoulder. "We love you too much for that."

CHAPTER 40

Sig

Track 40: "Paradise by the Dashboard Light" by Meatloaf

That evening, Kate and Phil offered to keep Roland company while Abby and I went out. It was a much-needed reprieve. Even though I liked her father a lot, it had felt a little claustrophobic in that house.

I'd made a reservation at the nicest restaurant in town, a seafood place by the water. Abby looked adorable in a white empire-waist dress, and she wore her long hair up, which she'd never done before. I appreciated the uninterrupted view of her slender neck, tempted at every turn to wrap my hand around it.

"At least Phil and Kate didn't seem too freaked out about us," she said as she placed her napkin on her lap. "You never had a chance to fill me in on how the talk went."

"We had a good chat. They're just as confused as we are, but they handled it well and will be accepting of whatever choices we make."

Abby stared into her water glass. "I would assume not much affects you when you've already been through hell like they have."

"That's definitely true. They're strong people. I was more ashamed of not having told them than worried about their reaction. They insisted I didn't owe them an explanation, but I believe I did."

Abby's gaze suddenly moved to something happening in the corner of the restaurant.

"What's wrong?" I turned around to look.

"You know that ex of mine, Asher?"

I stiffened. "Yeah?"

"Well, he's sitting right over there. He's the guy in the red shirt."

I turned again. The bloke had blond hair and sat across from another guy. He hadn't seemed to notice her yet.

"Do you want to leave?" I asked.

"No, of course not. I have nothing to hide. I mean..." She laughed and pointed to her belly. "I couldn't hide it even if I wanted to now."

"How badly do you care what he thinks?"

"I don't give a *shit* what he thinks."

"You trust me?"

She raised her eyebrows. "Should I?"

"Let's switch places for a minute." I moved to her chair. "Come sit on my lap."

She did, and I reached up to cup her face as I brought her mouth to mine, rubbing her stomach slowly and intentionally. I checked a few times to confirm whether he was watching. And eventually he was.

When a waitress approached, Abby hopped off of me and returned to her seat. We'd made a brief spectacle of ourselves, but if her ex had seen us, it was worth it.

We managed to enjoy our meal without focusing on him. Abby seemed relaxed throughout dinner and didn't appear to care about the presence of her ex in the room, which pleased me. At one point, though, her eyes veered off to the side again, and a look of discomfort crossed her face. "He's coming over here." She wiped her mouth.

The next thing I knew, he was standing in front of us. "Hey…I thought that was you," he said.

She cleared her throat. "Asher, how are you?"

"Good." His eyes darted to me. "You look nice."

"Thank you." She gestured my way. "This is Sig, my—"

"Baby daddy," I finished.

He looked down at her stomach. "Yeah, I noticed you were… Wow. Congratulations."

"Thank you."

He turned to me again. "You're English."

"How keen of you to notice."

"We met in England, actually," Abby said.

"I didn't realize you were over there." His eyes dropped to her stomach. "I guess there's a lot I didn't realize."

"Yeah. Life is unexpected. Thank you, I guess, for breaking up with me so I could experience it."

Nice.

He nodded. "I'm glad you're happy."

Abby sat straighter. "I am."

"Well, I'll let you get back to your dinner. Good seeing you and good luck with everything."

"Thanks," she said.

He walked away, and after a moment of silence, I smiled. "Well, that was brilliant."

"Yeah..." She looked a bit sullen.

My chest tightened. *Does she still have feelings for that bloke?* "Are you okay?"

"Yeah, uh, it felt a little weird to put myself in those shoes for a moment—where this was a simple, cut-and-dried situation. Of course you *are* my baby's daddy, but it's not that easy, right? Because it's not my baby."

"I'm sorry if I upset you by saying that."

"No, no, no. It was great. I wouldn't change a thing about that interaction. I guess it just..." She paused. "Made me wish it were true?" She shook her head. "I don't know. Sorry."

I cringed. *You're a genius, Sigmund.* I hadn't considered the implications of my statement at all. "I'm sorry I upset you."

"You didn't."

"I just wanted to stick it to that wanker who hurt you."

"He was definitely taken aback." She forced a smile. "It was perfect."

The air felt thick with tension for the remainder of dinner.

After we left the restaurant, I stopped short of starting the car. I was in no rush to return to the house, where Roland would likely still be awake.

Abby still seemed preoccupied, with a vacant look on her face. I knew she was thinking about us, all the things we *weren't*.

"Did you want to go straight home?" I asked, reaching over to caress her thigh.

"What else did you have in mind?" She smiled flirtatiously, bringing me great relief. Perhaps I hadn't totally wiped any joy from this evening.

I massaged her leg. "Anything involving you on top of me?"

"Where are we supposed to go? Phil and Kate are at the house. I just texted Dad, and he said they haven't left yet. I don't really feel like joining them."

"Why don't I book us a room for an hour or so? I'll go *anywhere* to be alone with you."

"That's a waste of money."

I patted her knee. "I'm good for it, Abby. I don't think I can stand to wait much longer. I've been dying for you all day."

She looked around, surveying the car park. "Why don't you park over there by that tree?"

"Are you suggesting what I think you are?"

"Sadly, I am."

I couldn't move the car to the empty side of the lot fast enough. We probably wouldn't get caught, but even if we did, I wasn't sure I gave a fuck. I'd wanted to be buried inside of Abby since the moment I woke up this morning. When I shut off the engine, my dick was already straining against my trousers, begging for an escape. I moved my seat back as far as it would go. "Come here," I ordered, unzipping myself and taking my rigid dick out.

Abby climbed on top, straddling me as she lifted her dress. In a split second, I sank into her, groaning so loudly that it was conceivable some of the patrons in the restaurant might have heard. "Fuck, Abby. Have you been this wet all night?"

"Maybe." She bucked her hips as she began riding my cock.

I rested my head against the seat, enjoying every second. "Look at me, Abby. I want to see you." I wrapped my hand around the back of her neck and thrust harder, urged on by the look of pure lust in her eyes as she bore down on me. "Give it to me, beautiful."

The car shook as our bodies rocked together. Suddenly she dug her nails into my shoulders and the muscles between her legs began to convulse around my shaft. I could feel her orgasm as she tightened around me and screamed. I came instantly, practically blacking out from the pleasure.

As the motion of our bodies slowed, she smiled down at me with her gorgeous, glassy eyes. The bun on top of her head was now a mess. And for the first time in what felt like forever, my soul was happy. *She* made me happy.

CHAPTER 41

Abby

Track 41: "London Boy" by Taylor Swift

The weeks after Sig went back to England were particularly hard. As much as his surprise visit had brought us closer, in some ways things were as unclear as ever—now with an ocean between us again. And I missed him even more than I had before he came.

The only thing truly clear after he left? I loved him. I knew that now, and it scared the hell out of me. I wasn't sure when my feelings had transitioned from infatuation to love—was it when he'd looked into my eyes at the airport and I could tell he didn't want to go? Was it when he'd steadied my dad as he noticed him losing his balance one evening after dinner? Or was it that crazy night in the shed? Regardless, I loved Sigmund Benedictus more than I'd loved any man before. And I feared it was one-sided. I knew he *cared* for me—his actions showed that. But love? The soul-shattering kind he'd shared with Britney? I wanted him to love me *that* way. Although I wasn't sure he'd ever be capable of it again, I could never accept anything less.

Dad was scheduled for lung surgery next week, and his recovery would determine whether I'd either be staying here in Rhode Island to deliver the baby or heading back to England. I needed to fly while the airline would still let me, since pregnant women weren't advised to travel by air after thirty-six weeks. At thirty-one weeks now, I was cutting it close. But still I crossed my fingers, hoping to give birth in England. I missed Lavinia, and Westfordshire, in general. Missed London, too. My heart ached to be back there, even if just for a short time more. I knew Sig would fly here for the birth, but from the time I'd made the decision to move to the UK, I'd always envisioned it happening over there.

On this early-December day, Dad had a pre-op appointment in Boston, so we'd been gone most of the afternoon. It was dark out now, and when we pulled into our driveway, I couldn't believe my eyes. For a moment I thought I'd pulled onto the wrong property, but it was definitely ours.

The entire house was lit up in Christmas lights.

How? Between my pregnancy and Dad's condition, neither of us had found the energy to decorate this year. So we'd nixed the idea.

"Did you have someone do this?" my father asked, looking up in amazement. The entire surface area of the house seemed covered.

"I wish I could take credit, but I didn't. I have no idea how this happened." As I stared up at the lights, I started to cry—happy tears. It wasn't until this moment that

I realized how sad I'd been, how scared about the future. From the impending birth, to my dad's health, to the status of my relationship with Sig, my life was filled with uncertainty. This, though, was a moment of joy. A moment to pause and appreciate all the good I had in my life. How lucky I was to be alive.

Then it hit me. Sig was the only person I'd spoken to about not being able to put up Christmas lights this year. This had to be his doing. But how the hell did he pull it off?

Once we got inside, I called him. He'd barely had a chance to answer when I said, "You did this? The lights?"

"Oh good. They didn't fuck it up."

"Whoever *they* are, they did an amazing job."

"Are they bright and obnoxious? That's what I asked for."

"They rival Clark Griswold's from *Christmas Vacation*. Pretty sure we might make the news tonight and cause a traffic jam from onlookers."

"Good. Good."

I sniffled. "How the hell did you manage this?"

"I hired a team to do it while I knew you were in Boston with your father. I wanted to surprise you."

"Well, you brought me to tears. I can't tell you how much this means to me—to us."

"I didn't mean to make you cry, beautiful. Besides, it's nothing compared to what you're doing for me, for Kate and Phil. I could never repay you. Just wanted to bring a little happiness to your day, because I know it's not going to be an easy week for you. You and your dad deserve lights this year more than any."

I wiped my eyes. "You know, Benedictus, you sure are ruining your prior reputation as a jerk."

Sig's holiday surprises didn't end with the Christmas lights. The following day, he sent me a text in the middle of the afternoon.

> **Sig:** I want to take you on a lunch date. Virtually. Can you swing it?

> **Abby:** Dad's sleeping, and I was just going to make myself something, but I would much rather go on a date with you.

> **Sig:** Eat something first. I'll call you in twenty minutes.

When it came time for our call, he appeared on the screen wearing a gray wool coat and scarf—so handsome. It was nighttime there, but I recognized the store in the background. "Are you at Marks and Spencer?"

"I might be." He winked. "It's the one not far from my flat."

Sig knew I loved shopping at the food hall there, might even call it an obsession. There was another one within walking distance of the office in London, and I'd often gone there to stock up on prepared foods before returning to Westfordshire in the evenings. I'd even bring a cooler with me, prompting much ridicule from Sig. Lavinia and I loved their pigs-in-a-blanket appetizer. They had so many tasty snacks that I couldn't get here in the US.

"They've put out all the Christmas items," he said. "I'm feeling bad that you have to miss their holiday displays. So I thought I'd bring everything to you tonight."

That made my heart squeeze. The idea of missing Christmas in London was hard to accept. I longed to experience at least one season there with him. "You're gonna kill me with your Christmas kindness, Sig. I was a blubbering mess last night with the lights, and now this?"

"I figured you could pick out whatever you want, and I'll ship it to you in a care package. Unfortunately, it has to be nonperishable, so the pigs in a blanket won't make it. But they have an obscene amount of chocolate."

"And you say you're not romantic. This is the most romantic thing anyone has ever done for me—second only to the Christmas spectacular you set up at my house last night."

"Keep this our little secret." He smiled, but then his expression turned serious. "I hate what you're going through with your dad right now. I just want to bring you some happiness, like you've brought me. This is the first Christmas I've allowed myself to acknowledge anything having to do with the holiday. Since Britney died, Christmases have been hard. But this year, I feel like celebrating. It's nice to get in the spirit again. You're the reason for that."

"You're gonna make me cry." The doorbell rang. "Someone's at the door," I said.

"Go answer." He smirked.

What else does he have up his sleeve? My heart raced. When I opened, it was a delivery guy with an order from Starbucks. I thanked him and closed the door. "What's all this?"

"We couldn't have a proper Christmas date in the city without hot cocoa, could we?"

I peeked inside the bag. "A chocolate croissant, too. My favorite."

"I know. Besides Devil Dogs."

Sig then proceeded to take me around Marks and Spencer on FaceTime, showing me the various holiday displays. It was almost as good as being there with him. Every time I expressed interest in something, he'd throw it in his cart. By the time he checked out, I knew he'd be shipping me a light-up house filled with chocolate, gingerbread cookies, and a London-themed smash cake with treats inside, among other things. I'd have enough sugar for a year.

My mouth hurt from smiling. "Are you taking me home with you now?" He'd continued our call after exiting the store.

"Yes. You're walking with me. I'd give anything for it to be real."

"I wouldn't get kicked out tonight, would I?"

"Absolutely not, love."

Love. It always gave me goose bumps when he called me that. Yet it was ironic, since *love* and true commitment were perhaps the only things he wasn't able to give me this Christmas. While it felt amazing to be spoiled like this, I would've traded it all for his heart.

That night after dinner, I watched as Dad ate the other half of the chocolate croissant I'd saved for him. He hadn't had much of an appetite for the chicken and potatoes I'd made, but he seemed to be enjoying the pastry, which made me happy.

After he went up to bed, I retreated to my room and decided to set up the laptop Kate and Phil had dropped off for me recently. Britney's parents had visited us a few times to help out since returning from Florida. I'd mentioned that I was shopping for a new computer since mine died, and they'd insisted on giving me Britney's laptop. They said it was virtually unused and had only been sitting around collecting dust. She'd apparently purchased it not long before she died. They'd brought it for me the last time they were here.

I had mixed feelings about taking it. I was grateful for the generous gift, but also felt incredibly guilty using something Britney should've been here to enjoy. I supposed there were *a lot* of things lately that made me feel that way. This laptop was nothing compared to what she was missing with the love of her life—who now also happened to be the love of *my* life, even if he didn't realize it.

I'd had the laptop charging in a corner of my bedroom for the past couple of hours. I unplugged it and brought it over to the desk to set it up. Britney's parents told me they'd copied all of her documents to a thumb drive, so most everything on the computer had been erased.

But when I clicked into the Gmail icon on the desktop, rather than prompting me to log in, it opened an existing account—Britney's account. I would have immediately logged out if not for something that caught my eye.

There were dozens and dozens of bolded, unread emails in her inbox, with the most recent delivery date being yesterday. And the sender on all of them?

Sigmund Benedictus

CHAPTER 42

Sig

Track 42: "Surprises" by Billy Joel

Christmas in London had come and gone.

Lavinia and I had spent the holidays with Leo, Felicity, and their kids, though we made a brief appearance at my parents' house on Christmas Day. My heart, though, was in the States with Abby. I'd offered to go there for the holiday, but she'd told me she preferred that I didn't. She'd insisted I stay here and not leave Lavinia alone. Lavinia didn't like to fly, so taking her with me wasn't an option. I might have gone to Rhode Island anyway, but I got the impression there was more to Abby's request, that she really did want some space.

She'd been acting a bit weird for the past month or so. I couldn't put my finger on it, but she seemed preoccupied. It couldn't have been solely the situation with her father, because his surgery had been successful. The worst was seemingly over with him for now, yet the change in her demeanor remained. During our nightly calls, whenever I asked if something was bothering her, she'd say no and move on to tell me something trite about her day. But when you're in tune with someone you care about, you can see in their eyes when something is wrong. She had a lot on her mind and was choosing not to share it with me. I tried to convince myself it was the stress of pregnancy, but deep down I knew better.

Her father's doctors remained optimistic, yet Abby had decided to give Roland a bit more time to recover before booking her return to England. Giving birth here was still the plan for now. While I could hardly wait to see her, the uncertainty in the air grew more palpable by the day, the closer we got to the baby's arrival.

There was so much we needed to work out. But important decisions about the status of our relationship were not going to get made over the phone. So if she wasn't able to come here soon, I'd be traveling to the US. I couldn't put it off any longer.

Today was January second. New Year, new me. While most days had seemed to drag lately as I counted them away, today was different. Today demanded all of my attention. I was finally going to tell my parents about the baby. Lavinia was right. I needed to have the decency to tell my parents *before* their grandchild was born. I stood by my decision not to divulge anything up to this point, however. I'd avoided months of unneeded stress and inquisition. Telling them now, with little more than a month to go, was my compromise.

I never would have admitted it to her, but Lavinia's presence today was most appreciated. She was my ride or die and always supported me, despite the stupid decisions I made. I could've come home and announced that I'd murdered someone, and Lavinia would reprimand me first, then help me cover it up. That was the type of friend she was. I'd chosen to have my parents meet me at the inn so Lavinia could be by my side at the table as a much-needed buffer.

She walked in as I paced in the kitchen, waiting for my parents. "How are you doing?"

I stopped in my tracks. "Good. I'm ready. I have nothing to hide." I inhaled a breath. "It feels like the right time."

"That's my boy." She smiled. "Fancy a drink to calm down?"

"No. I need to save that for when they're here. Although, believe me, the thought of getting totally pissed is tempting."

"Did you tell Abby you were going to talk to them today?"

"No. I didn't want to stress her. Or more, I knew she'd be stressed out *for me*. She knows I've been dreading it. I'll tell her when it's over so she doesn't have to worry."

When the doorbell rang, I took a deep breath and readied myself to greet them. I'd prepared lunch for Mum and Dad but planned to get right to the point before any eating. I clapped my hands together. "It's showtime." I headed to the door with Lavinia behind.

Upon opening, I nearly fell back a step from the shock of seeing Abby standing there—rosy cheeks, wind-blown hair, and *very* pregnant.

How?

"Oh my heavens!" Lavinia said.

"Abby!" I practically leapt forward, pulling her into a tight embrace—well, as tight as it could be with the massive beach ball in between us. "Why didn't you tell me you were coming?"

"I wanted to surprise you and Lavinia..."

I squeezed her tighter, not realizing until this moment just *how* badly I'd needed her back. There was nothing we couldn't work out as long as she was here with me. After a moment, I reluctantly loosened my arms around her, bustling her inside and closing the door.

"Lavinia!" Abby reached out to hug her. "I missed you so much."

"My dear, I'm so very happy right now. It's so good to have you back."

"It's good to be back. I wasn't sure I'd make it."

"Your father is okay?" Lavinia asked.

Abby nodded. "Dad's doctor gave him the all clear this week. And my sister is coming to stay with him for two weeks, which is basically a miracle. She should be arriving right around now. That's the only reason I felt comfortable leaving him."

"It's about time she picked up some of the slack," I grumbled.

Though Lavinia stood practically on top of us, I placed my hand around Abby's cheek and brought her mouth into mine. Her lips were cold from the air outside, and I did my best to warm them. She seemed to relax as she gave in to our kiss. My body ached for more.

Then the doorbell rang.

I froze. "Shit," I muttered, snapping back to reality. *Poor Abby.* She'd have to face my parents, too.

She turned to look at the door. "Who's that?"

I caressed her tousled hair. "My parents."

Her eyes widened. "Your parents?"

"I invited them over to finally tell them the news. I obviously didn't know you were coming, so..."

"Oh...gosh." She gripped her stomach. "Horrible timing. Should I leave?"

"Absolutely not. I have nothing to hide anymore. Unless you're not comfortable."

She licked her lips. "You know what? I'm good." Letting out a long breath, she nodded. "Yeah. Let's do it."

I felt horrible that she'd walked into this. Reaching for her hand, I brought it to my lips and kissed her fingers. Then I walked over to the door to open it.

CHAPTER 43

Sig

Track 43: "If You Leave Me Now" by Chicago

My parents were dressed as if they were going to church rather than a casual lunch at the inn. I nodded once. "Mum, Dad, good to see you."

My mother reached out to kiss each of my cheeks. "Always good to see you, son. And such a rare treat to be invited to lunch. Hopefully, Lavinia's not going tso offer us Fireball again, though."

"Your mother won't stop talking about that one." My father chuckled as he patted me on the back.

"Hello again," Lavinia spoke from behind me. "So lovely to see you both."

"And you." My mother gave her a once-over, likely horrified by Lavinia's Birkenstocks with socks. "You're looking...gorgeous."

"Ah, you're a fantastic liar, Rosemary. But I'll take any compliments I can get these days."

My father offered Lavinia a hug. "A pleasure to see you again."

My mother blinked when she finally looked over at the beautiful, young brunette standing behind Lavinia. "Hello." Her gaze fell to Abby's round stomach. "And you are?"

"I'm Abby." Abby swallowed. "Nice to meet you."

I hated that I was putting her through this. But there was no other way but through the fire at the moment.

"Abby. Very nice to meet you, too, dear." Mum tilted her head. "Are you a guest here at the inn?"

Abby nodded. "Yes, I am."

"You're American. Where did you travel in from?"

"Rhode Island."

"Is your husband here with you?"

As Abby's face reddened, I couldn't take it anymore. "No, she's not married," I jumped in. "Abby is not just a guest here, Mother. She's someone very important to me, and I need you and Dad to sit down so I can explain."

My mother's face paled as she connected the dots, likely assuming I'd gotten Abby pregnant the natural way. I wasn't sure which situation she'd consider worse.

I spent the next several minutes laying it all out—from the moment Phil and Kate had arrived at my apartment that morning to Abby's recent return from looking after her father in the US. My mother tried to intercept the conversation multiple times, but I insisted she let me speak. Abby and Lavinia sat quietly on either side of me, and when I finally opened the floor to my parents, my mother's first question came as no surprise.

"How could you not have told us before you decided to do such a thing?"

"Would you have been receptive to the idea?"

"Absolutely not," she huffed. "But—"

"Then why would you expect me to tell you? It wouldn't have changed my decision."

She looked over at Abby a moment. "It was a reckless decision. This child needs a mother. I don't know what Phil and Kate were thinking, making such a selfish decision."

"Rosemary," my father interrupted. "We have no choice but to accept it. You must save your breath and calm yourself."

"I can't calm myself when my son has been keeping such a monumental secret from me." She scowled. "What would your nan have thought, Sigmund?"

I shrugged. "I wouldn't have had a problem telling Nan. She was always more accepting than you, Mother. Much more open-minded. I'm certain Nan would've been overjoyed to be a great-grandmother again."

My grandmother had passed away several years ago. Leo and I had both considered her our confidante whenever we had a problem. She was also one of the few people who brought me any comfort after Britney passed, despite her already being in poor health at the time.

"I highly doubt your nan would have encouraged such a hasty decision," Mum countered. "Nor would she have approved of you hiring a complete stranger to carry your child."

My blood boiled. She could be angry at me, but negativity toward Abby was not acceptable. I needed to stop her before she said anything stupid.

I raised my voice. "Abby is not a stranger anymore, far from it. She and I are very close. And I couldn't have asked for a better person to carry this child."

"If you'll excuse me," Abby interjected. "I'd like to speak for myself, since I'm sure your mother has many false opinions of me right now."

A knot formed in my stomach, but I wasn't going to stop her. Abby had every right to defend herself, to be part of this conversation.

Her eyes fixed firmly on my mother's. "You don't know me, and I'm sorry you had to find out about this situation so abruptly. But I've known your son for quite some time now, and his decision was *far* from hasty. He was tormented by it, and nearly backed out in the beginning. But while he had reservations—strong ones—he made this decision out of love for his wife, to honor *her* wishes. And out of respect for her parents, who lost their only child. With all due respect to *you*, Mrs. Benedictus, you don't know what it's like to lose a child. You're very fortunate."

The table remained silent. Abby looked between my parents and continued. "And both of you are very lucky to have each other, to not have lost the love of your life so young, as your son did. You can't tell someone what they should or should not do when you haven't walked in their shoes. And perhaps you're thinking I'm some kind of opportunist out for money. Your son thought that at first, and believe me, he's learned quite a bit from you about mistrust." Abby gestured to her belly. "But I can assure you that no one in their right mind would put their body—or their heart—through this just for money. I wanted to help. And while that might be a foreign concept to you, it's the truth."

My mother remained speechless. I was both relieved and perplexed by that.

I thought Abby had finished, but then she spoke again.

"Your son is an amazing man. He's been through something no one should ever have to experience, let alone at his age. He's suffered much of the time in silence these past several years, something you probably didn't realize since he doesn't open up to you. Because you never took his marriage seriously to begin with." She looked my way and smiled slightly. "And as for his treatment of me? He's been protective, respectful, and has given me everything I could want during this process. I will never forget this experience. It is the most meaningful thing I've done with my life. And in the end, I'm going to go back to the States knowing I made a huge difference in several people's lives. And if I died, I would know I'd left my mark on this world."

"...back to the States..." That was all I heard.

She went on. "Don't waste your time picking apart this situation for all of the reasons you think it's wrong. Spend it giving your son the love he deserves, the love he needs that's been so desperately missing from his life since his wife's death." Abby shrugged. "You're going to be grandparents whether you like it or not. You already are. Congratulations to you both."

My stomach churned. Had Abby already made a firm decision that there was zero hope for us? I guess I'd given her no clear reason to assume otherwise. Was this what had been different over these past several weeks? I thought I might burst with the need to be alone with her, to tell her I never wanted her to leave. *Ever.* I couldn't have cared less about my mother's opinions right now. I wanted to kiss Abby for that speech.

To my shock, Abby stood from the table and walked out of the room.

I rushed after her. "What's going on?"

"I really need to take a drive—alone."

"But you just got here. I don't want to be apart from you."

"I know." She rubbed my arm. "Spend time with your parents. Talk it out with them. And I'll be back later."

"I don't understand. Where are you going?"

"Felicity's. I want to meet the baby."

I reached for my keys. "Let me drive you, then."

"No. You can't leave your parents. And I want to drive myself, okay?"

I scratched my head. "Will you...text me when you get there?"

"It's not that far, Sig. But of course, I can."

I had to ask. "Are things okay with us, Abby?"

"Yeah. Don't worry about me right now. Finish the conversation with your parents. Answer their questions. Make things right with your mom."

That was the last thing she said before she walked out the door.

I stood by the entryway for a minute, analyzing her bizarre exit. Or maybe it wasn't so bizarre. As I returned to the table, I knew I needed to make something immediately clear. "I won't accept any badmouthing of her," I announced. "Do you understand? Abby has been nothing short of an angel through all of this. She deserves your utmost respect, even if you don't realize it yet."

"Where did she go?" my father asked.

"She needed a break. Can you blame her?"

My mother clutched her necklace. "Are we that bad?"

"Do you want the honest answer?"

"Sigmund..." She frowned. "It's time to let me talk."

"Alright, Mother." I returned to my seat.

"While this is not a situation I would've chosen for you, I heard every word she said. Alright? As much as I might have been against this had I known about it earlier, there's no choice but to embrace it now."

"Are you saying you're gonna spare me any more of your opinions on the matter?"

"I'm saying...I love you. That's it, really. All we can do as your parents is give you our opinions. You're clearly an adult and make your own decisions, regardless of what we think. Ultimately, we just want you to be happy."

"Very well, then." I nodded. "Let's end on that note and not say another word about it."

"I do have one more question," she said.

"What?"

"You *are* aware that your *surrogate* is in love with you?"

Lavinia snorted.

Mum tilted her head. "Exactly how long have you been involved with her and what will this mean for your supposed business arrangement?"

"Too much information for one day, Mother. I can't begin to answer that question right now. But when I have everything figured out, eventually I'll let you know."

My mother grimaced. "Eventually."

"That sounds fair to me," my father said. "Let's leave the poor chap alone, Rosemary. We came for lunch. Let's proceed with that plan."

Lavinia interrupted, "I think we should all toast to your grandchild."

"That would be...lovely," my mother said.

"I don't know about anyone else, but I could *certainly* use a drink." My father laughed.

Lavinia grinned over at me. "I'll grab the Fireball!"

She knew damn well that my parents hated Fireball. The four of us got a good laugh out of that.

With this difficult discussion behind me, you'd think I would've breathed a sigh of relief. But tension seized my chest, tighter by the minute. *"...back to the States,"* she'd said.

CHAPTER 44

Abby

Track 44: "Ghost" by Justin Bieber

I held baby Eli in my arms. "I can't believe how big he is already."

"I know." Felicity smiled over at her son. "He changes every day."

Eli, now four months old, had dark blond hair like his father. For some reason, I'd assumed the baby would end up a redhead like Felicity and his sister.

Little Eloise was busy in the corner, playing with her toy kitchen set. I watched as she placed plastic muffins into the oven.

Felicity crossed her legs. "I can't believe you came here practically right after you landed."

"Yeah. My stomach and I barely fit in the Fiat now." I chuckled. "But it was worth dealing with the tight squeeze just to escape."

"I can't imagine how awkward it was to meet his parents for the first time that way."

"I said what I needed to say and got the hell out of there. I'm sure they probably thought I was rude, but it's what I needed."

"I think it was brave that you stood up for yourself. And I'm so glad you chose to come hang out with us. I've been lonely with Leo gone for the day. So this is perfect."

When the baby got fidgety in my arms, I went over to hand him back to her on the couch.

"Can I pry?" Felicity asked as she rocked him and I sat back down.

I rubbed my hands along my belly. "Okay..."

"We spent a lot of time with Sig over Christmas. He told us you'd been acting a bit differently recently. He seemed worried. It was the first time I realized how serious things had gotten between you. Are you regretting that?"

Felicity and I had kept in touch over the phone while I was back in Rhode Island, so she knew I'd become more than just a surrogate to Sig. But I hadn't told her anything about the current state of my head. And I hadn't told Sig, either.

"The only thing I regret is falling in love with him, Felicity."

She smiled empathetically. "Oh, honey... I'm sorry. I didn't know your feelings had evolved *that* much."

I nodded. "I love him. I love him so much. Even being around him today...that was part of the reason I needed a breather. It was overwhelming to see him after so much time apart and realize my feelings hadn't diminished even a little."

"I know he cares about you, too," she said.

Her choice of words stung a little. "That's the thing. I know he *cares* about me. But I need more. I won't accept anything less than his full heart. And if he can't give me that, I don't think we'd ever stand a chance."

"Have you told him you love him?"

"No." I shook my head. "I can't."

"Why?"

"Because I don't want him to feel obligated if he doesn't feel the same." A flash of panic set in. "And please, don't mention to anyone that we had this conversation."

"I won't." She shook her head. "I'll admit, Leo and I talk about you guys a lot. But if you're specifically telling me not to say anything, I won't. You have my word."

"Thank you."

"Anyway, why do you think that he's incapable of giving you his whole heart?"

"It's not that I think it. I *know* it, Felicity."

"He told you that?"

"Not me."

"I'm confused."

I looked behind my shoulder to make sure Nathan, the house manager, wasn't in the vicinity and lowered my voice, "I haven't told anyone this. So again, I need your utmost discretion."

"Okay..."

Breathing in, I let it out. "He's been writing to her. All this time."

Her brows knitted. "Who?"

"Britney."

"Britney..."

"Yes. Her parents gave me her old laptop when they found out mine stopped working. When I tried to log into my email for the first time, it opened straight up to Britney's account. And there were messages from him. The most recent one was from, like, the day before, and they went all the way back to right after she died."

"You read them all?"

"No." I shook my head. "I read one. Then I stopped myself. I know it's terrible, and I shouldn't have done it. I have no business reading his private thoughts to her. I told myself I could read one just to understand the gist of why he was writing her, and I wouldn't read any more."

"Okay...what did you see?"

"I clicked on a random email that was sort of in the middle. In his message, he counted the number of days she'd been gone, and he told her how he thinks of her every minute of every day. And he wanted her to know..." I hesitated.

Felicity leaned in. "What?"

"That he will *never* love anyone the way he loved her."

Felicity closed her eyes briefly and sighed. "Ah..."

"I shouldn't have clicked on that email." I looked away. "But in some ways, I'm glad I did."

"How long ago did he write that?"

"Honestly, I didn't look at the date. Like I said, I just clicked on one. But it doesn't matter." I sighed. "Anyway, I didn't trust myself not to open another, so I logged out of her account. Now I can never get back in, since I don't have the password."

Felicity nodded. "I can understand why reading that upset you. But people's feelings can change over time."

"Sometimes I feel like I'm competing with a ghost. That's awful to say."

She smiled sympathetically. "You can say anything here."

"Like, if we were together, it would only be because she's not here—not because we're soulmates or meant to be. If she miraculously walked in the door right now, wouldn't he run to her and leave me in the dust?" My chest tightened. "That's not a good feeling. And then I feel stupid for thinking about that, because how can I be jealous of a dead person?" I turned to her. "Be honest, am I crazy here?"

"I think it's very natural to want the person you love to love you back equally."

"Well, he hasn't said he loves me at all, so there's that."

The doorbell rang, interrupting our conversation. I could hear Nathan answering the door and then another man's voice.

CHAPTER 45

Abby

Track 45: "My Love Mine All Mine" by Mitski

I stood suddenly when I saw Sig at the entrance to the living room. My heart fluttered. "What are you doing here?"

"I got impatient. I wanted to see you."

I walked over and he cupped my cheeks and kissed me passionately, without any regard for Felicity sitting there. When he finally let me go, he kissed me softly on the forehead before turning to her. She seemed amused.

"What's that expression for, Ginger? Have you never seen anyone kiss?"

"I've never seen this side of you. It's nice."

I'd nearly forgotten that Felicity and Leo were apart while Britney had been here with Sig. Felicity had never met Britney, so she'd never witnessed what Sig was like in a relationship.

Felicity smiled at me. "Let me give you two some space. I've got to change Eli anyway." She wrangled her daughter. "Come on, Eloise. Come help me with your brother."

My eyes followed them as they headed up the stairs. When I looked up at Sig again, his gaze was warm.

"I was gonna head back soon, you know," I told him. "You didn't need to come all the way here."

He tugged gently at my shirt. "Do you have any idea how painful it was to see you for a matter of minutes after all the time we've spent apart, only to have you leave again?"

"How did it go with your parents after I left?"

"After your mic drop, you mean?" He grinned. "Pretty sure you saved the day. My mother softened a lot. Your passion is palpable, able to permeate even the toughest of hearts. We ended up toasting to the baby and managed to have a nice lunch together."

Relief washed over me. "Like so many things in life, worrying about the outcome was worse than the actual event. I'm glad they know now. You didn't need that looming over you."

He tucked a piece of my hair behind my ear. "We have enough looming over *us*, as it is, don't we? And I know much of it's my fault—for not being crystal clear about my intentions, for leaving so much up to an uncertain future. You've been upset these past few weeks. And I haven't helped the situation, haven't given you clear answers on where *I* stand, and yet I've asked you to open up to me. That's not fair."

"Where *do* you stand, Sigmund?"

He stared through me. "I'm terrified. Terrified of losing you. Terrified of becoming a father. Terrified of changing my mind and deciding to raise this child when I still don't know if I can handle it. I'm terrified of making the wrong decisions. I've been using our incredible chemistry as an escape from difficult choices. As we get closer, it's harder to escape into you and not worry about the rest. These months with you—both in person and through the connection we've built when we weren't physically together—have been some of the best of my life. This is the first time in a long time that I've been happy. I didn't think I was capable of feeling that way again. But I can't stick my head in the sand forever. I don't know what's best for this child. I don't know what's best for *you* anymore, a life with or without me." He wrapped his hands around my face. "But there *is* one thing I'm certain of, and that's that I love you."

My heart skipped a beat. I was not expecting those words. Not today. Not ever.

"I don't know whether that means I should love you enough to encourage you to go on with your life or beg you to stay," he continued. "I just know I love you, Abby. And I needed to tell you. That's why I couldn't wait for you to get back. It couldn't wait a second longer."

My eyes welled up as a bittersweet feeling rose within me. I wanted *so* badly to believe him, that he *truly* loved me. But the doubt was real. I still struggled with the worry that I was a consolation prize. And I could never admit that insecurity. It felt selfish and immature. It wasn't fair to make him compare. Not to mention, I could never admit that I'd read his private email.

I looked up and realized too many seconds had gone by in silence. But there was only one honest response. "I love you, too." I placed my hand over his, still cradling my face. "But I'm scared."

"I will never willingly hurt you." He leaned in to kiss me again, my stomach pressed against him. He jumped back as my belly suddenly twitched. "What was that?"

I laughed. "It was your baby kicking."

While he'd seen the baby kick on FaceTime, Sig had never been around to feel it before. He placed his hand on my bump and watched in awe as it happened again. "Oh my God."

"Surreal, right?"

He kept his hand there for a minute before the baby seemed to calm down. "You're amazing. How your body has been keeping this little alien alive while dealing with everything else—including me…"

"It's been my pleasure. All of it."

He pressed his forehead to mine. "Let me take care of you tonight."

My body stirred. "What did you have in mind?"

"Believe it or not, *that* wasn't the first thing." He winked. "It's up there, though."

After we said goodbye to Felicity, I followed Sig back to the inn. As usual, he insisted on driving in front of me to provide some light on the otherwise dark road.

Later, he made me dinner and told me to relax down-stairs with Lavinia for a bit while he went up.

When I heard the water, I suspected he was running me a bath. But I didn't expect the scene I actually found when I got up there.

CHAPTER 46

Abby

Track 46: "Small Bump" by Ed Sheeran

The lights were off. There were candles flickering. And the most relaxing spa music played on a Bluetooth speaker.

"What's all this?"

"It's my way of welcoming you home," Sig said.

Home. This did feel like home in so many ways.

"You coming in with me?" I asked.

"If you'll have me."

"I would love that. But will we both fit? Technically it's gonna be three of us in there."

"I'll make it work." He smiled.

After I slipped out of my clothes, he did the same. Sig got in the tub behind me and wrapped his arms around my body, placing his palms over my stomach. My back leaned against his chest. The plan was for me to relax, but it seemed the baby had other ideas. It started kicking pretty aggressively.

Sig laughed. "My goodness. What's going on in there?"

"He or she wants to come out and splash, I think." I giggled.

"Is the kicking more active than usual today?"

"Definitely. Maybe the baby senses my anxiety."

He kissed the back of my neck. "Talk to me, beautiful. Why are you still anxious? I'm doing everything possible to help you relax tonight."

"It's nothing you've done. But I still have a lot on my mind."

"Tell me what's going on."

I couldn't afford to keep my thoughts inside any longer. We were running out of time. "I don't know if I'm ready to be a mother," I blurted.

His body stiffened behind me. "You think me telling you I loved you meant I was expecting something more from you now? I wasn't, Abby. I was simply expressing my undeniable feelings. The conflicts we have yet to face don't change the fact that I've fallen in love with you. And my love for you doesn't change the fact that I still think what's best for you is to move on with your life. But it's impossible for me to encourage that anymore. I don't want you to leave. But no one is asking you to be a mother or expecting that." He expelled a long breath against my neck. "Incidentally, I'm nowhere near ready to be a father, so I can relate. I'm no more prepared for this situation because I'm the biological father."

Panic built inside of me. Even if he wasn't ready to admit it, I knew Sig would ultimately decide to raise his child. It didn't matter if he was ready, this was *his* child. He seemed at peace with allowing Phil and Kate to raise it, but once he saw his and Britney's baby, he wouldn't be able to let it go. And I couldn't allow this precious baby to get used to having me around, only to have my relationship with Sig fall apart once life after the surrogacy set in.

There were too many unknowns. Too many risks. Would his child with Britney be an everyday reminder of how much he loved her? Would whatever he felt for me pale in comparison? Would the stress of raising a baby put a damper on the love fog we'd been in? Would it change everything? The bottom line was, Sig would always be the baby's father. But if he and I didn't work out, I could break this child's heart. It wasn't fair. I was too scared to risk hurting this tiny soul, who meant more to me than anything in the world. We were too close to the end to ignore the inevitable any longer.

"When you were talking to my parents earlier, you alluded to going back to the US," Sig said, as if he could sense the turmoil in my mind. "Is that why you've been different? Have you been afraid to tell me that's what you've decided?"

That wasn't exactly what had been eating at me. But now that we were on the topic, I wasn't going to run away. "I do think it's best if I go back, that I don't get attached to the baby when its born. That I leave after."

Silence filled the room.

"You're sure..." he finally said, his tone filled with disappointment.

"No, I'm not," I admitted. "But as a wise and *old* man once told me, 'Sometimes you have to wager your best guess on the decisions you make, even if it doesn't feel a hundred-percent comfortable.' If I don't make this decision now, it's only going to get harder. My leaving was always the original plan, right?"

Sig was quiet for a few moments before he answered. "I've always said you need to do what's best for you. I will love and respect you forever, no matter what you decide. But I'm not going to pretend that losing you is something I can easily handle. I promise to support any choice you make despite that." He paused. "Under one condition."

"What?"

"Let me have this last month. Don't distance yourself from me because you're planning to leave. I need this time with you." He tightened his grip around me. "Please."

His request warmed me inside, and also made me uneasy. But there was only one answer, despite my mixed feelings. "Okay. I promise."

I turned to look at him and immediately regretted it. His eyes were red, like he was trying not to cry. My heart broke, because leaving England went against everything I truly wanted.

After we left the bath, Sig followed me into my room. There was no discussion about where he'd be sleeping tonight; he wasn't leaving my side. As painful as this day had been, the ache between my legs couldn't be tamed. I let my towel drop to the floor.

The desire in his hooded eyes grew by the second as he looked me over. "Fuck, you're even more beautiful."

He let his own towel fall, and his rigid dick bobbed, growing wet at the tip with arousal.

I lay down, and he crawled over to join me on the bed, positioning himself behind me and wrapping his arms around my waist. I felt the heat of his cock pressed against my ass.

He spoke low against my back. "If you're not in the mood to fuck, we don't have to."

Instead of responding verbally, I reached down and under, wrapping my hand around his shaft and guiding him inside me, showing him *exactly* what I was in the mood for tonight.

He groaned as he sank into me. "You knew what I needed, didn't you?"

"I need it, too," I panted, pushing my ass against him.

He gripped me possessively, as if he never wanted to let go. "I feel like it's been years," he muttered. "How the fuck do you feel even better than before?"

I had to agree. It felt better than ever for me, too. Maybe because it had been so long. Or maybe because through each powerful movement, I could feel his desperation as he filled me completely.

Sig's teeth grazed my shoulder, his body rocking against mine. As his breathing quickened, I lost control, my muscles spasming around his cock. His stomach tightened behind me as a deep groan escaped him, his hot cum spilling into me.

Sig stayed inside of me long after we'd finished, holding me and kissing my back, repeating over and over in different ways how beautiful I was. I'd never felt safer, more cherished. It made me doubt everything I'd supposedly decided earlier about leaving him. Planning to go back to my life was sensible in theory, but my heart would always be here...with them.

After he finally pulled out, I turned to face him. Before I could say anything, he leaned in to kiss me. Running my index finger along his beautifully angular chin, I said, "You know, the weekend Phil and Kate came to visit my dad, when I first offered to be the surrogate, I was supposed to have been away in New Hampshire with my friend Allison."

"Really?"

I nodded. "But she flaked on me at the last minute, so the trip got canceled. If I hadn't been at my house, I would've never bonded with the Alexanders the way I did. They might've found someone else. And I never would've met you. I can't believe how close I came to never knowing you, never having this experience."

"I can't believe how close I came to fucking it all up with my attitude."

I brushed his hair off his forehead. "If you weren't so damn handsome and intriguing, you might've."

"Every second of every day matters. Every single choice." He thought for a moment. "When I met Britney at that airport, she'd literally bumped into me. One bump. That was all it took. We were on the same flight, but if I'd just gone to the bathroom and somehow not knocked into her, I might've never started arguing with her, might never have met her. And how strange is it now to think that one bump also brought me to you. A matter of seconds could've changed my entire life as I know it."

I searched for his hand and placed it on my stomach. "That bump brought you this bump."

He smiled. "It did."

"You're gonna do great, Sig."

His eyes narrowed. "What are you talking about?"

"Raising this little human. You'll be an amazing father."

"You know something I don't?"

"I guess in my heart, I do."

"Well, that's news to me, love."

"You're the most protective person I know. You won't let anything happen to him or her."

"I'm much more comfortable with this baby safe inside of you." He rubbed the skin along my hip. "In fact, I'd love to freeze this moment in time: the baby safely protected and you here with me."

I curled into him, and we lay in silence for a while.

"What if I can't do it?" he asked.

I looked up into his eyes. "Take care of the baby alone?"

He shook his head. "Live without you."

A chill ran down my spine. "You'll know where to find me if you can't."

He examined my face. "So you're saying even if you go back, the invitation is open to come and steal you away?"

"I don't think I'll ever be able to say no to you, Sigmund Benedictus."

"So, let's say I find out from Phil and Kate that you've met someone. You're engaged. Getting married." He sucked in a breath. "God, just thinking about it, I want to murder him—whoever he is."

I smiled as I threaded my fingers through his hair.

"You'd be open to me showing up on your wedding night, asking you to cavort with me in your father's shed, burying my head between your legs, and ruining everything for you?"

"If you must..."

"No." He shook his head. "It doesn't feel right—thinking of you with anyone else. Just talking about it makes me vengeful. You're still the only woman who's ever made me feel this kind of jealousy." He cleared his throat. "Alright. I'll stop. I'm not making this easy." He ground his teeth. "You told me tonight you're leaving. I'll find a way to accept it, if that's what you want."

But the look of sadness in his eyes made me unsure of my decision.

CHAPTER 47

Sig

Track 47: "Pray" by Sam Smith

Over the next couple weeks, I made some necessary changes to maximize my time with Abby during the last weeks of her pregnancy, the biggest of which was working remotely until she delivered.

Abby hadn't returned to her position at Covington. We'd had to fill her post when she'd left for Rhode Island to take care of her father. And with her being at the inn every day, I decided I should be, too.

If there was an emergency, I could always head into London, but I wasn't going to waste these precious days staring at my office wall when I could've been back at the inn staring at *her*, when I wasn't on my computer. I shut it down at exactly 5 PM each night and insisted that Abby go for walks with me, since her doctor said light exercise would be good for her circulation.

These days were absolutely my favorite of the entire experience, even if still laced with uncertainty. Every bittersweet moment spent with her felt like a gift:

Early breakfasts together before I had to log in for work.

The way she'd curl up next to me during my conference calls.

Lying next to her every night.

My favorite time was the period after dinner before bedtime. I'd rub Abby's feet while she and Lavinia put something stupid on the telly. Abby would look at the telly, and I'd look at her. And when she caught me now, I didn't even try to deny it like I used to.

I'd fallen more in love with her each day but hadn't repeated the sentiment aloud since that day at Felicity's. I didn't want to make things worse when she'd made her decision to leave. The need to tell her I loved her felt constant, though. I needed to convey it in a way that didn't seem like I was putting pressure on her, trying to sway her into doing something she might never be ready for. But my feelings had only grown since the first time I'd said those words. And she needed to know that.

One evening after I finished giving Abby a foot rub, she fell asleep on the couch. Lavinia chuckled as she looked over and noticed Abby out like a light.

As a light snore escaped through Abby's dainty nose, I marveled at her beauty. "Isn't she exquisite?"

I didn't realize I'd posed the question aloud until Lavinia responded. "Indeed, she is."

Abby stirred, and her eyes blinked open. She held her hand out for me to help her off the couch. "I have to pee." She wobbled over to the washroom just off the kitchen.

When Abby reemerged, she clutched her stomach with a troubled look on her face.

"Abby?" I shot up from the sofa. "What's wrong?"

"I'm getting the worst pain all of a sudden. It's mostly in my back. But it definitely doesn't feel normal."

My pulse began to race. "Shall I call your doctor? He gave us his mobile."

"Yeah." She nodded, her breaths uneven. "You should."

I took out my phone and sent an urgent text to Dr. Bonner, explaining that Abby was experiencing severe pain. He directed us to Reddington Hospital in Westfordshire. I would've preferred London, but we couldn't afford the ninety-minute drive. Reddington was only about ten minutes from the inn.

Abby held her back. "I should bring the hospital bag I packed."

"Uh...yeah," I said, feeling disoriented. Remembering she had that bag in the corner of her room, I ran to fetch it before booking it downstairs again.

Lavinia's voice shook as she saw us to the door. "What can I do?"

I looked her straight in the eyes and whispered, "Pray."

I'd never driven so fast yet so carefully in my life, down the long, winding road through Westfordshire. Certainly, I'd never driven with my heart in my throat like this. Holding Abby's hand, I kept insisting everything was going to be okay, even if my fear grew each time her pain worsened.

When we arrived at the hospital, I hadn't a clue how we'd gotten there. Everything was hazy, the ride blurred by the intensity of my fear. Almost as soon as we passed through the sliding glass doors, Abby looked down at herself.

"There's blood," she cried.

"Blood?" A shooting pain passed through my body as I, too, saw red.

She clutched her stomach. "Oh God, I'm so scared."

"We need to be seen immediately," I yelled, my voice trembling.

Someone rushed over.

"She's pregnant and bleeding!" I explained. "We don't know what's happening." My voice shook as I begged, "Please."

It took everything in me to hold it together, and all I could do was wrap my arms around Abby as we waited, helping her stand when she seemed so weak.

"Come right this way," a nurse said, leading us down a hall and into an examination area.

Abby lay on the bed. More people entered the room in a frenzy.

"How far along is she?" someone asked.

I wracked my brain. It was January twenty-first. Abby wasn't due for another few weeks. *Not far along enough* was the answer. "She's due February tenth."

Hospital staff surrounded her. And a doctor arrived to do a vaginal examination. After a moment, the doctor turned to me with a look of urgency. "We're dealing with a placental abruption."

"What does that mean?" I asked, my heart pounding.

She stood, removing her gloves. "It means she's losing blood fast, and we need to get this baby out immediately." She turned to her staff. "Prepare the OR."

CHAPTER 48

Sig

Track 48: "Angel" by Sarah McLachlan

Feeling completely helpless, I caressed Abby's hair as we waited for the next step. "Everything will be okay. They're gonna get the baby out. And everything's going to be fine."

Terror filled her eyes. "I'm scared."

"I know. I know, love. But I'll be right here with you. I won't leave you. I promise."

A rush of people reentered the room. The next thing I knew, they were lifting Abby onto a bed with wheels.

I held her hand and walked in sync with the rolling of the bed, my pulse going a mile a minute as we headed down a hallway. When we got to the operating suite, a woman stopped me as I tried to follow them in.

"You're gonna have to stay out here."

"What?" I shook my head. "No! I can't leave her. I promised I wouldn't."

"I'm sorry, sir. We can't have anyone besides medical staff in the operating room. Hospital rules. You can stay right here outside the door and someone will keep you updated."

"I need to be in there!" I yelled.

"Their lives could be in danger, sir. We need as few people in that room as possible so the doctor can do her job."

Their lives?

Abby and the baby.

Their lives.

What. Is. Happening?

"Please. I can't lose her." My voice trembled. "Do whatever it takes to save her." When the cold and heavy steel door closed, I shouted, praying she could hear me. "I'll be right out here, Abby."

I began praying and praying and praying under my breath. Praying to God. Praying to Britney. I'd never prayed to Britney before. I'd never asked her for anything. But I desperately needed her help. It felt like my soul had been sucked out of me and transported into that operating room.

I frantically googled placental abruption on my phone. Before a few minutes ago, I'd never heard of it. How had I not known this was a possibility? The words on the screen knocked the wind out of me.

Life-threatening complications.

Hemorrhage.

Possible death of mother, child, or both.

I had to exit out. I didn't even want those words in my head right now. Shutting my eyes tightly, I began to pray again. When I'd told Lavinia to do that earlier, I'd had no idea how badly we would need prayers tonight. There were times in this process where I'd thought of Abby losing the baby. But never had I imagined I could lose *Abby*. And losing both? Incomprehensible.

If anything happened to either of them, I wouldn't survive it.

God help me.

God help us.

Please.

For the first time, I thought to text Kate and Phil. *Shit.* They needed to know we were here. Thankfully, they were already in England, staying at the flat they owned here in anticipation of the birth. It would take them a while to get here from London, and it was late. They were probably sleeping.

My hands shook as I typed.

We're at Reddington Hospital in Westfordshire. Abby had a placental abruption and is having an emergency c-section as we speak. Don't know anything more. They won't let me in the OR. Get here as soon as you can.

The door suddenly opened. My heart jumped, and then it nearly leapt out of my chest as a nurse approached, holding a baby—a baby whose arms and legs were moving around, a *live* baby.

"Your son is here. His vitals are good. We're taking him back to the recovery room."

My son.

A son.

As she placed the whimpering infant in my arms, I looked down in a daze. This should have been the most monumental moment of my life. But it felt like I was experiencing it from outside my body. This moment had been hijacked by the dark cloud of fear looming over me.

"What about Abby?" I asked.

The nurse's expression darkened. "Abby lost a lot of blood. She's going to need a transfusion. But they're doing everything they can to stabilize her."

Looking down into my son's precious eyes—Britney's almond-shaped eyes—I began to sob. I'd lost the woman I loved before. It was excruciatingly painful, but I'd had time to prepare. By the end, we knew it was coming, and as awful as it was, we were able to properly say our goodbyes, say everything we needed to say. But this? Losing Abby like this would be crueler than anything I could imagine.

The nurse's voice barely registered. "Although he likely won't need to stay there, we'll be taking the baby down to the NICU as a precaution. Everything checked out fine thus far. I assume you'd like to stay here until you know Mrs. Knickerbocker's status?"

The words coming out of her mouth sounded muffled. I felt dizzy. "Uh..."

"Are you alright? Can I get you some water?"

"No, thank you."

She reached for my son. "I'll take him down to the NICU now."

I handed him over. "Thank you."

Cold swept over me the moment I let him go. I wanted so badly to give my child the attention he deserved as he entered this scary world, but I couldn't think straight until I knew Abby was going to pull through this.

A couple of people in protective gear brushed past me carrying units of blood. I closed my eyes again and prayed.

Please don't let anything happen to her.

Please.

It was the most painful wait of my life. Nearly a half an hour had passed, and I'd gotten no additional news. I wanted to burst in there but was too afraid to disrupt things or draw attention away from the task at hand for even a second.

Then the steel door finally opened.

CHAPTER 49

Sig

Track 49: "There Goes My Life" by Kenny Chesney

The doctor removed her mask. "Abby is stable. She lost a lot of blood, so we had to give her three units."

"She's going to be okay?" I asked.

"I'm optimistic that she's going to be just fine."

Oxygen returned to my body for the first time since we'd left the inn. What felt like a thousand-ton weight lifted from my chest.

"And we didn't have to do a hysterectomy," the doctor added.

Hysterectomy? My chest constricted. "I didn't realize that was a possibility."

She nodded. "That's sometimes necessary with placental abruption. So she's very lucky. If you'd waited any longer to bring her here, I'm not sure that would have been the case."

My lip trembled. "Can I see her now?"

"Not in the operatory. But why don't I take you to recovery? That's where they're bringing her."

"Alright."

She took me down there, and I paced as I waited. When they finally wheeled Abby in, her eyes were closed.

My beautiful Abby. To think she'd nearly lost the ability to have children—or worse—was unthinkable. But for once, God had answered my prayers, and I was so very grateful.

"It's going to take a while for her to fully wake up. But she's conscious," the nurse said.

Abby's eyes gradually opened.

Glued to her bedside, I spoke softly. "Hi, love. It's me."

"Who?"

"Sig."

Her voice was hoarse. "Oh. Yeah. You looked like Voldemort for a moment..."

What? I chuckled. "Alright."

"Wait... I see you now. You look nice."

"Thank you."

"Handsome."

I wiped my eyes. "Thank you," I said, half-crying, half-laughing.

"What happened?" she asked, as awareness seemed to slowly replace the stupor of anesthesia. A look of alarm crossed her face. "Is the baby okay?"

"Yes. You had a boy. Everything is good with him. And you're gonna be fine, too."

"Where is he?" she rasped.

"He's in the NICU right now, but only as a precaution."

"A boy?" Her eyes filled with tears.

I brushed my hand along her hair. "Don't cry, Abby. You've been through so much."

"Why aren't you with him? He needs you."

"He's in good hands. I'm right where I need to be."

She cleared her throat. "What happened to me?"

"How much do you remember?"

"Everything until they took me into surgery. I heard them say I was losing blood."

I nodded. "They had to give you a blood transfusion. It saved your life."

"I can still have kids?"

"Yes. They didn't have to take anything besides the baby out, thank God."

She burst into tears. "I was so scared I would never see you again."

"Don't cry, love. You're here. You're fine. The baby is fine. Don't think about any of that right now. I want you to think happy thoughts. You've been through too much and you need to recover." I sniffled as I caressed her hair.

"Why are *you* crying, then?"

I had no suitable answer.

Before I could come up with anything, she asked, "What does he look like?"

"He has Britney's eyes. My dark hair. And your fighting spirit."

"Wow." She smiled, but then it faded. "He shouldn't be alone, Sig."

"I don't want to leave you yet."

"Do I look like I'm going anywhere?"

I smiled, squeezing her hand. "I'll go check on him and come right back."

She frowned.

"What's wrong, Abby?"

"I want to see him, too."

"I'll bring him straight to you, if they let me."

"Please," she begged. "I want to meet him."

"Alright." I bent to kiss her.

I stepped out and addressed one of the nurses. "Can someone direct me to the NICU? I want to check on my son."

"Of course." As she led the way, she said, "We'll be moving Abby to room two-ten shortly, so she likely won't be in recovery when you return."

"Two-ten," I repeated, burning that into my memory. "Okay. Thank you."

"This is Baby Knickerbocker's father," she told the woman at the desk as we entered the neonatal intensive care unit.

I realized that because of the emergency, we hadn't had a chance to explain the surrogacy. They'd assumed Abby was the baby's mother and assigned him her last name.

"He was just moved to the newborn nursery." The woman smiled.

"Why was he moved?" I asked.

"He graduated out of this joint. Didn't need to be here."

I breathed a sigh of relief.

"Follow me," the nurse said as we exited.

We walked down a different hallway into another room with dim lighting. A nurse tended to a baby in the corner, who I assumed was my son. We walked over, and he lay in what looked like a clear plastic bassinet on wheels.

"Baby Knickerbocker's father is here," the nurse again announced.

The woman who'd been taking care of him smiled. "Let me get you a bracelet, so you don't have any trouble taking him. Hang on." She printed a label before sticking it on a white plastic strip. She then wrapped it around my wrist. I looked down at the bracelet, which had a numeric code, his birth date, and Abby Knickerbocker written on it.

My son was swaddled in a white cotton blanket with blue and pink stripes. She carefully lifted him out of the bassinet and handed him to me. He felt warm. Though I'd held him right after he was born, this felt like the first time. I was fully present. I hadn't been able to appreciate the magnitude of meeting him before.

"Hi," I whispered.

He made a sound, seeming to respond to my voice. He looked at me for a brief moment before his eyes began wandering around the room.

"Look at you. You're perfect." I brushed my thumb along his tiny fingers, marveling at his long fingernails. "I have to apologize for a couple of reasons," I told him. "One, because *I'm* the dad you're stuck with. And also because I don't know what I'm doing. I'll be bothering your uncle Leo and aunt Felicity a lot for help and advice. We're going to have to figure this out together, you and me. But I promise to try my best."

My heart filled with a kind of love I'd never experienced before. It made me feel as though every second of my life until now had been meant to get me to this moment. "I also have to apologize because your mum, Britney, isn't here. It wasn't my idea to bring you into this world without her. But I'm damn glad I didn't stop you from being here. Now that you're with us, I can't imagine anything else. Because look at you. You were meant to be, weren't you? They were *all* right—everyone who ever told me I wouldn't be able to let you go once I saw you. I can't imagine handing you off to anyone, not even your grandparents." I brought his little face to mine and kissed his tiny nose. "So...unfortunately for you, you're stuck with me." I smiled. "I'm Sigmund, by the way. But you can call me Dad. Or That Prick. Call me whatever you want. It won't change the fact that I'm your father."

He whimpered.

"There's a beautiful woman who gave birth to you. She wants to meet you. Should we go to her? I think we should. Perhaps that's why you're looking around so much. You're wondering where she is, that warm body you've been camped out in all this time, eh? Wait until you see her. She's a bombshell."

I kissed his forehead. "God, I love you, little mate."

Then I heard a voice behind me.

"Is he taking visitors?"

I turned to find Phil and Kate standing there.

"Hey." I beamed with pride.

"Oh my God." Kate covered her mouth as she leaned in to look at her grandson for the first time. "He looks like you." She laughed.

"Poor little bastard, right? But at least he has Britney's eyes."

"You're right. He does," she said, her voice going wobbly with tears.

Phil looked down at the bracelet around my son's wrist. "Knickerbocker, huh?"

"We didn't have time to explain anything, so they gave him Abby's last name based on her ID when we checked in. Everything happened so fast. I didn't have the energy to go into it and didn't want to cause confusion." I offered the baby to Kate. "Would you like to hold him?"

Her eyes widened. "Is the sky blue?"

I chuckled and carefully placed him in her arms.

Phil leaned over her shoulder. "Hey, little buddy. It's your grandpa."

"Your grandad is a ballbuster. I hope you're ready." I rubbed the back of my hand against my son's cheek. "Did you see Abby yet?"

"We went straight to her room when we arrived. She looks good, considering the hell she's been through."

"We could've lost her. And him. We got incredibly lucky." My eyes began to sting again. "I couldn't have survived losing another woman I love."

"Wow." Kate smiled up at me. "You love her. That makes me so happy."

"There's still *a lot* to figure out, Kate. But I'm certain now that I want to raise my son. I hope that's okay."

"We knew that, Sig." Phil laughed.

"You did?"

They looked at each other and smiled.

"Yes, of course we did," Phil said. "We would've been thrilled either way, but in our hearts, we knew. We're planning to be here most of the year to help you. We'll all get to enjoy him and experience this together."

My heart swelled, and I couldn't wait any longer. "I need to take him to Abby. She hasn't met him yet."

"Go." Kate handed me back my son. "Have your private introduction with Abby. We'll be here, if you need us. We're booking a room at the hotel down the road for the next couple of days. We'll go grab coffee and meet up with you in a bit."

I called over to the nurse. "I'm taking him to see Abby. Is that alright?"

"As long as you have that bracelet on, you're good to go anywhere on the premises with him." She stopped me before I left. "He's going to need to eat. Do you know if Abby plans to breastfeed?"

"I don't think so, no."

She held out a bottle of what I assumed was formula. "Give this to him sometime in the next ten minutes or so. Let us know if there's a problem with feeding."

I took it. "Thank you."

As I headed down the hallway in search of room 210, I felt like I was in the middle of a dream, one that had started as a nightmare before turning into something amazing.

"Ready to meet her, little guy?"

CHAPTER 50

Sig

Track 50: "A New Day Has Come" by Celine Dion

The door to Abby's room was slightly open.

"Knock, knock," I said softly before entering.

Abby struggled to sit up. "You took long enough..." Her hands trembled as she held them out to receive the baby. "I can't believe how nervous I am."

I placed him carefully in her arms.

She looked down at him, speaking softly. "Well, hello there, handsome. Do you remember me?"

My son's eyes opened and seemed to focus in a way I hadn't seen yet. *Wow.*

"You're so beautiful," she whispered. "I wish I could take credit for it. But I'm just the incubator." She smiled. "I hope you enjoyed your stay, little man. I did my best, even if everything went haywire at the end." Her voice quivered. "I don't know what I would've done if anything happened to you."

He continued to look nowhere but at her. I was certain he recognized her. She pressed her face against his and closed her eyes. A tear fell down her cheek. This woman had nearly given her life for him. I hadn't fully grasped that.

"I love him so much," she confessed. "Am I allowed to?"

My heart filled with love for her. "Out of everyone allowed to love him, you're at the top of that list." I ran my hand along her hair. "He's only here because of you. You're my hero, Abby."

She rocked him gently. "We've all been through a lot together in a short amount of time, haven't we?"

"Look at the way he's looking at you. He knows it's you." I stuck my pointer finger out, and he curled his little fingers around it. "I'm keeping him, by the way," I announced.

"I know."

"You do?"

"Yes, Sigmund. I never doubted that."

"Everyone seemed to know that but me."

She looked over at the bottle I was holding. "Are we supposed to give that to him?"

"The nurse told me he needs to eat."

She reached for it. "Let me try."

Abby placed the nipple of the bottle near his mouth, rubbing it gently over his lips, but he kept moving his head from side to side, refusing to take it. Then he started crying. It was the first time I'd heard my son cry. Even when they'd brought him out to me the first time, he hadn't been crying. I must've missed that part since I couldn't be in there when he came out.

Abby handed me back the formula, but even with the evil bottle out of sight, he kept crying. After a few minutes, he started rubbing his face along Abby's breast.

"Is he searching for it?" I asked.

"I think so." She turned her attention from him to me. "Should I try to feed him?"

"Would you do that?"

She nodded. "I want to."

"That would be brilliant."

Abby opened her hospital gown and took out her beautiful breast, which looked ready to burst. She placed her nipple against his mouth, and to my amazement, he took it, latching on and beginning to suck.

"Oh my God." Abby's jaw dropped. "He's doing it. It's working."

Aside from seeing him for the first time, this selfless act was the greatest miracle I'd ever witnessed.

Abby and I both fixated on this suckling little guy. Love for him and for the two women who'd made him possible rushed through me. It was a powerful trifecta of love multiplied, and I felt so undeserving.

Eventually, the baby fell asleep with her breast still in his mouth.

"Well, that went well." She turned to me. "What do we do now?"

"He likes the juice." I shrugged. "I can't give it to him. I guess this means you'll have to stay in England." I tucked her hair behind her ear. "But not just because of that. Because I'm desperately in love with you, Abby. Before tonight, I was trying to figure out a way to convey how badly I needed you to stay without my seeming selfish. I don't care if I look greedy anymore. I need you, not for him—for me. I can't imagine my life without you. I love you so much. I've never been more scared than when I thought I might lose you."

"I love you, too." She brought her hand to my cheek. "And I love him. I wasn't sure how I was going to feel after I gave birth. But I feel like he's my son, Sig. I don't even want to give him back to the nurse, let alone get on a plane and leave him behind altogether. I think if you didn't want to be with me, I might've had to steal him." She laughed.

"And if you didn't want to be with me, I might've had to take him to the States in a carrier on my chest, while I did everything to win you back." I kissed her cheek. "I want to do this with you, Abby. We'll take it one day at a time. Figure it out together. I've already had a talk with our son. He knows to expect me to fuck up. Hopefully he'll cut you the same slack."

She chuckled. "He's gonna need a name, you know."

Ah! That would be nice, wouldn't it? "I have no idea what to name him," I admitted.

"I do." Abby smiled.

"You do?"

She nodded. "I think we should name him Alexander—Britney's last name and a strong first name for a boy."

"We can call him Alex." I looked down at my son, who was starting to wake from his milk coma. "Yeah. It's perfect."

"Perfect like he is." Abby smiled down at him. "Hey, Alex. You like your name?"

He opened his eyes, and I whispered in my son's ear, "I told you she was a bombshell."

"You guys were talking about me?" Abby grinned. "You never told any of the hospital staff that I'm a surrogate, did you? They've all assumed I'm his mom. And I haven't told them otherwise."

"No. There was no opportunity. It's none of their business anyway, right?"

A nurse came in. "I was just coming to check on things. Did he take the formula?"

"It won't be necessary, at least for now," Abby said. "I breastfed him. He latched on pretty easily, and now he seems full."

"Ah. That's great. Your husband didn't think you'd be doing that. I'm glad you had luck with it. So many new mums have difficulty. We have a lactation consultant on staff who can make herself available, if you need her."

"Thank you," she said. "Hopefully we won't."

"Abby's a natural," I said.

"I didn't do anything but take my breast out." She shrugged.

"Always works for me, too." I winked.

The nurse cleared her throat. "I'm gonna leave the paperwork here for his name and birth certificate. Someone will be by to check your vitals soon."

After the nurse left, I picked up the paperwork and pen. "Shall I?"

Abby nodded. "Go ahead, *husband*."

I began entering the information. At the spot for the middle name, I wrote *Knickerbocker*.

Alexander Knickerbocker Benedictus

Abby's eyes widened. "You're giving him my last name as his middle name?"

"Bringing this little man to life was a three-person effort. His name needs to reflect that, our three last names. His two mums and his dad. He wouldn't be here without all of us."

Her eyes watered. "Thank you."

"Thank *you*, my love. For everything. For making the dream I didn't even realize I had come true."

She wiped her eyes and pointed to the corner of the room. "Can you bring me my hospital bag?"

"Yeah." I stood. "Of course."

I opened the bag and faced it toward her as she reached in to pull out a soft toy. "I had this made for him," she said, handing it to me. It was a little giraffe with a floral print.

"When did you have the time to do this?"

"I ordered it back in the States."

"Giraffe..." I said.

"I remember you saying Britney used to call you that. The material for the outside is from her pajamas. I found this woman on the Internet who makes stuffed animals from clothing of loved ones who've passed away. I asked Kate for something of Britney's so I could make something for him. I know it's kind of a girly pattern, but I didn't know we were having a boy at the time, and her mom said those were her favorite PJs."

Swallowing the lump in my throat, I looked down at the giraffe. "This means so much."

Abby set the toy next to Alex. He turned his face toward it and took the giraffe's nose into his mouth.

CHAPTER 51

Abby

Track 51: "Endless Love" by Diana Ross and Lionel Richie

It felt so good to be dressed in normal clothes, even if I wasn't allowed to leave the hospital yet.

Sig's parents had just gone after they'd come by to meet Alex. It had been a surprisingly pleasant visit. Rosemary seemed to have softened. I suppose meeting your grandchild for the first time would do that to you.

Sig returned from seeing them out and sat down in the chair across from me by the window. So much more rested after a couple of days in the hospital, I finally felt ready to address something with him. "I have a confession..." I began as baby Alex lay napping in my arms. "There's something I never told you. It was the reason my mood was a bit off starting around Christmas."

He blinked, looking concerned. "Alright..."

"You know how Kate and Phil gave me Britney's old laptop?"

"Yeah?"

"Well, when I logged into my email for the first time, *her* account popped up."

"Oh." He closed his eyes briefly, as if he knew exactly where this was going.

"Yeah," I continued. "She was still logged in. I saw dozens of emails from you. It wasn't any of my business, but I clicked on one only."

He swallowed. "What did it say?"

"You told her you would never love anyone the way you loved her. That stuck with me. I had myself convinced that no matter how much I loved you, I would only ever be a consolation prize."

He opened his mouth, but I stuck my finger out. "Let me finish."

Sig nodded somberly.

"I don't feel that way anymore. It wasn't fair for me to use your private words to her as a gauge for how you might feel without even talking to you about it. I was very hormonal and scared for the future at that time, certain I was destined to lose you. I love you so much and was afraid you could never love me back the same way."

"Why didn't you tell me what was going on?"

"Honestly? I didn't want to admit that I'd read one of your private emails." I shrugged. "And I suppose I also didn't want to hear that there might have been truth to my fears. That scared me more than anything."

Sig stood and came to the bed, placing his hand on my cheek. "It is true that I won't ever love anyone the way I loved her. But it's *also* true that I won't love anyone the way I love you. It's not an either-or situation. My love for each of you is parallel, mutually exclusive and different in ways that could never be compared." He exhaled. "Writing to Britney has been my way of keeping her alive, in a sense. It's helped me to gather my thoughts and release my emotions when I didn't feel comfortable talking to anyone else. I obviously never thought anyone would know about those emails."

"I think it's beautiful." I took his hand. "And you don't have to explain it to me."

"It's important that I show you some of the recent ones."

"You don't need to do that, Sig. It's none of my business."

"I *am* your business now." He looked into my eyes. "We are each other's business. You nearly gave your life to deliver Alex. There's nothing you haven't the right to know or see, Abby. Truly."

He took out his phone and scrolled through before handing it to me.

"Read as many of them as you'd like. I have nothing to hide from you. I actually wrote to her last night while you were sleeping. Start with that one and take your time." He stood. "I'll go get coffee, give you some space."

He left the room before I could protest. I looked down and hesitantly clicked on his most recent email to her.

Dear Britney,

Where do I begin?

Congratulations, Mum. Our son is here. His name is Alexander, after your last name. We plan to call him Alex. But you likely know all this. I've never felt your presence more strongly than in the past forty-eight hours.

He has your eyes. It's like looking into your soul again and getting to see you looking back at me. It's the most amazing feeling. The light at the end of the tunnel after the second-hardest but most beautiful day of my life—the day he was born.

We could've lost him. We could've lost Abby. I'd never been so scared, but perhaps I made it through because I knew in my heart that your spirit was with me the entire time. I prayed, but I lost a lot of trust in God when He didn't save you. So I wondered whether He was listening. It seemed He was. Or was it you? Did you pull some strings up there when you weren't cavorting with your childhood crush Heath Ledger?

As I watch our son sleeping right now, I wonder how it was ever possible that I tried to stop this from happening. I was only ever scared to bring him into this world without you here. But you are here, aren't you? You're in him. Alive in him. None of this would've been possible were it not for you. I'll never know why you were meant to be an angel, and I was meant to soldier on here. But I'm so grateful to continue to be blessed by your spirit.

I wouldn't put it past you to have sent me Abby, either. Only you could have known who would be perfect for me. Only you could have known the person I needed to bring me back to life.

After all, were it not for you, I never would've known what love was, wouldn't have recognized that it's love I've been feeling for Abby for quite some time.

How lucky am I to have been blessed with two loves in my lifetime? What did I do to deserve that?

I promise you our son will always know who his mother was, how much his father loved you. How you loved Alex even before he was here when you told your mother you wished to live on through your yet-to-be-born child. As I look at Alex sleeping now, I'm overwhelmed with love for you. And I'm overwhelmed with love for the woman sleeping right next to him, the woman who brought him—a piece of you—into this world. A piece of you back to me.

Britney, my love, when you knew you were close to leaving this world, you made me promise that I would be open to love again someday. I looked you in the eyes and told you that would never happen, that it was impossible. At the time, that's what I believed. I now realize I didn't have a choice in the matter. As much as I didn't want to fall in love with anyone else, I have. Very deeply and unconditionally. Please know that in no way diminishes what you and I shared, the love I have for you. You made me the man I am today. You made me capable of loving.

I will spend the rest of my life making you proud as I raise our son to be the best man he can be. Don't worry, I'll teach him to do the opposite of everything I did when I was younger.

I promise to write soon and keep you updated every step of the way.

Goodbye for now, my angel.

Your love,
Sigmund

CHAPTER 52

Abby

Track 52: "I Do" by Colbie Caillat

Sig took a while to come back. He must've thought I was sifting through all of those emails, but I'd only read the one. It didn't matter what the others said because I'd seen everything I would ever need to see. That most recent message said it all.

With Alex still sleeping in my arms, I closed my eyes and let the emotions evoked by his honest words flow through me.

When Sig finally returned, his voice broke me out of my meditative state. "I brought you some crackers from the vending machine, if you want them."

"Thanks."

He stood by my bed, coffee cup in hand, seemingly waiting for me to say something.

"I'm touched that you wrote to her about me," I said, placing a waking Alex on my breast. "But you didn't need to show me the emails to prove you love me."

"Based on what you told me before I left, it seemed I did."

"While it's true that I was feeling insecure after I came back from the States, a lot has changed in these last few weeks—the way you've cared for me, the panic in your eyes when you thought you could lose me, the way you begged the doctors to do whatever it took to save me." I smiled. "I heard what you told them before they put me under. I remember all of it now, Sig. And I remember thinking that if something *did* happen to me, I would leave this Earth knowing that not only had I made an impact, if they could just save Alex, but also knowing I *was* loved by you. True love for one person doesn't need to be compared to love for another. Because there's no finite amount that you can love someone. It's infinite."

"Oh, my sweet Abby." He wrapped his arms around me. "I do love you infinitely."

"Also...random..." I said after he let go. "I promised myself that if I did make it through, I would write a book about this. It's interesting the things you think of when you could be dying."

"It would make *quite* the story."

"It's a love story in the end."

"It is, isn't it?" His eyes sparkled.

There was a knock on the door.

"Come in," he hollered.

In walked Phil, Kate—and Lavinia.

"Special delivery," Phil said. "Look who we brought."

Lavinia looked so cute in her black coat and pink hat.

"Thank you for driving her," I said.

Lavinia clapped her hands. "You know I've been champing at the bit to meet little Alex."

I handed the baby to Sig, who walked him over to Lavinia. "Here he is." He placed Alex in her arms. "What do you think?"

"He's even more handsome than his father." Lavinia looked down at Alex lovingly. "Oh, how I've longed to meet you, little one." A tear rolled down her cheek.

"Don't cry, old woman. You need to save your energy to help me take care of him," Sig cracked.

"Well, if I drop here in this hospital, at least I'm in the right place and can say I lived to see the day you had a son. It wasn't looking good for a long while, Sigmund. But I am so very happy for you..." She looked around the room. "For all of you. I love you as if you were my son. And that makes him my honorary grandson."

I glanced over at Sig. "Lavinia, actually, I was thinking...since my mom isn't here anymore, Alex is going to need an *actual* grandmother representing my side of the family. I was wondering if you wouldn't mind if he called you Nan."

Lavinia's eyes turned glassy as she fended off more tears. "I never thought I'd have a grandchild. That means so much to me."

Sig rubbed her back. "We love you, crazy lady."

Phil and Kate smiled from ear to ear, and a few seconds later, Leo and Felicity appeared at the door.

Felicity held a giant bouquet of flowers. "Hope now is a good time?"

"Hey!" I waved them over. "Come on in!"

They went right to Lavinia, who was still holding Alex.

"I can't believe I'm looking at your son, Sigmund," Leo cracked. "Hell has frozen over, in the best way."

While the entire room congregated around our son, my cell phone rang. It was a FaceTime call from my father. I answered, and his face popped up on the screen.

"Hey, Dad. You're on speaker with a room full of people, so don't say anything incriminating."

"Ah, you know me too well. Is that prick with you?"

"He is."

Sig walked over so my father could see him.

"Hey, Sig." My father waved.

Sig's eyes widened. "I believe that's the first time you've said my actual name."

"Well, we're family now, sort of. So...figured I'd let the nickname go."

"No need. I quite like it. It's fitting in any case."

"How are you feeling, Abby?" my dad asked.

"Still a bit hard to walk around, but better every day."

"I'm so sorry I wasn't there, sweetheart."

"It's okay, Dad. No one could've predicted that Alex would come early. That's his name, by the way. I don't think I told you. We'll see you soon enough when you come in a few weeks."

I'd chosen not to let my father know how close I came to losing my life. He knew I'd had to have an emergency c-section, but I didn't want him to worry, since he was still vulnerable health-wise. Someday I'd tell him about the placental abruption and blood transfusion, but not anytime soon.

"Alex is a wonderful name. How's he doing?" he asked.

"He's doing great, Dad. But I need to let you know something."

"Okay..."

My father and I had spoken right after I gave birth, but I hadn't told him all the latest developments.

"I've decided to stay here in the UK. I'm in love with Alex. And I'm in love with Sig. They're my family, and they need me here."

My father didn't immediately say anything, so I feared he might be upset.

"Does that mean you don't get the money?" After a few seconds' pause, he burst out into laughter. "I'm kidding. I'm kidding."

"Don't worry. I'll compensate her *very* well—with Devil Dogs and kisses."

Dad beamed. "That's great news, honey. I'm happy for you."

"Well, I'm relieved you feel that way. I figured maybe you'd be a little sad, even if you're happy for me."

"Abby, I saw this coming a mile away."

"It means I can't be there for you the way I want to be. And it also means my dream of reopening the store will have to die."

He shook his head. "You owe me nothing. Your mother would be so happy for you right now. The last thing she'd be thinking about is the store. I'll start calling some of the other vendors in the area to see what stock we can unload on them. Don't you worry about anything except that little baby."

"I hope we can get you to move here once you retire. Alex needs his Grampy."

Phil leaned over me to speak into the phone. "You can be Grampy. I'll be Grumpy."

"Never thought I'd share a grandchild with my best friend." My father's eyes looked glassy.

Phil grinned. "Crazy how life comes full circle, huh?"

"I'm honored to be his Grampy," my father said. "And I certainly will have to get my ass over there because I don't want to miss all the important milestones."

"There's one milestone you're *not* going to miss, Roland," Sig interrupted. "Because it's about to happen right now."

"What's that?" Dad asked.

I looked over at Sig, confused.

"While I have you on the phone, I need to ask something," Sig said.

"Okay?"

He sucked in a breath. "Can I have your permission for your daughter's hand in marriage?"

My heart lurched. *What?*

Dad's eyes went wide. "Are you serious?"

"I am." Sig let out a shaky breath. *He's nervous.* "I know this is normally done in private," he told my dad. "But I can't wait. I'd planned to call you tonight. But since you're on the phone now and since most of the people who are important to me are here, I figured, why not? Anyway, I can't do it without your blessing."

Dad chuckled. "I don't think your biggest obstacle is me, buddy. Of course you have my blessing, if this is what Abby wants. But I think you need to ask her and find out."

"If you say so, sir..." Sig reached into his pocket and took out a small, black velvet pouch.

Oh my God. Is this really happening now?

Sig turned to me. "Abby, I know you weren't expecting this today. And honestly, I was going to wait for us to be home and settled. But with your dad on the phone, there's no time like the present." He knelt by my bed. "As I was walking my parents out earlier, I told my mother there would be no more secrets between us. I let her know I planned to ask you to marry me. She said she knew you were the one for me when you stood up for us that day she came to lunch and found out about the pregnancy. Without even knowing my plans, my mother brought something to give me today." He loosened the strings to the pouch. "She likely didn't expect me to propose today, either. But this ring has been burning a hole in my pocket. It belongs on your finger, and I don't want to wait to give it to you." He took out the sparkler. "This is a family heirloom. My nan's wedding ring. Our grandmother was very special to me and Leo. Nan was one of my biggest supporters. She was devastated after Britney died and naturally very worried about me. She apparently gave this ring to my mother before she passed away. She specifically instructed Mum to give it to *me*, should I fall in love again. She told my mother she believed it would take a very special person to make that happen. She wanted her wedding ring to go to that woman." He turned to Leo. "And clearly this proves once and for all that I was Nan's favorite."

Leo chuckled and stuck up his middle finger.

Sig returned his attention to me. "She would've loved you." He held the ring out. "*I* love you, Abby, with all of my heart and soul. You saved my life and made me happier than I could've imagined. Alex and I are so lucky to have you. He needs you as his mother. And I need you as my wife. Will you marry me?"

Looking around at all the smiling faces in the room, I soaked in this moment. Then I turned to Sig, never more certain of anything in my life. "I love you so much. I can't think of a better way to spend my life than with you two. Of course I will."

My hand quivered as he placed the ring on my finger. It was the most beautiful ring I'd ever seen—a yellow gold band with an antique filigree design and a large, oval-shaped diamond that seemed flawless. I wrapped my arms around my beautiful man and felt the rest of the room fade away. For a moment, it was just him and me.

"Welcome to the family, Abby," Leo said.

"I couldn't be happier for you guys!" Felicity added as she came over to hug me. "And I'm so happy *I* get to keep you, too."

The diamond sparkled in the overhead lights. "I keep thinking I'm gonna wake up from this dream," I told them.

"I couldn't help but overhear," said a nurse I hadn't seen enter the room. "Congratulations. I assumed you two were already married."

"There's a lot you've assumed, actually, but we're fine with it." Sigmund winked at me.

CHAPTER 53

Abby
Seven Months Later

Track 53: "Somewhere Over the Rainbow" by Israel Kamakawiwo'ole

"Go write," Sig said shortly after he walked in the door from work.

Alex squealed in laughter as his dad lifted him into the air and swiftly brought him back down. Our son was seven months old now. With his dark hair growing out, he looked more like Sig every day, despite having Britney's eyes.

"Are you sure?" I asked. "I could make you a cocktail to relax first."

"No need. You've been home all day with him. Go now while he's content and happy to see me."

If there was one thing I'd learned since becoming a mother: when an opportunity arose for a break, I needed to take it.

I escaped into Alex's nursery and sat in the comfy blue rocking chair in the corner. This had become one of my favorite writing spots. Ever since Alex was about a month old, I'd been writing a book about my surrogacy journey. Without a whole lot of time to write, I had to sneak in words whenever I could.

When Sig and I brought Alex home from the hospital, we decided to settle in his London apartment rather than making the inn our permanent home. The guest room here became Alex's room. While we'd need a bigger place long term, being in the city for now had its advantages. I loved living near some of my favorite stores and restaurants. I'd enjoy being here as long as I could until we eventually moved to a more family-friendly place, probably somewhere in the countryside. We just needed to find the right property.

About a half hour into my writing time, the door to the nursery slowly opened.

Sig entered alone. I moved my laptop to the ground as he knelt by my feet. He placed his head in my lap and kissed his way from my torso to my breasts to my lips.

"I thought I was supposed to be writing," I murmured as he nuzzled my neck.

"I realized I never got my kiss after I came home, so I put Alex in the mechanical swing and came to collect."

"He does love that swing. It's the only way I can make lunch or go to the bathroom during the day." I stood. "Sit." When he did, I positioned myself to straddle him on the rocker.

He put his hands on my shoulders, pushing me down against him. "I missed you today."

Grinding over him, I moaned. "Yeah, I can tell."

"If I wasn't certain Alex will tire of the swing soon, I'd take you right here on this chair," he rasped. "Anyway, these rocking chairs aren't meant for the kind of fucking I want to do."

"I'm gonna get it tonight, aren't I?"

"If you want it, yeah."

"I love how you don't hold back now that I'm not pregnant anymore."

"Not pregnant...*yet*," he teased.

"Oh, you're bad."

"You have no idea how badly I want to be with you right now."

"Well, this surprise visit to my writing cave is definitely a highlight of my day."

"The best part of my day is always coming home to you." He looked up at me. "I do worry about you being alone all day. I don't want you to get depressed."

"Are you kidding? Alone? Every other day Phil and Kate pop in, and half the time you come home on your lunch break for a quickie while Alex is napping. It's really not all that much alone time. And even then, am I *really* alone with Alex?"

"As long as you're happy. But if you're not, you'll tell me, right?"

"You still think I'm gonna leave and go back to the States or something?"

"If you left and went back to the States at this point, I'd be right behind you."

I laughed. "That's true. I have a brigade now, don't I?"

"The Benedictus Brigade."

"I can't wait to be a Benedictus."

We planned to get married sometime in the next year, a traditional wedding with a slew of guests and all the fanfare. I'd already picked out my dress. We just needed to set the date and get our shit together. We'd been too busy adjusting to our new life.

"Speaking of you becoming a Benedictus," he said. "There's a possible wedding venue in Westfordshire I'd like to show you. Maybe in the next couple of weeks."

"Oh, that sounds like fun. Can we scoop up Lavinia? I miss her."

Since we stayed in London during the week and all of Alex's things were here, we only got out to the inn about every other weekend. My old bedroom there had been converted into a weekend nursery for Alex.

"Of course we can," he said. "We'll take her to the pub for lunch, too."

As much as I loved London, anytime we went back to Westfordshire, I felt nostalgic. It felt like my English home.

A couple of weeks later, we finally took that drive out to the countryside. After scooping up Lavinia, we stopped at a property in Westfordshire that looked almost like Leo and Felicity's. It had acres and acres of farmland surrounding a large brick house.

"This is right down the road from Leo's, isn't it?" I asked.

"Yes, about a half mile," Sig said.

"This is the most similar property I've seen to Brighton House. They're renting it out for weddings?"

"Not exactly."

"They're making an exception for us?"

"Actually, it's not really a venue. It's a residence."

"Whose house is it?"

Sig flashed a crooked smile. "Ours."

"What are you talking about?"

"I bought it."

"How could we afford this? I mean, I know you do well, but this is..." The words escaped me.

"We can more than afford it." He looked over at Lavinia. "But I was also thinking of selling the inn."

Lavinia's ears perked up. "Selling the inn?"

"Don't worry, old woman. I won't do anything you don't want. But I was thinking you might prefer to live here with us, in the guest house. It's next to the main house. You'll have your own space, but it's close enough to walk over if you need something. You don't need the responsibility of the inn anymore. And I know Abby would love your company without having to trek everything to the inn every other weekend."

Sig and I had talked about eventually having Lavinia move in with us.

She looked between Sig and me. "You want me to live with you?"

"Only if it's what *you* want," he said.

"Of course I would want to live on this beautiful farm. But why are you so good to me?"

Sig placed his hand on her back. "I'm not doing you any favors, Lavinia. I *want* you here. But if you must know... You were there for me in a way no one else was at the time in my life when I needed someone most." He winked. "Besides, like I always say, you're a good drinking chum."

"Well then, I'd love to."

"I thought you might." Sig turned to me. "There's plenty of room for your dad, too, should he ever decide to move here. There are six bedrooms in the main house, more than we would know what to do with."

My father wasn't quite ready to retire yet, but I was hopeful he'd decide to relocate here when he finally did. I shook my head. "I never imagined getting to live in a place like this." I adjusted my son's sunhat over his face. "And Alex will get to grow up close to his cousins Eli and Eloise." My excitement grew with each second. "Can we get animals?"

"Of course! What's a property like this without animals?" Sig scratched his chin. "But you're assuming there aren't any here already."

I looked around. "Are there?"

"There's one, actually."

"There is?"

He lifted his chin. "Follow me."

Sig led us to a small fenced-in area out back that featured an open, three-sided shelter. There was a lone, large...bird standing in it. It had beautiful dusky, grayish-brown feathers that were black at the ends.

I covered my mouth. "Is that an ostrich?"

"An emu, to be precise. A while ago, you said if a man were to gift you with an outrageous animal like Leo did Felicity, you'd choose an ostrich. Unfortunately, come to find out, ostriches are quite violent animals. They attack with their beaks. I didn't want you to get your finger bitten off in the name of love. The emu is a much nicer alternative." Sig brushed his hand along the bird's feathers and said, "Meet Loco."

"That's his name?"

"Yeah. His previous owner named him."

"Where the hell did you get him?"

"That's a story for another day. Let's just say, I owe someone a huge favor in Australia. Loco's been here for a week now."

"Who's been looking after him?"

"I've been borrowing Nathan from Leo and Felicity to come over and feed him."

My mouth fell open. "Out of all of the crazy things we've experienced together, this emu takes the cake. I absolutely love him, though." I reached over to pet him. Alex's eyes practically bugged out of his head. "You love him, too, don't you?" Alex kicked his legs as if he wanted to fly out of my arms to touch the animal. "Look at that smile."

We spent the next hour touring the inside of the house and walking around the property. Then Lavinia stayed inside to rest while the three of us went back out to the yard.

Just as we stepped outside, a massive rainbow appeared in the sky. It was the first rainbow I'd seen in England and probably the most vibrant rainbow I'd witnessed in my life.

"Rainbow, Alex!" I pointed toward the sky. "Look at the rainbow!"

He stared up at the sky, mesmerized. "Mama," he babbled.

It was the first time he'd ever said it, though I'd been practicing it with him, trying to get him to utter that sound.

Sig and I looked at each other in amazement. There were no words. Regardless of whether it was true, we knew what the other was thinking. *Britney.*

"Yeah." I bounced him. "That's Mama coming to say hi, isn't it?"

EPILOGUE

Sig
Four Years Later

Final Track: "And I Love Her" by The Beatles

Holding my daughter's hand and carrying my infant son, I stood at the entrance to a quaint bookshop in Notting Hill.

Abby had contacted a number of bookshops around London, trying to get one to stock the book she'd self-published. This one was the only shop that bit, and the owner, Shepley Van Zant, had been nice enough to offer Abby a Saturday-afternoon slot to sign her books. He'd even created a poster advertising the event.

I snuck up behind Abby and Alex at the table where she'd set up a stack of books to sign. There was no line.

"Mummy, are we just going to sit here all day?" Alex asked.

"Well, I hope at least a few people show up. But I don't mind hanging out with you, even if nobody comes."

I cleared my throat to announce our presence.

Abby turned to find the three of us behind her table. "See? There they are now! My fans!"

"Those aren't fans," Alex corrected. "That's Daddy, Miriam, and Henry."

"Are you kidding? We're her *original* fans," I said, handing Henry over to his mum. "Look, he's so excited he's drooling over her."

Five years ago, I could never have imagined being a father of three. Alex wasn't even a year old when Abby became pregnant with our daughter, Miriam, who was now almost three. I guess breastfeeding isn't as foolproof a form of birth control as we'd assumed. Miriam, named after Abby's mother, was the spitting image of Abby. Thank God, because both boys—with the exception of Alex's eyes—looked just like their dad. Our son Henry had been born six months ago. Our hands were very full.

"Where's Lavinia? I thought you were bringing her," Abby asked.

"She wasn't feeling up to coming."

Our kids' honorary nan was getting older but still kicking. I'd planned to bring her here in a wheelchair, but she'd caught a cold and didn't want to get anyone sick. Lavinia still lived in our guest house, although we'd had to bring in help for her lately. But she always perked up when the kids were around.

Leo and Felicity entered the book shop and approached with their kids, Eloise and Eli.

"Hey!" Abby waved them over. "See? I have even more fans."

Alex hopped out of his chair. "Mummy, can I go to the kids' section with Eli?"

"What happened to being my assistant?" Abby teased.

"It's boring."

She laughed. "Sure, go on."

"Can I be your assistant now, Mummy?" Miriam took the seat next to her mother.

"Of course you can."

Felicity looked over at our boys playing in the kids' section. "Those two are like peas in a pod."

Leo turned to me. "I just hope they don't get into as much trouble as we did, right, cousin?"

"I pray every day that Alex is nothing like me." I chuckled.

"Have you signed any books, Abby?" Felicity asked.

"It's been slow." Abby shrugged. "And by slow, I mean...no one's come by. But it's still nice to have been invited to sign here. My goal is for one person other than friends and family to show up. If I can impact even one person, I'll know writing the book was worth it."

"I could never have done it," Felicity said. "People live their whole lives talking about writing a book and never follow through. You should be proud of yourself."

"I couldn't be prouder of her." I rubbed my wife's back.

With Henry on one arm, Abby rearranged the small stack of books in front of her. "Well, you guys are biased, but I'll take your praise."

Henry began tugging on Abby's shirt. "Shit. He's hungry, huh?" She stood. "You think my line of fans would mind if I went in the back and fed him? Gonna find a private place to take him."

After she left, I planted myself next to Miriam. "You be my helper if anyone comes to buy Mummy's book, okay? You can take the money, and I'll do the talking."

"Okay, Daddy." She smiled up at me, nearly melting my heart. Nothing like seeing your wife's face transformed into the likeness of a cherub.

Felicity and Leo took off to browse while our sons played quietly in the corner.

Then a woman approached the table. She was already holding a copy of Abby's book. *Well, doesn't this just figure?*

"Hello. I was looking to meet Abby Benedictus." She grinned. "I take it you're not her?"

"I'm not. I'm her husband, Sigmund."

The woman blushed. "Oh goodness. It's so great to meet you. I'm sorry. I'm just a bit flustered."

Her nerves caught me off guard. I introduced my daughter. "This is Miriam."

"I know. Well, I figured from the book." The woman smiled shyly. "Hello, Miriam."

"Hello," my daughter answered.

"My wife is in the back feeding our son. She should be out soon."

"I'll wait. I want to tell her how much this book meant to me."

The woman waited patiently for about five minutes. I finally looked over to find Abby walking toward the table with Henry. "Here she is now."

"Oh, hello." Abby handed Henry to me and straightened the wrinkles in her skirt. She seemed nervous to meet this lady, which was quite adorable.

"You almost missed your first reader," I said.

"You might be my first and last reader today, but you've made my day. Thank you for coming. It's great to meet you," Abby said. "And you are?"

"Connie." The woman clutched a somewhat worn copy of the book to her chest. "You have no idea how wonderful it is to meet *you*. The pleasure is all mine. I'm the one who should be thanking you. You see, my husband and I were unable to have children due to my cancer treatments. We used a surrogate with a donor egg from my sister. I know it's a bit of a different scenario than yours, but in the beginning, I struggled with the fact that my son wasn't actually mine and whether that would somehow affect our bond. I found your book—or rather, I should say, it found me. I happened to see it sitting in one of those Little Free Library boxes in my neighborhood. I'm so happy I found it—because I'm certain it was meant for me. And I want to support you, so I'd like to purchase another copy here...to have you sign, of course."

A look of pride crossed my wife's face. "I appreciate that so much."

Abby didn't know it, but *I* was the one who'd placed her book in that Little Free Library. In fact, I'd ordered dozens of copies online without Abby knowing and had driven them to every Free Library box I could find around London, in all different neighborhoods. There was a website that listed some of the locations for those boxes, and I'd used that as my road map.

After the woman purchased a book and left, Abby turned to me. "At least I can say I have a biggest fan."

"She's not your biggest fan." I nudged her. "I am."

"You know, my favorite part of this book is the part I didn't write," she said.

"Ah, yes. Too bad it took me as long to put the foreword together as it took you to write the entire book."

"It was worth the wait." Abby kissed my cheek and held out her hand to Miriam. "Come on, sweetie. Let's go pick out a book for you since you've been such a good girl." She turned to me. "Just holler if anyone shows."

Henry was now asleep in my arms, sucking on his binky.

Left alone at the table, I picked up one of the books and admired it.

One Bump by Abby Benedictus

I opened it to the dedication.

> *For Britney,*
> *Rest easy. I've got them.*

Feeling warm inside, I turned a couple of pages to the foreword I'd written, which I hadn't read since I'd submitted it to Abby a year or so ago.

Dear Reader,

As I begin the process of writing this foreword, my wife is asleep in the chair across from me. She's holding a cup of tea and somehow managed to conk out mid-sip. I keep looking at her, waiting for the tea to slip out of her hand, the porcelain cup to shatter on the floor. I'm fully prepared to clean it up, if need be. But it seems somehow, even in her sleep, Abby has things under control.

It's no surprise that she wasn't able to stay awake long enough to enjoy it. From the mo-

ment our son was born, she's given every bit of herself to him. And when our daughter came sixteen months later, so began the juggling act. After long days with the children, she's devoted any free time she had to this book. At the time that I'm writing this, she's pregnant with our third child, a boy we'll name Henry. We've decided three children will be it for us. This will be her third c-section, and her body needs a break. As you'll find from reading this book, we almost lost her the first time. And that's made every pregnancy since riskier than the last. The thought of ever losing her terrifies me.

When I met Abby, I was a lifeless shell of a man—a widower who had himself convinced there was no chance for happiness after loss. I'm here to tell you that while life is never the same after you lose someone you love, there is hope. You'll never get the same life back, but if you're blessed with the right person, you can reinvent yourself. And I was so very lucky to have been granted a second chance at happiness.

But enough about me. Let's get back to the subject of this book and the beautiful soul who wrote it. This is the story of how she became my surrogate, how I nearly flubbed it all up, and how despite that, it turned into an unexpected love story—not just about Abby's and my love for each other, but the unconditional love she's given to our son, while also respecting the memory of his biological mother.

We decided Alex should know the truth as soon as he could understand. Abby bought him a book called My Mommy is An Angel *for his first Christmas. And these past few years, we've explained as best we could in simple terms how he came to be. He tells everyone he has two mums, one here on Earth and one in heaven. He looks for his angel mum in rainbows and sleeps with his favorite toy, a cuddly giraffe he knows is made from her pajamas. He's handled it all so well, and I'm very proud of him. So proud of Abby, too, that she's unselfishly made space for my son to appreciate and be proud of how he came to be.*

I hope you read this book with an open heart, offering me grace for having made several mistakes along the way.

Writing our story was not only cathartic for my wife but helped her discover a passion for writing I hope she'll continue. I'll be here cheering her on, every step of the way. Writing is her passion. I'd been searching for my passion until I met her. Now, she's my passion. Our family is my passion. Being a father is my passion.

Abby, my love, congratulations on the completion of this book. I'm so very grateful to be a part of this story—not only because you brought me our son, but because he brought me you.

Your love,
Sigmund

Did you miss Leo and Felicity's epic love story?
The Aristocrat (a standalone novel)
is available for sale now!

OTHER BOOKS BY PENELOPE WARD

ACKNOWLEDGEMENTS

I have to start by thanking my beloved readers all over the world who continue to support and promote my books. At the time of writing this, I've been publishing for more than a decade and am so very grateful to still be here. To all of the book bloggers and social media influencers who work tirelessly to support me book after book, please know how much I appreciate you.

To Vi – My right-hand woman. I don't remember a time without you. I'm so lucky to have you to vent to every day. You're the best friend and partner in crime I could ask for. Here's to the next ten years.

To Julie – Ten toes in the sand! Cheers to a decade of friendship and Fire Island.

To Luna –When you read my books for the first time, it's one of the most exciting things for me. Thank you for your love and support every day and for your cherished friendship.

To Erika – One of these days, we'll hit a Mrs. Roper Romp together. Thank you for your love, friendship, and summer visits. It will always be an E thing.

To Cheri – It's always a good year when I get to see you, my dear friend! Thanks for being part of my tribe and for always looking out and never forgetting a Wednesday.

To Darlene – What can I say? You spoil me. I am very lucky to have you as a friend. Thanks for making my life sweeter, both literally and figuratively.

To my Facebook reader group, Penelope's Peeps – I adore you all. You are my home and favorite place to be.

To my agent Kimberly Brower –Thank you for working hard to get my books into the hands of readers around the world.

To my editor Jessica Royer Ocken – It's always a pleasure working with you. I look forward to many more experiences to come.

To Elaine of Allusion Book Formatting and Publishing – Thank you for being the best proofreader, formatter, and friend a girl could ask for.

To Julia Griffis of The Romance Bibliophile – Your eagle eye is amazing. Thank you for being so wonderful to work with.

To my assistant Brooke – Thank you for hard work in handling all of the things Vi and I can't seem to ever get to. We appreciate you so much!

To Kylie and Jo at Give Me Books – You guys are truly the best out there! Thank you for your tireless promotional work. I would be lost without you.

To Letitia Hasser of RBA Designs – My awesome cover designer. Thank you for always working with me until the finished product exactly perfect.

To my husband – Thank you for always taking on so much more than you should have to so that I am able to write. I love you so much.

To the best parents in the world – I'm so lucky to have you! Thank you for everything you have ever done for me and for always being there.

Last but not least, to my daughter and son – Mommy loves you. You are my motivation and inspiration!

ABOUT THE AUTHOR

Penelope Ward is a *New York Times, USA Today* and *#1 Wall Street Journal* bestselling author.

She grew up in Boston with five older brothers and spent most of her twenties as a television news anchor. Penelope resides in Rhode Island with her husband, son and beautiful daughter with autism.

With over two million books sold, she is a 21-time *New York Times* bestseller and the author of over forty novels.

Penelope's books have been translated into over a dozen languages and can be found in bookstores around the world.

Subscribe to Penelope's newsletter here:
http://bit.ly/1X725rj

SOCIAL MEDIA LINKS:

Facebook
https://www.facebook.com/penelopewardauthor

Facebook Private Fan Group
https://www.facebook.com/groups/PenelopesPeeps/

Instagram
@penelopewardauthor
http://instagram.com/PenelopeWardAuthor/

TikTok
https://www.tiktok.com/@penelopewardofficial

Twitter
https://twitter.com/PenelopeAuthor

Made in the USA
Monee, IL
21 April 2024